'You deserve more than I can give you.'

It was a warning Kadlin wouldn't heed. 'You don't decide what I deserve any more than our fathers decide who I marry. I am in charge of myself.'

Gunnar's lips had hardened into a determined line, but deep in his eyes lurked the longing of the boy he had been.

It nearly broke her heart, so she softened her voice. 'I've dreamt of the night you would come back to me for a long time. Come…' She tugged him gently. 'Lie down with me.'

She had more than dreamt of it. Gunnar was the only man she had ever thought to spend her life with. He was the one for her—the only one—so it seemed entirely natural that this night had finally come.

Author Note

I've always had a soft spot for wounded heroes. Gunnar holds a particularly special place in my heart because his emotional wounds, stemming from his childhood, are almost as severe as his physical wounds. He is not the perfect hero, but he is a very *real* hero. He's a perfect example of how love can touch us all and help us strive to become something better than we were. While I don't envy Kadlin the task put before her, her (almost) unwavering faith in the power of love is the one glimmer of hope that Gunnar needs to become that person.

I am a firm believer that each and every one of us is deserving of love and its power to heal. I hope you enjoy reading about Gunnar and Kadlin and their journey to discover this as much as I enjoyed writing their story.

ONE NIGHT WITH THE VIKING

Harper St George

First published in Great Britain 2016
By Mills & Boon, an imprint of HarperCollins*Publishers*
1 London Bridge Street, London, SE1 9GF

Large Print edition 2016

© 2016 Harper St. George

ISBN: 978-0-263-26296-4

3475900x

Harper St George was raised in rural Alabama and along the tranquil coast of northwest Florida. It was this setting, filled with stories of the old days, that instilled in her a love of history, romance and adventure. At high school she discovered the romance novel, which combined all those elements into one perfect package. She lives in Atlanta, Georgia, with her husband and two young children.

Visit her website: harperstgeorge.com.

Books by Harper St George

Mills & Boon Historical Romance

Viking Warriors

Enslaved by the Viking
One Night with the Viking

Digital Short Stories

His Abductor's Desire
Her Forbidden Gunslinger

Visit the Author Profile page at millsandboon.co.uk.

For Joseph

Chapter One

She was the only woman he had ever loved.

The realisation washed over him in a single instant, a tingling chill that started at his fingertips and worked its way up his arms and on to the rest of his body. If he'd seen her even once in the past few years, he might have recognised that love sooner. Or if he had allowed himself to even dream that such a sentiment was possible, he would have attributed it to her. But he'd tried to make himself forget her. It was easier to pretend she didn't exist. If he didn't think about being with her, he wouldn't long for her. If he didn't remember how it felt to hold her, he wouldn't have to face the reality that she wasn't meant to be his. That he would never hold her again and his hands wouldn't ache from the emptiness.

Only Gunnar had never really stopped imagining her face. Every woman he'd ever touched had become her in the black of night.

From his hidden niche in the forest, he watched Kadlin follow the path from her home to the stream, her cheeks pink with the cold and her long-limbed stride graceful and swaying. She leapt a snowdrift and her younger brothers followed suit, both of them squealing and laughing as one of them tripped and fell into the icy snow bank. Her mongrel barked and joined the fray, bouncing in merriment. Gunnar found himself smiling as he quickly stepped back to hide behind a tree when she turned abruptly to join in their laughter. The precious sound of it reached him where he hid in the forest and dislodged the weight he carried in his chest. It had been years since he'd heard her laugh. He'd forgotten how good it felt to hear it.

The sound brought back memories of their childhood frolics through this very forest. He stood for a moment with his eyes closed as he let the images come to him: Kadlin pelting him with a snowball, Kadlin lying in wait for him on a low-hanging branch as he looked for her and then tackling him to the ground, Kadlin boxing his ears when he'd called her a girl. But then their happy voices began to fade, so he followed to keep them within sight.

If not for the presence of her younger brothers, he would have approached her at the stream. But he remembered the last time he'd visited her and the harsh words her father had said to him, so he kept his distance. There would be time to visit her later that night when everyone slept. He'd made that trip often enough in the past and knew just how to gain entry without being seen. He kept his place in the seclusion of the forest and watched them.

Twin braids hung down to her waist. He'd been fascinated with her hair for as long he could remember. It was a rare silvery blonde he'd never seen on another. As a child, he'd sneak into her bedchamber on the nights he'd been too bruised and dispirited to find solace in his own bed, unravel her long braids and let the waterfall of silk cascade over him. And he could vividly recall her startling clear blue eyes watching him as he did it. The acceptance he saw reflected there was the only refuge he'd known. Rejected by his father, who was a bitter and spiteful man, and then by his mother when she had abandoned her bastard child to marry, he'd never known tenderness and approval, except from Kadlin.

He'd been a fool to not recognise the depths of his feelings for her back then. But he'd also been a child and what did children know of love? He only knew that he had gone to her when his own life had become unbearable and she had offered him comfort. He didn't quite understand what had compelled him to push her away. Perhaps it was because she had been meant for his half-brother and he didn't want to face the inevitable pain that would follow when she chose Eirik over him. But he recognised now that she filled some place in him that had been empty without her and his life would be infinitely better with her in it.

It was unfortunate that his life was taking him across the sea in mere days. Yet even as the thought crossed his mind, he recognised that going away was the best thing for her. She deserved someone as honourable and good as she was. Someone who would be able to do more than take from her. Someone who could return a modicum of all that she had to give a man. He wasn't that man and he knew that he could never aspire to be. He was darkness to her light. He would only take from her. But he would see her tonight, talk to her one last time, hold her in his arms. It would have to be enough to keep him for the rest of his life.

Kadlin awoke to the disturbing knowledge that she was not alone in her bedchamber. She lay perfectly still, listening for some sound that would betray the intruder, but she failed to hear anything past the pounding of her heart. The fire had reduced to only a smoulder, so she blinked, urging her eyes to adjust to the absence of light. There was a heaviness in the room, a presence that wasn't her own. She was certain that it wasn't a trick of her imagination. The presence prickled her skin and sucked out the air in the small chamber.

Where was her dog? The realisation that her faithful companion had abandoned her set off a cold flare of terror and her heart froze in her chest. If someone had been able to take Freyja, then—

'It's only me, Kadlin. Don't be afraid.'

Gunnar! She would have known his voice

anywhere. The deep cadence was followed by a spark of orange as the fire flamed back to life. Its warmth caressed his beloved features, making his wolfish amber eyes appear to glow at her from across the small distance. The flickering flames highlighted the deep red of his hair and drew her attention to the angular planes of his face as they played hide-and-seek with the light. He was the fire god come to life.

But he was Gunnar, decidedly flesh-and-blood male. Her heart resumed its pounding, but for an entirely different reason. She'd not laid eyes on him in well over two years; he'd been gone, fighting across the sea. Even before that, her knowledge of him had become sparse and relegated to stolen glimpses and awkward meals when their fathers met. They had still been children the last time he had made the long trek, alone through the forest, from his home to her bed.

Now, he had the broad shoulders of a seasoned warrior, made even wider by the fur cloak draped across them. She could barely tear her gaze from their solid strength, but he prodded the fire and she noticed how large and strong his hands had become. Much different than the hands that had held her so many years ago. A trembling began somewhere deep within her.

'I didn't know if I would see you again.' Her words came out a bit breathless so she forced herself to take a deep breath as she sat up in bed. She wanted to touch him, to reassure herself that he was really there and this wasn't some dream, to know the feel of his shoulders beneath her hands so she could compare it to her dreams. She wanted to reach out and hold on to him before he left and she never saw him again. To shake him for taking himself away from her.

But it had been so long since they'd enjoyed the easy camaraderie of their youth and he seemed so fierce and remote from the boy she had known. 'You returned with Eirik in the autumn.' They could have had the whole winter to know each other again. She didn't give voice to the words, but the accusation hung silently in the air between them. 'Why have you stayed away?' A shadow moved in the corner behind him and she realised that her dog had been given a large hank of dried meat to chew. Gunnar had come prepared, it seemed.

He took a deep breath and seemed to come

to some decision, because when his gaze lit on hers, he looked at her so directly that she was left speechless. There was no jesting there, no artifice, or even a veneer of civility. There was just a restless energy that he seemed determined to harness so that it focused completely on her. When he finally spoke, his voice was textured with longing. 'You were betrothed to my brother. If I saw you again, I knew that I would have challenged him for you.'

He finally released her from the captivity of his stare, his intense gaze flicking over her tousled hair and down to her breasts, making warmth bloom in her chest. He dropped one last piece of wood on the fire and rose to his full height so that he seemed to take up most of the space in the room.

Her skin prickled from the intensity of his attention. She'd imagined this very scenario many times over the years, awakening to him in her room, but the reality of his presence was nearly overwhelming. His acknowledgement of his desire for her, coupled with the intensity of his stare, set her body to life in a way she'd been unable to imagine. Heat prickled her skin, so that every part of her was aware of him. When he took a step in her direction, her belly fluttered in anticipation. To rein herself in, she offered a challenge to his words. 'You would have allowed your brother to marry me? Knowing that you wanted me for yourself?'

There was no mistaking that heated look in his eyes. She'd seen it enough in other men who had come to ask her father for her hand, though she'd never once welcomed it. But from him, it was like the light of the spring sun warming her skin after a particularly brutal winter. He was the only one she had ever imagined herself marrying.

'I believed that he was your choice.' He came to a stop at the edge of the bed next to her.

She rose to her knees before him, leaving her blanket to pool on the bed, and fought her desire to touch him. Apparently he had harboured some affection for her all of these years, but she found it difficult to believe, when he could have had any woman he wanted. Or perhaps she was afraid to believe it, afraid that even knowing that, it would change nothing. That he still wouldn't be hers. 'You must know that Eirik never owned my heart. He is a dear friend, but…not in the way that I would require for marriage.'

'I passed the winter away from home, in places that would make you shudder with revulsion.' He shook his head. 'With horrible people…because I didn't want to return to my father's home and see you as Eirik's wife. Every night I imagined you in his arms and it was torture. When I returned home to find that you hadn't married him, I came to you as soon as I could.' He paused, his lips curving in an attractive smile. It lit his eyes, giving her a glimpse of the boy she had loved. His strong hand reached out to catch the end of one of her braids and curl it around his finger. They both watched as the light caught it and turned the blonde strands to silver. 'Leave it to you to thwart the wishes of not one but two jarls, your father and mine.'

Her lips curved in a slight smile at his jest, but she was reluctant to get away from the confrontation. '*He* was not the man I wanted.' His breath hitched, but he didn't shift his attention from the strand of hair he caressed. 'Why have you ignored me all these years, Gunnar?' she whispered.

'Nay, Kadlin, you were never ignored. There was never a moment when I wasn't aware of you. Any time you were near, I felt it even without seeing you. My body knew you were there and I couldn't help but hear you, smell you.' He brought the strand of hair to his lips and closed his eyes as he breathed in her scent. 'I could never forget the way you smelled and the way it felt to sleep with my face buried in your hair when we were children.'

'But you've stayed away. Why?'

He groaned and pulled back only enough to look at her. 'The boy you knew died a long time ago, Kadlin. I am not what you need.'

She took a deep breath to steady her nerves. This man, this *warrior* standing before her, so forbidding and brutal, was *not* the boy she remembered. But he was no less attractive for the change that his harsh life had wrought. To the contrary, he carried an edge that somehow served to make him desirable with that mystical allure taken on by all things forbidden. Despite that, he still seemed so familiar to her. Unable to avoid touching him any longer, she let her palms rest on the backs of his hands. Did he feel the magic that happened when their flesh touched, the invisible flame that sparked between them?

Her hands moved restlessly up and down the length of his forearms, unable to stay still when the urge to touch him was so powerful. They were as solid as iron beneath her palms. Taking in the broad expanse of his chest, she suspected that all of him would feel that way. A jolt of unexpected excitement moved from her fingertips to her belly. 'I don't care, Gunnar. You are what I want.' Truer words had never passed her lips. In the few minutes he had been there, she felt like a part of her had come back to itself. There was no more aching where her heart had been. He was meant for her and she knew it now more than she had ever known it before. Only now, she knew that deep in his heart he felt the same way.

His eyes glowed with a sudden fierceness that might have frightened her only moments earlier. 'You should be careful of the things you say to me.'

'Why?' she challenged.

He grinned, but it was wicked and full of all of the dark things that she very much wanted to experience with him. A wolf's grin. His fingers loosened their grasp on her hair so that his hands could settle gently at her hips, clenching the light fabric of her nightdress in a show of restraint that caused a strange pulse to begin between her thighs. 'Because I've spent every moment in this chamber trying to convince myself that I came only to bid you goodbye.'

'You didn't truly think that I would let you go so easily?' Her body warming beneath his touch, she allowed her hands to finally settle on the solid expanse of his chest. He was so hard and strong. Her fingertips tingled as she touched him, tracing over the dips and planes. But that wasn't enough, so she let them delve beneath the edges of the fur cloak to be closer to his heat. His words had started a throbbing deep within her and it begged to be closer to him.

He shook his head at her teasing words and gave her a heavy-lidded stare. 'You don't understand what you do to me, innocent.'

She might have uttered those same words to him. He made all thoughts of censure and convention flee her mind. In fact, he made her gladly throw them away if it meant that he could be hers. With her palm over the restless pounding of his heart, she leaned towards him. His eyes widened slightly in surprise, but he didn't pull away when her lips touched his. Kadlin closed her eyes and let her tongue stroke his bottom lip, tasting the mead that he had drank, before slipping inside the silken heat to find his. When his tongue, both soft and rough, stroked against her own, it caused an ache in her that wanted more from him. Her fingers worked up his chest to delve into the hair resting at his nape and pull him close. Finally succumbing, he groaned, his fingers curling tight around her hips as he pulled her flush against him.

The kiss quickly escalated from delicate exploration to ravenous need, until he finally drew back and took a deep breath. Kadlin tried to stifle her smile, but she couldn't because she was so happy to have finally kissed him as she had dreamed about for years. It was even better than her dreams. Clearly discomfited and aroused, he was the most singularly attractive man she had ever seen. His allure came from the wildness that he exuded, the untamed quality that defied explanation. Only, she had seen deep inside to the heart of the man within that wild creature and he wanted her.

'I understand, Gunnar. You do the same to me.'

The heated look he gave her threatened to make her go up in flames. His hands tightened almost involuntarily on her even more as he held her hips against his, allowing her to clearly feel the extent of his hard desire for her as it pressed firmly into her belly. 'You deserve more than I can give you.'

It was a warning she wouldn't heed. 'You don't get to decide what I deserve any more than our fathers decide who I marry. I am in charge of myself.' His lips had hardened into a determined line, but deep in his eyes lurked the longing of the boy he had been. It nearly broke her heart, so she softened her voice. 'I've dreamt of the night you would come back to me for a long time. Come…' she tugged him gently '…lie down with me.' She had more than dreamt of it. Gunnar was the only man she had ever thought to spend her life with. He was the one for her, the only one, so it seemed entirely natural that this night had finally come.

Letting him go, she moved back to her place on the bed, her fingers slowly going to the ties of her nightdress. His eyes hungrily followed her every move and his breathing became faster. Her belly fluttered as his gaze licked over her skin. She released the string so that the fabric fell down her shoulders, revealing the tops of her breasts.

He glanced to the door, but when his gaze came back to her, it was hot and fierce. She trembled with excitement when he reached up and untied the thong holding the fur cloak in place across his broad shoulders, so that it fell to the floor.

'I've only ever wanted you,' she encouraged him. 'Come claim what is yours.'

Chapter Two

Kadlin closed her eyes as she turned over in bed and fought the waves of nausea that rolled through her. She pressed her forehead against her arm and waited for it to pass. It had been the same every morning for the past week. Wake up to let Freyja out and then stumble back to bed, too dizzy to stand upright and fight the nausea that threatened to make her empty the contents of her stomach. Even before the nausea and vertigo, her breasts had been very sore. She had tried to attribute the strange soreness to her monthly ague, only the bleeding had never started, and now, she couldn't deny it any longer.

It was time to admit that she was with Gunnar's child.

The acknowledgement made her flop on to her back and stare at the ceiling. Her hand went to her belly, hoping to find some evidence of their child. It was a ritual she had repeated nightly in her chamber from the first moment she had even begun to suspect. So far, it seemed as flat as it had ever been. But that was all right, because today she could finally admit the truth to herself. Today made seven straight mornings of nausea.

When she'd invited him into her bed, she'd only thought that she'd been risking her heart, not a child. How naïve she had been. A laugh shook loose from deep in her belly and escaped past her lips as she threw her head back. Freyja scratched at the door to get in, startled by her mistress', voice, but she ignored her. Her sweet maid, Edda, was a fool. Kadlin didn't know the specifics behind the girl's service to her family, but she had long suspected that Edda's father had grown impatient with the young woman's promiscuity and sent her away to toil under the watchful eye of Kadlin's mother. His plan had met with little success, because the girl left a string of admirers in her wake. Thinking that Edda must be knowledgeable in the ways of men and women and child-making, some time ago Kadlin had asked her if it was possible to avoid motherhood while still enjoying a man. Even then, Kadlin's thoughts had been of Gunnar. She'd been so certain that if she could seduce him, then he would admit his heart belonged to her. Edda had assured her that a virgin couldn't get with child her first time with a man. That terrible logic had seemed so profound and true at the time. Now it just seemed horribly stupid and irresponsible.

She should have never listened to her. Kadlin frowned as she recalled exactly what had happened that night and realised that perhaps she was being unfair, perhaps it wasn't entirely Edda's fault. She had pulled Gunnar down for more kisses and had touched him until he had hardened again beneath her palm. It had been her own whispered pleas that had coaxed him to take her again…and then yet again. Perhaps it had been the second or third time with Gunnar that had done the trick and not the first.

Not that it mattered. He wouldn't care. He wasn't here and he would never be here. She had been so sure that once they had lain together, he would admit his love for her.

Pressing her palms to her forehead to ward off the tears that threatened, she squeezed her eyes shut tight and tried to stop the painful memory of how their night had ended. Yet it refused to be stopped and brought with it a fresh wave of pain, jagged along its edges so that it tore at her anew. She'd dozed and awakened to find him dressing, his back to her as he pulled up his trousers. Still floating in the lingering aura of bliss, she had asked him to stay.

'I never made you any promises.' Those words still made her wince. When he'd turned, his eyes had been flat and cold, as though he was looking at a stranger. She hadn't thought that promises had been necessary. Deep in the marrow of her bones, she knew that Gunnar was meant to be her husband and she was meant to bear his children. It was a truth as obvious to her as her own name. There was no doubt that he felt it, too, so she hadn't even expected him to attempt to deny it.

'We were meant for each other.' Her words only amused him. His lips tipped up in that infuriating smile he had perfected long ago.

'I'm not meant for you. I'm leaving, Kadlin, and I won't be back. Go on with your life and marry a man who wants you.'

What happened afterward remained a blur. She was sure that she had protested, had argued that he didn't mean those words, but nothing had chipped away at the wall he had so quickly erected between them. In mere moments, he had left her life as quickly as he had returned to it.

Her face flamed with the memory and a pain-filled groan escaped her chest. *She* was the fool. She had been too confident that his love for her was as true as her love for him. He'd given her no reason to put her faith in him, but she'd done it anyway. And now he was gone and she would have his child. Her eyes fell closed and she imagined snuggling the babe to her breast while Gunnar looked on, his eyes bright with love and tenderness for them. She would give anything to have him there. To be his wife. To tell him the joyous news of their child and watch him smile as he drew her into his arms. There was no one else she wanted as husband and father to her children. No one. Gunnar had always been the one to fill that role in her fantasies.

Soon, she would have to tell her parents. She didn't want to dwell on the look of disappointment sure to cross her father's face. But she didn't have to tell him yet, so she vowed to simply enjoy the knowledge that Gunnar's child slept in her womb beneath her heart. Later, she would decide what to do.

But later came much sooner than she expected. Kadlin was scarcely able to savour the pregnancy for three weeks before a decision was made for her.

'Hush, little one, Mother comes.' Her baby brother fussed and sucked at his fist as Kadlin swayed and bounced, trying to find a rhythm that would soothe him until their mother could free herself from the children that ran around her. Kadlin smiled as she watched her four little sisters, the youngest one only three years old, chase their mother across the field. They were like beautiful miniatures of the woman as they ran in descending order of size. What had been a berry-picking excursion had quickly become a game of chase the mouse. Just last year her two brothers would have joined in the fun, but they considered themselves too old for such nonsense now, though they watched closely from their place guarding the baskets.

Kadlin laughed from the shade of the birch and cuddled the baby close, her thoughts on her own child. Though she was still happy, she was no closer to determining a solution. It would be later in the summer before a boat left so that she could send word to Gunnar, but even as she thought it, she realised it wasn't something that she could do. He had left her and made it clear that he wouldn't return. He wouldn't care about a child and she was too prideful to risk yet another rejection. Try as she might, she couldn't forget the hardness in his eyes that night.

'You are beautiful with a child in your arms, Kadlin.'

The unwelcome voice made her gasp as she turned around to face the one who'd intruded on her privacy. A man with a blade-straight nose and vivid blue eyes approached. Since many of the men were across the sea, the jarl had thought it prudent to send out a contingent of men to help keep order on his lands. Her father had appointed Baldr to lead those men and he must have compensated him well to make him stay instead of seeking out his fortune like the others. Baldr frequently sought her out, making her wonder if he and her father had ever discussed her hand as part of their arrangement. Though he was handsome, there was a cruelty in his face that made her unconsciously hold her breath every time she spoke to him.

'Hello, Baldr. I wasn't aware you had returned.'

'Just late last night. I looked for you this morning, but didn't find you. Were you ill?'

Kadlin swallowed and spoke the lies that were coming too readily to her lips. Everyone noted her morning absences. 'I've been unwell, but as you can see, I'm feeling much better.'

He nodded and smiled a smile that was a bit too knowing. When his gaze swept over her torso, lingering on the extra fullness of her breasts, she adjusted the infant to hide them. 'Aye, that's what your pretty maid said.'

Her heart sank. Nay, Edda, not him. Edda was the only one who had begun to suspect that she was with child. Kadlin had caught the maid sneaking glances at her waistline more than once in the weeks since her morning sickness had begun. No one else had even bothered to question her chastity, but the girl had every reason to suspect. That very morning, she had come in late with Kadlin's washing water, knowing that Kadlin would still be abed. Edda had looked dishevelled and flushed, making Kadlin wonder if she'd just come from a lover.

She took a step backwards and couldn't stop her eyes from cutting as harsh as her words. 'Do you think bedding my servant will make you more appealing to me, Baldr?'

He laughed, a short hissing of breath that barely escaped his chest, and took slow steps towards her. He stopped just before her and reached to touch her hand, a lock of glossy, dark hair falling across his forehead. 'Men bed her because her beauty is second only to yours. But you must know that they also do it because they know it's as close as they'll get to bedding you.' His fingertips trailed from her hand to the expanse of flesh exposed above the bodice of her gown.

She jerked away, causing his smile to widen. 'But that isn't really true any more, is it? Someone bedded you and now his seed has taken root.'

'You're depraved.'

'I want you as my wife, Kadlin, even with that bastard in you. I'll accept it as my own. That's more than you'll get from anyone else. More than you've got from the bastard's own father.'

Those words cut a little too close to the truth. 'Leave my sight!' The infant startled at her harsh words and then began to cry. She held him tighter to her chest, but didn't take her eyes from the man before her. 'I will never want you, Baldr. Never!'

He glanced behind her to the others who had surely noted her outburst. 'It matters not what you want, Kadlin. If it's the jarl's wish, you'll accept me into your life.' His lustful gaze raked her body before settling on hers again. 'And into your bed.' With that promise, he turned on his heel and left.

Fingers shaking with a mixture of anger and fear, she handed the baby over to her mother only moments later. She was out of time. Her father would know before nightfall and she had no idea what to do. The worst of it was that she couldn't even dispute what Baldr had said. Gunnar wouldn't acknowledge their child. He didn't want them.

Ignoring her mother's questions, she ran all the way back to the longhouse and shut herself in-

side her chamber where she gave in to the despair
that had threatened her all along. And waited for
the summons she was certain would come from
her father.

It came later that night.
'What have you done?'
It was the second time her father had asked that
question, but she still had no answer for him. She
stood just inside the door of her parents' chamber; it was closed tight behind her to keep the
conversation as confidential as possible in such
close quarters. The only sounds were the sighs
of the baby sleeping peacefully on the bed and
her mother's soft sobs from her chair beside her
father. Seeing the tears on her mother's cheeks
made her throat ache with her own unshed tears.
'What man did this to you?'
She risked another glance at the face she held
so dear, only it wasn't the kind face of the father
she cherished. His cheeks were aflame with his
fury, and his greying, golden hair was dishevelled, as if he'd raked through it with his hands
countless times. Everyone said that he indulged
her, that he favoured her too much, and perhaps

they were right because she'd never seen him so angry.

'Leif, calm yourself. Can't you see that she's afraid?' Her mother's soft voice broke the tension and she held out her hand to Kadlin, but Kadlin couldn't make her feet move her forward to accept it.

The jarl cursed under his breath and raked a hand through his hair. When he looked up at Kadlin, the anger had receded a fraction, replaced with concern. 'Were you forced?'

Kadlin shook her head and found her voice. 'Nay, Father, I was not forced.'

'So it's true.' He sighed as if he'd been hoping that the information he'd been given was wrong. 'Seduced, then?'

Again she shook her head, nay.

The anger returned. 'Give me his name.'

'What will a name do? He's gone, across the sea with everyone else.'

'Oh, Kadlin.' Her mother brought a hand up to cover her lips as she processed those words before continuing. 'Why? If there is someone you favoured you could have come to us and we could have arranged a marriage before he left.'

Addressing her mother, she spoke evenly. 'Because you would not have arranged a marriage for us so easily. And because I wasn't even certain of him myself. I hadn't seen him in years.'

The jarl shook his head. 'I have brought countless men before you and you've eschewed them all. All of them! Even Eirik. And you ask me what will a name do? I want to know this paragon of masculinity who stole your good sense and virginity when not one of the men I brought before you even turned your head. A name, Kadlin.'

She drew herself up to her full height and took a deep breath. It wasn't as if her father could kill him now, and besides, he was gone, never to return. She would never see him again, never touch him, never laugh with him. The ache in her throat threatened to choke off her words when she spoke. 'It was Gunnar. Gunnar is the father of my child.'

Her parents sat in a stunned silence that was only broken when her mother broke down into sobs again. Her father was unnaturally still before he finally spoke. 'You gave yourself to a bastard?'

'He is acknowledged, Father. It's not as if he's

without a family. Besides, he cannot be blamed for the manner in which he was conceived. I want to marry him.' Nay, that wasn't right. Not any more. When would she learn to think of him as part of her past? 'I *wanted* to marry him. I don't know why this comes as such a surprise. As a child, I spoke often of marrying him. But it's been years since I've seen him and I needed to see him again to be sure.'

But her father shook his head. 'Kadlin…he is not for you. Aye, his father has acknowledged him and raised him, but he has no future. No lands, no place in the world except to swing a blade and count his treasure.'

'Aye, Father, that's right. He has treasure from his excursions. He leads his own ship. He has the means to support me and a family. Why was he such a bad choice?' Not that it mattered now with him long gone, but she couldn't stop the unreasonable well of anger that rose within her. If her father had sanctioned her choice all along, perhaps this wouldn't have happened. Perhaps they could have married years ago.

'Why was he such a bad choice? Tell me this, Daughter. Where would you live with him? Does he have a home? A hall to keep you warm in the winter, a place to keep your children protected as they grow? He is not that type of man, Kadlin. He's transient. He lives on only what his father's good conscience has provided for him and when that ends he will pass his winters in hovels or whatever place he has managed to come by through pillaging, where he will live in constant fear of being killed. And one day he will be killed and what do you suppose would become of you? You would be passed to the next man in line, or perhaps taken as a triumph of his murderer, and you would live with him until he, too, is killed and so on and so forth until you, too, are gone. By then your children will have been scattered to the whims of life. Is this how you envision your future?'

Kadlin shook her head to deny the harsh future he described. 'Nay, you are wrong.'

'Am I? Then let us go back to the essential question. Has he offered you marriage?'

She swallowed past the ache in her throat and forced the word out. 'Nay.'

'He beds a woman like you, a prize that every

bachelor wants, and doesn't even have to speak of marriage to do it?'

'Stop it, Father!' She held her hand up to ward off his words. 'None of this matters now. I loved him and he left me! Does that make you happy? There will be no marriage. I gave myself to him and he didn't want me.' Her voice broke on that last word and tears spilled down her cheeks as she wrapped her arms around her middle in some attempt to hold herself together, as the pain threatened to rip her apart. Her mother's arms joined her own and she turned into the woman's embrace, seeking some nameless solace from the pain of the gaping wound in her heart.

'You'll marry Baldr.'

'No—'

Her father shook his head. 'Don't attempt to sway me, Kadlin. He's offered and I see no other choice. Your child needs a father, a name.'

'Please, Father.' Pulling away from her mother, she ran and fell to her knees before him, bringing his hand to her cheek. 'Please, not him. I don't like him.'

He smiled wryly and brushed his fingers across her cheekbone, the anger momentarily gone from his eyes. 'You don't like any of them, Kadlin. But you must accept that your child needs a father. Do you want him to be a bastard like Gunnar? You've seen how difficult his life is. Do you want your son to have the same life? Always at a disadvantage because of the accident of his conception?'

She closed her eyes against the pain of his words, more tears escaping down her cheeks. 'You know I don't.'

'Then marry Baldr. He has promised to care for you and the child.'

'Nay, Father. He is a cruel man. He frightens me.'

The anger completely left him then to be replaced by something that was even worse. Pity. He cupped her face with both hands and placed a kiss on her forehead. 'I would do anything to spare you from this pain. If he were here now, I would kill Gunnar myself for leaving you to face this alone. It only proves that I was right about him.' Taking a deep breath, he ploughed ahead. 'You will be married now. You have no choice.'

She trembled as a deep, wrenching sob struggled to find purchase in her throat. Her father's words hinted at a truth she had tried so hard to deny. Gunnar must have known that a child was possible. He must have known that she loved him. He must have known how his leaving would destroy her. But she had to make a choice for her child now. 'I'll marry Dagan, but not Baldr.' Dagan was a childhood friend she had known almost as long as Gunnar. He was kind and good, a fine warrior who planned to leave for the Saxon lands before winter. Though the thought of marrying anyone except Gunnar tore out her heart, if she would marry anyone else it would be Dagan. He would understand that she needed time before...before she could truly be a wife to him. The very thought of it caused another tear to leak down her cheek.

'Dagan?' Her father looked pensive and then nodded. 'He's from a strong family. He will agree to this?'

'Aye,' she whispered. Dagan had hinted at the idea of marriage before and she had turned him down gently.

Her father nodded. 'Before the next moon you will be married.'

Chapter Three

Two years later

Gunnar squinted into the grey dawn and tried to make out the figure he was sure he had seen just over the ridge. It had been a quick movement, but too large for a small animal. Though the signs of spring were all around—the frost losing its grip on the earth, the small white flowers peeking out of the dead foliage on the forest floor—it was too early in the season for the larger animals to be out. It must have been a Saxon. The smell of their unwashed bodies wafted across the distance.

It was time for battle. Absently, his fingers reached into his tunic to stroke the lock of silvery-blonde hair he kept tied on a leather thong around his neck. It had become a habit before battle, one that he couldn't break, even though he had determined to stop thinking of her. More than once, he'd found himself doing it and resolved to cast the lock into the nearest fire, but he never could bring himself to do it. As paltry as it was, the memento was his only link to Kadlin—the only link he would ever have. Stroking it never failed to make him remember how good it had felt to become a part of her that night, to claim her and make her his. Or how her scent, like sunshine mixed with wildflowers, had stayed on his skin for days afterward; and how in summer, when the afternoon sun shone through the clouds after a rain, it reminded him of her scent and would never fail to arouse him.

One night would never be enough with her, nor would a lifetime. He could touch her every day for the rest of his life and it would never be enough. She was the only light able to penetrate the coldness inside him. He'd willingly warm himself for an eternity in her light.

He wanted her. By the gods, he wanted her with him more than he'd ever wanted anything in his life. Her absence left a gaping wound inside that no one could see and it festered worse every day. But she wasn't meant to be his.

Leaving her after taking her body, after hearing the sweet words she'd whispered in his ear, had been the hardest thing that he'd ever done. He'd lain with many women, but he'd never experienced the overwhelming wave of possessiveness that had overcome him when he'd risen to dress and looked down at her. With his seed glistening on the tender flesh of her inner thighs, he'd felt as if he'd branded her, marked her as his in a primal ritual as old as man. It had taken every ounce of will he possessed to walk away.

He'd only been able to do it because he'd convinced himself that leaving was best for her. She deserved a life where she would be surrounded by those she loved. She was meant to be a jarl's wife, not the wife of an unwanted bastard. Not the wife of someone incapable of loving and protecting her as she deserved. It was only that memory of how he had failed in the past that had given him strength to ignore the darkness within him that urged him to take her away with him, to leave her to her peaceful life without him.

When his ship had set sail, he'd known that he was entering some of the darkest days of his life. The years away from her had been black; he had no reason to believe that the ones ahead of him would be any better.

The soft crunch of dry twigs alerted Gunnar to his friend's presence behind him just before Magnus spoke. 'What do you see?'

Gunnar opened his eyes and tried to shake thoughts of Kadlin away. If he wanted to live, he couldn't afford distractions. That was the very reason he needed to get rid of that bloody lock of hair; it was a distraction. Nodding to the small break in the trees, he spoke softly. 'I saw a Saxon. Just there.' They were both silent, waiting for another movement. After a few minutes, they were rewarded as the figure of a man darted across the opening.

Magnus grumbled in disgust. 'They should come fight us like men instead of hiding in the trees.'

'They already tried that and realised they couldn't win,' Gunnar muttered as he scanned the treeline, looking for more. Earlier in the week, he and his men had come across a ragtag group of Saxon men. There had been a fight, and when it had become apparent that his men were the stronger warriors, the Saxons had scattered. His men had found some of them, but the rest had escaped and had regrouped and followed them. He didn't like their cowardice in hiding and his blood pumped furiously at the thought of crushing them. 'They won't approach. They're waiting. We'll have to root them out.'

Magnus nodded his agreement. 'There are at least two score. If they met with others, there could be more.'

'I'll take some men and ride in behind them. Drive them out into the open.'

'Why not wait them out? We can handle them.'

Gunnar shook his head, the need to fight outweighing his patience. 'Nay, we'll fight them now.' He turned to go back to camp. They needed to strike fast.

'Wait, brother,' Magnus said as he put a hand on his arm. 'Let us wait. We don't know how many men are hiding. We don't need to fight now.' He paused and when Gunnar seemed unmoved by his logic, he added, 'It could be suicide.'

'I know,' Gunnar replied and kept walking the path back to camp. It could be suicide, but not in the way Magnus suspected. He'd never risk the lives of his men. He intended to go alone, to figure out what they were dealing with before leading his men in. He'd gained a reputation for recklessness, but every chance he'd ever taken had paid off. It was why the men under his command had quadrupled in size. They wanted the treasures and accolades those fighting beneath his command had accumulated over the years.

The truth was that he no longer cared if he lived or died. He could have stopped fighting. Eirik had offered him numerous opportunities to take over command posts. He could have become a jarl in this new land in his own right by now, commanding the battle from afar at times. And while that idea had originally held some allure, it had come too late. He'd learned that Kadlin was married to someone else now.

The night he had come face to face with her husband was the night he realised that some part of him had still held out hope. It wasn't until that moment that he knew he had lost her for ever. And nothing seemed to matter any more. *That* shouldn't matter. She'd already been lost to him, but the thought of her touching another was like a knife blade taken to his already shredded heart.

Though he tried to stop it, the memory of that night came back sharp and crisp. The meeting had happened during the first snowstorm of his first winter here. New arrivals from home had only recently joined them so the hall was crowded. Somehow, through the din of multiple conversations and revelry happening around him, her name came to him.

Kadlin.

It took his eyes only moments to identify the one who had spoken it. A man on the other side of the fire had been regaling anyone who would listen about the beauty of his new wife. Gunnar's heart had stopped for one endless moment when the newcomer described her long blonde hair. Before he'd even realised what he was doing, Gunnar had found himself standing in front of the fool who had only smiled up at him.

'You have married, Kadlin, eldest child of Jarl Leif?'

The fool had barely managed to offer an acknowledgement before slumping to the floor, knocked cold by Gunnar's fist. He'd wanted the man to stand and fight him. Blood had pumped through his body, urging him to kill the man for daring to lay any claim to her, but he turned and left the hall instead.

The vision of her with someone else only made the pain in his chest so great that it escaped in a cry of rage that echoed in the sudden silence of the hall. No one was brave enough to approach him. Even Magnus and Eirik only hung back, waiting to see if any of the man's friends were foolish enough to chase him. Not one of them did. Though he was looking for a fight, he couldn't blame them. He must have looked like a madman. He was a madman.

Any flickering hope he'd carried within him that he might one day claim her had died out that night. He'd been a fool to let it persist as long as it had. There was nothing left of him. Death was the only cure for the excruciating pain. He'd let out one last bellow of rage and then hung his head as the snow fell around him, collecting on his hair and shoulders. His father had been right. A warrior is all that he was ever meant to be. So a warrior he would be. From that moment onward, his entire life became the fight and nothing else mattered. He had pushed Kadlin from his mind as much as he could and waited for death to claim him.

It hadn't helped that he knew losing her had been his own fault, somehow. Gritting his teeth to stifle the cry of rage that the memory brought with it, he rammed his left fist into the base of a fir tree and watched the bark splinter beneath the impact. He cradled the hand against his chest and threw his head back to take a deep breath as he savoured the momentary numbness before the pain exploded in his hand. The tree was a poor substitute for the crunch of bone a Saxon nose would have provided—he knew he should have waited for the upcoming battle to vent his anger—but the pressure in his chest had been too great to carry into a fight. There was an aching relief to be found as the pain shifted from his chest to his hand. Blowing out through the pain and then sucking in a deep, wrenching breath, he made his way to his men and forced Kadlin out of his mind.

Motioning a boy over to wrap his hand, he gathered them all to go over the plan for battle. In moments, he was mounted, leading the small group to their location behind the Saxons. He knew the forests in this land so well now that he rode on instinct, knowing the best place to attack, knowing exactly where they would be hidden even if he didn't know how many there were.

The scream came from nowhere and then it was all around him at once. The Saxons had been circling them, preparing an ambush. His horse, though well trained, reared in surprise just as a spear broke free from the trees. It landed in the beast's chest, making him scream in pain and lose his balance. Gunnar was unable to jump free as the horse fell backwards. Pain exploded in his legs and head when they landed, then everything went numb and quiet. A strange peace crept over him as he watched the Saxons flood out of the forest to surround his own men. He smiled because he knew that they had given themselves away prematurely and Magnus would surely crush them with his larger group of warriors.

Blackness pulled at him, but it didn't take his smile. It might not have happened with a sword in his hand or a sword in his belly, but he was dying in battle, a welcomed relief. He closed his eyes and waited for Odin to greet him.

* * *

Light flashed behind his eyelids and sent shards of pain shattering through his skull. Or it should have been pain, like every other time he'd awakened to pain so sharp that it had sent him hurtling back into unconsciousness. Instead, it was darts of light that roused him enough to open his eyes and it took an extraordinary effort to accomplish that minor task. Almost too much effort, as the need for slumber pulled him under again. But the sensation of falling was enough to make him finally open them. The light that had teased him before had disappeared to a hazy golden crest on the horizon. It was dawn or perhaps dusk and he was floating in the sky, which was absurd.

Gunnar turned his head to the left and then the right and realised that it wasn't him that was floating, but everything else around him. The horizon wobbled as if the world itself had shifted. A man's head drifted into his line of vision and then moved out again. Soon, more heads followed, but none that he recognised. These weren't his men.

The realisation brought with it the awareness that he was on a ship. Only it wasn't his ship, because these weren't his men. His gaze travelled over the vessel, trying to identify it, but he was having trouble keeping his gaze steady to look for markings. There was no figurehead on the prow.

'Where are we going?' he called to the man nearest him. He hardly recognised his own voice and it was delayed when it came to his ears.

'Up the coast, Brother.' Eirik knelt beside him, his face looking solemn and grim in the morning light. It must be morning if they were setting sail.

Gunnar jerked, not expecting to see anyone appear so close before him. *Brother.* The word rang around in his head and he had trouble holding on to it. 'Brother,' he whispered the word as if he'd never heard it before. As it found purchase, he was able to capture it on his tongue. 'You are my brother.'

'We haven't been good brothers, not in a long time. I regret that.'

Gunnar smiled, though he couldn't understand his compulsion to respond in that way. Perhaps it was because his body was finally numb from the endless pain that had gnawed at him, though he had no memory of what had caused the pain. He felt heavy and weightless all at the same time. He raised his hand and, after an attempt or two, it landed on his brother's shoulder. 'Aye, Brother. But there's not much comfort in regret. What use is it?' The soft leather of a well-worn tunic met his fingers, not the chainmail of battle. He thought it curious Eirik wouldn't arm himself properly for battle and he meant to comment on it, but another figure he'd not noticed before materialised at his side. 'Vidar, little brother. You are a man now. Do you go to this fight with us?'

Vidar glanced at Eirik before shrugging. 'I go, but Eirik is staying.'

The unfamiliar smile stayed on Gunnar's face and he couldn't make it leave no matter how he tried to summon a scowl. He struggled to keep his eyes open as that strange heaviness tried to claim him. His head drooped and he noticed that his legs were covered in furs. Did they think he'd go to battle like a woman, wrapped in blankets and furs? His legs wouldn't obey his command to kick them off so he yanked at the coverings. And then he stared because one leg was wrapped tight in rags and appeared twice as big as the other. But that didn't seem possible, so he considered the fact that the appendages weren't his legs at all but something foreign from his body entirely.

Eirik grabbed his hand, drawing Gunnar's attention back to him. 'I thought you'd like this back.'

Gunnar frowned down at the lock of hair Eirik had placed in his palm. He immediately recognised it as Kadlin's, but wondered how it had become separated from his tunic. A feeling of unease sat heavy in his stomach. 'How did you get this?'

Eirik was quiet for a moment, drawing Gunnar's wavering attention back to him. Only then did his brother raise his troubled eyes from the blonde lock. 'I never knew Kadlin meant so much to you. I should have realised.'

An image of her beauty swam before his eyes, bringing back that bizarre smile he couldn't seem to shake. 'She is everything.'

Eirik looked down. Something was troubling him, but Gunnar had no idea why that would be true. He'd gone off to battle numerous times without this concern from his brother. Deep down, he realised that it must be linked to the strange memory of pain, but he couldn't hold on to the thought long enough to formulate a question. Finally, Eirik met his gaze again and said, 'I want you to live, Brother. Remember that when you awaken.'

Gunnar intended to ask what he meant, but then Eirik pressed a small wooden barrel of mead to his side and draped Gunnar's arm around it. It was the kind they would strap to their horses when out on a short campaign. He pulled out the cork and pressed it to Gunnar's lips. Gunnar obliged him and took a long draught, but something didn't feel right.

'Drink more if you feel pain.' Eirik put the cork back in and rested the barrel against Gunnar's side.

'Where are we going?'

'I do this for your interest, Gunnar.'

The ship rocked and he recognised that it meant they were leaving the dock and heading towards the sea. But there was a disturbing hole in his memory and his time with Eirik was fading. The blackness was settling around his vision and threatening to overpower him again. He grabbed Eirik's cloak and pulled him back. 'Where are you sending me?'

'Live, Brother.' Then he pulled away from Gunnar's grasp with ridiculous ease and seemed to disappear.

Gunnar tried to sit up, but his head swam and began to ache, so he laid back and allowed the comforting blackness to claim him.

Gunnar floated the entire trip, his body lightened by the strange sense of weightlessness that followed him. There were times when he realised something was odd, that his limbs weren't responding as they should, that his thoughts were muddled, but he couldn't find the strength to care. The allure of sleep was too much to resist. Its relentless pull on him was the only thing that grounded him. That split second before it overcame him was the only moment when he felt as if his body was connected to the world around him; it weighted him down and pressed his back solidly to the wooden platform that had become his world.

Most of the time his dreams were nightmares, clawing at his mind with their vicious memories of the past. As always happened when his mind turned dark, it took him back to that night he'd spent with Kadlin. He remembered how he'd spent hours gazing down at her beautiful face, peaceful in sleep. He'd wanted to remember it for ever, because he'd known the horrible words that would have to be said before he left her. He'd known that he had to push her away, even as it had turned his stomach to mar something so precious.

Then the nightmare shifted to that sunny day as an adolescent when he had finally acknowledged that he was as worthless as his father liked to claim. It was the day he had tried unsuccessfully to strike from his memory; the day that he and Eirik had been attacked. A small group of criminals had found them fishing and had overpowered them, tying them up and taunting them with promises of their dark intentions. Gunnar had managed to escape his bonds and had run until he found a washerwoman who sent her son to get their father, so Gunnar had returned. Except he'd been too young and powerless to do anything except hide and listen to Eirik's screams as the men tortured and violated him. He'd made himself listen, absorbing every scream as if it had been his own, each one a confirmation of how contemptible he really was. Confirmation that had only been reinforced once his father had arrived and saved Eirik only to sneer at his bastard for not intervening.

At times Eirik's screams would become the hounds of Helheim hunting him down. At other times, the bays of the hounds would become his father reminding him of his many failures. Or the screams of his father on those nights when he'd imbibe too much mead and seek Gunnar out to rail at his son for making Finna, his mother, leave them. He'd awoken many times with a blackened eye from those encounters. They'd begun to happen so often that he'd run to Kadlin's home when he knew his father was in one of those moods. So, naturally, when his nightmares conjured up those memories, he would escape the nightmare and find himself in her arms. Only this time they weren't children.

The dreams were so vivid that he was sure that he was finally with her. He twined his hand in her flaxen hair and felt the silk sliding through his fingers; he felt the softness of her mouth beneath his thumb as he rimmed her lips and pressed inside the moist heat just as he had claimed her body; he sang songs to her that he had never even heard before. It was what he had hoped would happen if he died. If not for his occasional awakenings and nightmares, he would have thought the battle had killed him. Though he couldn't actually remember the battle, just riding towards it. He'd never admit it, though. What warrior would admit to forgetting an entire battle?

Finally, a new voice woke him enough to make him realise that he wasn't floating any more. The world had stopped and a real beast bayed in the distance.

'Freyja!' a woman's voice called out. The word crashed through his brain and he struggled to understand it. 'Freyja!'

When he was finally able to make his eyes open, a mongrel's giant snout appeared in his line of vision, just before a large, wet tongue stroked his face. He grimaced at the sensation, but then sobered when he saw that Kadlin loomed over him, her hair loose and flowing around her shoulders, the sky a fair blue behind her. She looked angry, vengeful. Not his sweet Kadlin. Then it dawned on him what he should have known all along. He *had* died in battle. Instead of spending eternity in Valhalla, Freyja had claimed him instead. Eirik had sent him off on his journey to Folkvangr. He laughed with bitterness. It seemed appropriate that the goddess would look just like Kadlin.

Death hadn't provided a relief to his torment after all.

Chapter Four

Gunnar looked as close to death as she'd ever seen anyone look with a beating heart.

'Get him inside.' Kadlin forced the words past a throat that threatened to close and stood back out of the way so that Vidar and the two men he'd brought with him could unload Gunnar from the wagon. If not for the distinctive red of his hair and the fact that Vidar accompanied him, she wasn't entirely sure that she would have known who had been delivered to her door. Gunnar's cheeks were hollowed and his frame shrunken from that of her memories. His skin had taken on a grey, unnatural pallor that twisted her heart. This was not the powerful warrior she had known.

The men hoisted him and walked past her to the sod house. His strange laugh lingered behind him, making her shiver from the unnaturalness of it. She was no stranger to the smells of men newly arrived from sea, but she covered her nose and mouth as she followed them inside and directed them to place their burden on a large bench in an alcove off of the main room. One of the men pressed a small barrel to Gunnar's mouth so that he drank, spilling a good bit of it down his neck.

Kadlin stared down at the man she had loved, afraid to touch him, afraid that it would wake her from this bizarre dream where nothing seemed real. One minute she had been hanging the freshly washed linens and the next Vidar was calling to her. He'd ridden ahead of the cart and she'd heard Gunnar's name, but had been so overwhelmed she hadn't understood the rush of Vidar's words. Even now, with him lying before her, she could barely believe he was there.

His head fell back to the bench and lolled to the side. Whatever animation he'd had, the drink had taken it from him, leaving him unnaturally still. She might have thought he was dead if she hadn't just met his eyes with her own. His flesh was so drawn and pale that she didn't know how he had survived the journey across the sea. Perhaps he hadn't. Perhaps he'd only come here to die.

'What's happened to him, Vidar?' As the boy spoke, she imagined what he described. Gunnar, fallen in battle, lying trapped beneath his dead horse while the fight raged around him. His crushed leg crudely bound at camp and his head wound cleaned, but it had taken days to get him back to Eirik's hall. A fever had raged for even more days and he'd yet to regain consciousness for more than a few minutes at a time.

Yet, he had stirred when the men had lifted him from the wagon and she was sure that he had recognised her. It gave her hope, even though he had now settled into a laboured sleep. His breath came harsh and uneven.

'What does Eirik think of his leg?' The right leg of his trousers was intact, but the left had been cut away to allow for wood and bindings to keep his leg stabilised.

Vidar shook his head. 'The leg is ruined.'

She had spent many late nights cursing Gunnar, but she had never wanted this to happen. Kadlin blinked past the sudden haze of tears in her eyes and focused on the dirty linen binding his leg. The bandage, along with his clothing, had likely not been changed since the men had set off on their journey. His tunic hung from him like rags and his hair was a tangled mess. She decided that the first thing to do would be to get him clean.

'Go help yourself to broth and ale.' She looked at the two men who had accompanied Vidar and waved them towards the front room and the pot bubbling on the fire. Turning her attention to Vidar, she said, 'Help me undress him.' But Vidar didn't move when she reached for the hem of Gunnar's tunic. 'Lift him up a bit,' she urged.

'Kadlin…' He glanced towards the men who had moved to do as she had bidden, then lowered his voice. 'I don't think you should be the one to undress him.'

'Have I shocked your delicate sensibilities, Vidar?' She gave him a wry smile and tugged on the tunic. 'He's filthy. Someone needs to bathe him.'

'But—'

'It's not as if I've never seen a man before. Help me!'

He sighed and when Gunnar groaned at a particularly harsh tug, he relented and lifted his brother's shoulders to help her divest him of the tunic and undershirt. Fabric was tied tight around his torso, making her suspect he had at least one broken rib.

'I can do the rest. Fetch me a bucket of the water by the fire and then go and get Harald.'

Eirik owned the farm where she lived and his farmer-tenant Harald lived across the field. He had experienced a similar leg injury as a young man, so she hoped that he would be able to provide some guidance. When Vidar left, she was alone with Gunnar, except for the two men who had accompanied them. But they were famished and drank their broth by the fire, not paying her any attention.

This was not how she'd imagined meeting Gunnar again. Any number of scenarios had crossed her mind and they varied from angrily smashing a tankard over his head to holding him tight and vowing to never let him out of her sight again. Her emotions regarding him had been wild and unrestrained. Much like her love for him had been.

She brushed the grimy hair back from his face with her fingers, noting that it was tangled and would likely need cutting. His beard, too, was caked with grime and would need to be shaved.

It was a task she looked forward to, because she'd always preferred him without one. It obscured the sculpted beauty of his high cheekbones, which was the very reason she suspected he liked it. Men weren't supposed to be beautiful, but he was. A Christian monk had once wintered with her family years ago and told them stories of angels and demons. She had always imagined Eirik to be beautiful like one of that God's angels, full of light. But not Gunnar. He had always been wicked. He was one of the dark ones, a fallen and wrathful angel.

Fishing the washcloth from the bucket, she rung it out and began wiping the grime from his torso, careful of the bruise over his left side. She tried to work in a perfunctory manner and not linger on the scars he'd acquired since she'd last seen him. But she couldn't help but stop to wonder how he'd come by each one as she found them. Try as she might, she couldn't stop the flood of memories that came over her. Their days of running wild through the forest as children and their evenings spent inside playing *hnefatafl*, when he would tease her mercilessly as he tried to break her concentration while she stared at the board, contemplating her next move. The first time he'd kissed her when they'd been children, when she was just beginning to understand what it meant. How strange and wonderful it had felt to have the weight of his body pressing down on hers, even though she'd not understood her own re-action. The years afterward when he'd become almost like a stranger to her, but she would still watch him and feel her breath catch when his gaze would lock on hers.

He'd held a strange power over her even then and she could feel it now trying to take her over. It wanted to make her soft where she had tried so valiantly to harden herself against him. She was seized by a nearly overwhelming devasta-tion that their lives should have turned out differ-ently. She thought she'd squelched that longing and the anger that accompanied it, but it rose up inside her anew. Tears stung her eyes, but she was able to blink them back and shake the mel-ancholy from her head. Her task was to get him clean before Harald arrived and then to make sure that he wasn't lying on his deathbed. Then she would see him gone, back across the sea or wherever he longed to be, somewhere away from her, before he could destroy her again.

A short while later Harald arrived. Kadlin averted her eyes from the crutch the man held and the stilted but efficient way he moved with it. She immediately felt ashamed, because it had never bothered her before, except that now she could only imagine Gunnar walking in that same crippled manner and it filled her heart with sadness. Together with Vidar, they unwrapped the wounded leg to examine it. It was horribly discoloured, but Vidar thought that it looked less swollen than when they had set sail. Harald confirmed that it had been broken in more than one spot, so they were careful to hold the wood in place to minimise any movement, but Gunnar still roused from the pain. Vidar was quick to supply him with the small barrel of mead he'd been clutching in the wagon. She gave it a harsh study, suspecting that it contained something much stronger than mead, but held her tongue.

After Gunnar settled down again, they wrapped his ribs and then the leg in clean linen and she grabbed a knife to cut away the rest of his trousers so she could finish cleaning him. Harald stopped her with a hand to her shoulder.

'Let me do this part.'

She frowned and shrugged him off.

'Kadlin, do you think he would want you to bathe him? He'll have trouble enough when he awakens. Don't do more to take his dignity away.'

Her eyes froze on the grime-covered trousers and she realised that he was right. It would likely embarrass Gunnar if he knew that she had tended to him so intimately. 'I'll wait by the fire.'

He nodded and took the knife from her, so she left him and Vidar to finish washing him and went back to the front room of the sod house. The fire warmed the space comfortably. It was small, but she never failed to experience a wave of satisfaction at how she had managed to turn the house into her home in the year that she'd been there since her husband had been killed in battle. Benches dressed in cosy blankets surrounded the perimeter of the room, while the stone hearth sat in the middle. Off to the side were shelves and a table used for eating and preparing food. It had given her sanctuary when she'd needed it and it appeared that it was to be Gunnar's sanctuary, as well. Picking up the empty bowls the two men had left behind, she intended to wash them, but she couldn't concentrate. So she abandoned the bowls to the bucket of water and moved to the bench where she usually did her sewing, lighting upon it briefly before standing again to pace the length of the hearth. Her gaze repeatedly went to the alcove just off the hallway until Harald and Vidar finally emerged.

'How bad is he really, Harald?'

Harald shrugged. 'Hard to say. If the fever has passed and doesn't return, he should live, but he won't ever have use of that leg again.' He indicated the large crutch he leaned against. 'At least not without one of these.'

She couldn't face that just yet, so she didn't think about it. 'How long before he…before he can attempt walking?'

He shrugged. 'That's largely up to him. A couple of months, maybe more.'

Months. How would she survive being so close to him for months? Yet her heart wouldn't let her send him away. 'Thank you for coming. Stay for a while and have supper.'

He shook his head. 'I've already supped. I'll

come back in the morning to check on him.'
Vidar rose from his seat on a bench to escort
Harald home, but the older man waved him back
to his seat. 'I've crossed that field many times
without you, boy.' He smiled and made his way
out the door, stopping outside to talk with the
men who had accompanied Vidar in the wagon.
Their voices rumbled through the wooden door,
speaking of the battle across the sea with an excitement that baffled her.

'Has he been awake at all?' she asked Vidar.

'Merewyn's Saxon witch made a potion of laced
mead. Eirik gave it to him before they set his leg
and he's been drinking it since. We thought it was
best for the pain. It makes him sleep. He's been
awake a few times, but he's not very lucid.'

'Don't give him any more of it. He needs nourishment now more than he needs oblivion.'

'But, Kadlin, he's in pain.'

'No more, Vidar. He's wasting away.'

Vidar sighed and nodded from his seat on the
bench beside her, exhausted. 'All right. He's in
your care now.'

She frowned at his resigned expression. 'Why

has he been sent to me? Wouldn't it have been better to let him rest and recover at Eirik's home?'

'Perhaps, but Eirik believed that he had no will to survive his injury. I agree. He would have died had he stayed and he still may.'

She crossed her arms and held them tight to her belly, trying unsuccessfully to hold back the pain. Seeing Gunnar again had caused the old wounds to fester and it was taking all she had to keep them from reopening. 'Why does he think that?'

'Gunnar has changed.' Vidar glanced to the alcove where his brother slept, seeming to weigh his words. 'He fights with recklessness, without thought for his own well-being. Like a madman. It's true that he was reckless before, but now he's even more so. It's clear to anyone who knows him that he fights with a longing for death.' He paused as if trying to determine how much to reveal. 'I once saw him walk into a camp of Saxons, alone, and draw his sword. He fought them all with a smile on his face. The men who fight beneath him have tripled in size, because he's amassed a fortune, or so the stories claim. But he doesn't use that fortune for anything except to purchase his boat from Father. He hasn't bought himself a manor so that he can become a jarl. Most men fight bravely to die with valour and glory—Gunnar fights so that he won't have to live.'

She imagined the danger that Vidar described and couldn't control the anger and fear that made her hands shake. Had he even once thought of her and considered making a future together? If he'd settled himself in a manor, even across the sea, he could have come for her. Her father would have put up some resistance, but he wouldn't stop her if Gunnar could prove that he could provide for her. But Gunnar hadn't done that because he didn't want her. He'd said as much before and it was even clearer now. 'Why send him to me? What does Eirik suppose that I can do?'

Vidar shrugged. 'You are the only one with some connection to him, the only one who can bring him back, according to Eirik.'

'That makes no sense. If that were true, he would have come back long ago.' There was a time she might have agreed with Vidar, but Gunnar had proved her wrong.

Vidar shrugged again.

'Go. Eat your fill and then take your rest. You must be beyond exhaustion.' She waved him to the pot on the fire.

* * *

'Where is my mead?' Gunnar grumbled and felt for the ever-present barrel, but the bedding beside him was empty. 'Vidar!' His voice, hoarse from disuse, carried through the hovel where he had been dumped, but no one answered. Opening his eyes to the meagre light that filtered in, he could barely make out the shadowed opening of the alcove where he lay. Uncertain of the distance, he pushed himself up on a shaky elbow and reached out. The opening floated before him, out of reach, but if it were feet or mere inches away he could not fathom.

A sweat breaking out on his brow, he lay back down and closed his eyes to wait for the sudden nausea to subside. Images swam across his mind. If they were from the past days, weeks, or hours, he didn't know. The faces of Magnus and Eirik came to him and it seemed they were saying something important, but he had no memory of their words. He remembered opening his eyes to Vidar replenishing his mead on several occasions, but the world might as well have been black behind him, because he had not seen past the boy's face. He did remember Kadlin, another dream in a long line that featured her. Clearly, she was not a goddess because he was not at Freyja's table. If this was Sessrumnir then the goddess needed lessons on hospitality. A fallen man should not be without his mead.

'Gunnar? Are you awake?'

He opened his eyes to see that his tiny world had righted itself and stopped floating. Vidar stood framed in the narrow arch of the opening. Nay, he finally admitted, he was not a fallen man. He was sure that a fallen man wouldn't feel this much pain. His entire body ached from the roots of his hair to the bottom of his feet. His leg throbbed, with the pain seeming to centre around his left knee and shin. 'Where is the mead? It's not here.'

Vidar's face was grim as he set the humble, wooden bowl that he held, with its single candle, on the stool beside Gunnar's bed. The flame wavered, causing a drop of fat to sizzle where it fell in the bottom of the bowl. Vidar glanced down the passageway, running a hand over the back of his neck before looking back at Gunnar. 'There's no more mead. I can bring you ale or fresh water. I've just brought it back myself from the stream.'

'No more mead?' As long as he could remember there was mead. Every jarl kept a steady supply and it was a practice Eirik had adopted. Even his uncle Einar, who spent months at a time in the countryside waging battle, managed to keep a supply of mead to give out after battles. The men expected it after victory. Of course ale was often given out, as well, but generally to the lesser warriors, the younger ones who had yet to prove themselves.

Gunnar tried to sit up again and noted how his forearms trembled with the effort. How long had he been unconscious? Had he been injured? Aye, his leg throbbed with pain. He searched his memory for what had happened, but his last clear thought was forming the battle plan with Magnus and his men. But it seemed so long ago. Everything else was a fuzzy, disjointed mass of memories that he couldn't piece together. He looked around the alcove and realised he couldn't place it. It didn't seem to belong in Eirik's home.

There had been a boat. He was sure that he had travelled in a boat.

Then he realised something strange in what his brother had said. 'Why are you fetching water?'

While Gunnar still thought of his brother as a boy, the truth was he was old enough now to fight in battle and work on a ship. Fetching water was a task relegated to little boys and servants.

Again, Vidar looked away rather than meet his gaze. Alarmed, Gunnar clenched his teeth to control the nearly overwhelming urge to bash an answer out of the boy. 'What has happened, Vidar? Where have you taken me?'

'You were injured. Eirik thought it best that you recover here.'

Gunnar looked down at himself to ascertain the truth of his brother's words. His entire body felt as though he had been pelted with stones, but his head ached the most. Nay, his leg ached the most. He raised a hand to prod a tenderness on his scalp. Pain lanced through him so sharply that he hissed and closed his eyes to the light dancing in his skull. Slowly opening them, he looked down his body to find other injuries. There were scrapes on his hands, but they seemed older—mostly healed, in fact. The pain had gathered itself together and settled in his left leg, blazing through the appendage like fire. He threw off the blanket with disdain and stared.

The leg was at least twice as big as his right one, but if that was its true size or not he couldn't tell, because it was wrapped in a linen binding. Only when he grabbed the binding to pull it off did he realise that wooden splints had been put in to keep it stable. 'By the gods, what happened to me?'

'Your horse was killed in battle. When it fell, your leg was caught beneath. Do you not remember any of it?'

Gunnar searched his mind for some memory of that, but he shook his head. There was nothing coherent after discussing the plan for battle. 'How long ago?'

'Weeks, Brother.'

The pity in his brother's voice made rage crawl up his throat, but he bit back the bitter words that would have spewed out. It couldn't be that bad. If it had been weeks, then it could have healed by now, regardless of the pain. 'Move, I'm getting up.' He waved his hand to push Vidar aside.

'Nay, you shouldn't get up yet.' Vidar moved to keep him down, but Gunnar swung his right leg over the edge of the bed and grabbed a hold of his brother's tunic to pull himself up.

'I've a need to take a piss and I won't do it here like an invalid.' But the words were barely out of his mouth when his weight moving forward pulled his injured leg off the bed and his foot crashed to the floor. Pain like he'd never felt sliced up his leg and reverberated throughout the limb. His breath caught. A strong wave of nausea rolled over him as darts of light flashed before his eyes. Just as he felt himself falling to the floor, he saw a vision of Kadlin. She stood behind Vidar, eyes wide and arms out as if to help him, but that's all he saw before he fell unconscious.

Chapter Five

When Gunnar next awoke it was to the warm, soothing strokes of a washcloth moving slowly across his chest. A woman hummed and the soft sound would have lulled him back to sleep if his head hadn't begun to ache. But he didn't want to acknowledge the pain, so he kept his eyes closed to enjoy the music a moment longer. It was pleasant, something a woman might sing to her child as she bathed him. He wondered if his own mother had ever sung to him like that as she held him close. He only had vague recollections of the woman: long red hair, dark eyes. She had been a shadow behind his father and Eirik's mother, lurking, or perhaps banished, to stand behind the dais at meals, to serve rather than be served. Then one day she had disappeared altogether. He could remember the child he had been, wandering from one chamber to the next, from one outbuilding to the other, looking for her.

Nay, she had probably never sung to him. He didn't know why the ridiculous question had even come into his head. To ponder those memories only made his head ache more, so he opened his eyes instead of facing them. But he wasn't prepared for the dream in front of him.

Kadlin.

It took a moment for his eyes to focus in the flickering light of the single candle, but he knew it was her. Even with her gorgeous hair subdued in braids and pinned to her scalp, he knew it was her. He'd seen her beloved face in dreams enough to know that he had woken from one dream only to be thrust into the next. Or perhaps he was awake now, as the pain in his head would suggest, but he had finally gone mad and was seeing her when he knew that her presence was impossible. It didn't matter. He'd gone beyond caring if he was mad, especially if it meant that she would be with him.

'I dream of you often, you know.' The timbre of his voice was rough from disuse. He didn't even recognise it; more proof of his unconscious state.

Her blue eyes shot to his, widened in surprise, and just as quickly returned to their study of his hand as she drew the cloth between his fingers. 'That sounds like a sentimental endeavour. Surely too sentimental for a warrior such as you.'

He smiled and waited for her to finish, enjoying the feel of her gentle-but-sure strokes. Though he was becoming aware of the way his entire body thrummed with pain, focusing on that small pleasure helped him to push the discomfort to the back of his mind and he didn't want to say or do anything to make her stop. Eventually she finished and went to place his hand gently back at his side, but, instead of letting her go, he turned his hand and captured hers. It was warm and small in his own. He caressed his thumb across her knuckles and then laced his fingers with hers. It had never been like this before. In all of his dreams, he'd never been able to recreate the heat and spark of excitement that warmed his belly from her touch. He glanced at her long, graceful fingers to make sure that he actually held them. 'A warrior such as me? I fear you're mistaken. Warriors are required to swing their swords in battle and recite poetry over the fire at night.'

She gave a soft laugh as if she were humouring him. He didn't care. He loved her laugh, even if it was given to placate him. She smiled as she said, 'You've never recited a poem in your life, Gunnar.'

'Nay, I suppose I haven't.' He loved the pink of her lips, the vivid blue of her eyes, the stubborn tilt of her chin. All of his other dreams had never got her completely right. There was a challenge in her eyes now that he'd left out before. It wasn't a mistake he'd repeat. She was captivating, truly the most becoming woman he'd ever seen. 'But it's a testament to my sorry ways. I should have said a poem for you every night of my existence. Perhaps that's why you haunt my dreams, a recompense for my wrongs.'

A shadow passed over her eyes, stealing the joy that had sparked there and he was sorry to see it go. When she would have pulled her hand free, he held tight and reached for her other one with his free hand. She pulled that one back, though, so his dropped limply to his side. 'You're angry. I'll accept your anger if it means you can stay with me and not dissipate as you have before.'

'You're not dreaming and I'm no phantom to disappear.'

He smiled. 'You've said that before. It's a trick that rouses me to waking, but I've not fallen for it in a long time.'

'Believe as you wish, but I need my hand to finish bathing you.' Her eyes softened again as she tugged gently on her hand.

He reluctantly let her go, but only because she promised more of that wonderfully soothing caress, and he watched her closely as she fulfilled her promise. But when she had finished his left arm and hand and moved to draw back the blanket, he moved quickly to grip it tight and hold it in place. The abrupt movement caused a sharp pain to lance through his head and left leg. It was so bad that he disgraced himself by gasping aloud.

'Please, you must keep yourself still.' She rose over him and pressed his shoulders to the bed at his back.

'I'll not let you bathe me there like a child,' he panted, when he caught his breath.

'All right, I won't, but you must be calm before you injure yourself further.'

She wasn't a dream! As waves of pain crashed through his body, he realised with unyielding clarity that he was awake and not dreaming at all. He remembered Vidar explaining his injury to him and he had a vague recollection of getting to his feet and falling just as he saw her. None of this was a dream. He had been gravely injured and then Vidar had accompanied him on a journey to…to where? He didn't even know where he was.

'Has Vidar brought me home?' But that didn't seem right. This wasn't his chamber and he knew the chambers and alcoves of Kadlin's home enough to know that he wasn't there. Another thought—an excruciatingly horrible one—pounded through his head: that he had been delivered to Kadlin at her husband's home.

She had turned her head, as if searching for someone to help, but looked back at him after his question. 'Aye, Eirik believed that your recovery would best take place here.' One hand stayed on his chest, but the other stroked his face to calm him. 'We are at Eirik's farm. Do you not remember it?'

He blinked and tried to look past her, but had

trouble pulling his gaze from her face. It seemed so unbelievable that she was with him, after all of their time apart, that he had trouble believing she wouldn't disappear on him if he looked away. Besides, she held him mesmerised, the stroke of her fingers on his cheek like a balm. Then he realised that there was nothing between the flesh of her hand and the skin of his face. He raised a hand to his chin, expecting to feel his beard there, but there was nothing. 'You shaved me, woman?'

'Aye, you were quite disgusting when you came here. I cut your hair, too. You can thank Vidar that it's not shaved, as well. He refused to let me.'

'Then it's true? The battle? My horse?'

She nodded. 'So I'm told. You arrived here the day before yesterday, but already your colour is better. We've tried to get some broth in you, but without much luck. I think if you can begin to eat, you could make a swift recovery.'

She was being evasive. He could plainly see the false way her eyes lit up with the hollow optimism. Before she could think to stop him, he tore the blanket back from his legs, uncaring that he was nude beneath it. He could only see the binding wrapped around his left leg. When he rolled his foot to the side, a shard of pain sliced through it.

'How bad is it?' he asked with the perfunctory tones of a commander, as if he were talking about the injury of one of his men. There was a part of him that couldn't accept that the injury was his and he couldn't even begin to contemplate what it meant for his future.

When she hesitated, his gaze jumped back to hers. 'Tell me, Kadlin.'

'Harald says that it is broken.' She moved slowly and held her hand above an area of his shin. As if anticipating her touch and the pain it would bring, it began to throb. But she held her hand aloft. 'Here. Though only a fracture, not a clean break. It is the knee that sustained the most damage. Magnus told Eirik that the limb was a bit twisted under the horse and pulled it out of place. I don't know if there was a break. It was wrapped so tight and seemed to be so painful when we tried to unbind it that we can't examine it. Also, you have a few broken ribs.'

He watched her soft, full lips form each word, but even that wasn't enough to keep the despair at bay. He'd never walk again. No one had to tell him that. One look at the swollen appendage and he could plainly see it for himself. The useless limb was damaged beyond repair. They should have just cut it from his body so he wouldn't have to look at it. He flopped back down, grimacing from the shard of lightning that lanced through his torso, and closed his eyes as he tried to imagine what a useless leg would mean. He'd never command a ship again; he'd never be able to stand with the rocking of the vessel. That would hardly matter, though, none of his men would follow a lame master. None of them. He'd be seen as unfit to lead. He *would* be unfit to lead.

The worst of it was that Kadlin would see him like this. He was lamed and deformed and she would witness it all. There would be no peace in believing that she would never know of his weakness. There was no hope that she would only hear of his good and heroic deeds and imagine him as the warrior that she had known. His weakness, once seen, couldn't be unseen by her eyes. It was why they were lit with a false light; she was trying to hide her disgust. He couldn't blame her for it.

'There is no recovery for me. I'll be broken like

Harald. Unfit to wield a sword.' *Unfit to call my-self a man.* Now Kadlin—the one person who had always refused to see the bad in him—would be forced to see how useless and unworthy of her he really was. Perhaps being sent to her was his one last punishment. He'd get to watch any tenderness she felt towards him slowly leave her eyes to be replaced with pity. He refused to submit to that.

'Leave me.'

She rose to her full height, but hesitated to go. 'I'll bring you some food. You need it to recover.'

He shook his head and then grimaced from the pain. 'Send it with Vidar, if he's still here.'

'Mama!' Her son toddled into the house, a smooth river rock held out in his small, chubby hand. 'Treasure!'

Kadlin scooped him up and exclaimed over the treasure he had found. 'It's beautiful. We can add it to the collection.' She set him down so he could go put it in the basket holding the other rocks he had found and deemed suitable for his collection. She smiled as he gave the alcove a quick glance and a wide berth as he went past it. She'd added a heavy blanket as a curtain as soon as Gunnar had been settled inside, so the child had only heard the strange noises coming from it. It was no wonder he was frightened.

'Thank you, Ingrid.' She turned and smiled at Harald's daughter who had followed her son inside. 'Could I get you something to eat?'

'No, thank you, ma'am. I need to be getting home.' With a nod, the girl left.

'Come, Avalt, let me feed you.'

The boy was too busy admiring his collection to pay her any attention, until Vidar emerged from the alcove. He stopped playing and looked up, waiting until Vidar met his gaze before running to his mother. She laughed softly and scooped him up, cuddling him close as he intently watched Vidar's approach. He'd been excited to have a man in the house and had generally welcomed Vidar with the enthusiasm of a young child fascinated with someone new. But the fact that he had emerged from the mysterious alcove had set the toddler on edge.

'Can we not give him more of the laced mead?' Vidar scowled as he set the empty bowl on the hearth. 'He's as irritable as a bear.'

Kadlin stifled a sigh of relief that Gunnar had drunk it all. She'd been worried that he would deny himself nourishment or that his stomach would rebel against the contents, since he'd apparently had nothing in weeks except for the mead concoction.

When she didn't answer immediately, Vidar brushed past her with an accusatory look. 'The Saxon witch sent plenty, enough to last for many more weeks. His leg pains him and his head is unbearable.'

'Nay, he's had enough. His head wound has healed. I believe it pains him now only because his body has grown to crave the mead. Once he's gone without it a few days, that will improve. Besides, did you see him?' Though his shoulders were still broad, Gunnar had lost the heft that came from fighting and his ribs shone through his skin. Even his face showed how gaunt he was; his cheeks had hollowed a bit and dark circles surrounded his eyes. 'He's wasting away. He won't eat unless we wean him from the mead and he needs the nourishment more than he needs the relief from the pain.' Though the groans from his pain still echoed in her ears and they tore at her. As much as she had tried to harden her heart against him in the years since his abandonment, she couldn't bear the image of him in pain.

'It's cruel. He needs relief from his pain. Nourishment or not, he'll never walk again. He'll never carry a sword or stand a ship. Let him have his solace from the pain. What does the rest of it matter?' It appeared that he had more to say, but he stopped when she rounded on him.

'What does it matter? That is your brother lying in there. Are you saying that his life isn't worth anything without that leg to support him? Are you saying that we should leave him to his mindless solace instead of trying to heal him?'

'You heard Harald just as I did. Gunnar will not use that leg again. You know him as well as I do, or even better, I'd wager.' He indicated the baby in her arms with his dark, flaming hair so like his father's.

Kadlin stifled a gasp of surprise. She'd known that her son resembled his father, but she hadn't realised exactly how much until she had seen Gunnar again. Apparently, the resemblance was visible to those who had a reason to suspect.

Vidar had the presence of mind to seem chastised and lowered his tone. 'You know that he wouldn't want to live with that leg.'

She couldn't deny the truth of those words. The despair Gunnar had felt upon seeing the injury was imprinted on her mind for ever. He would think it was a weakness, an unbearable flaw that wasn't to be overcome. 'That choice isn't his to make. Eirik sent him to my care, so I will see that he recovers. I hope to make him see that his life can still be good.'

Vidar grunted and walked to the front door, but stopped to turn to her. 'You haven't a chance, but I wish you luck. I'm going to see if Ingrid needs an escort home.' He grinned and walked out.

'Vidar!' She waited until he'd popped his head back in before lowering her voice. 'Please don't tell anyone your suspicions.' It was widely assumed that her son's father was her late husband. No one except her parents knew that it was Gunnar.

Vidar looked towards Avalt and nodded. 'I won't say a word.' Then he left, running to catch up to Ingrid.

Kadlin hugged her child tighter and buried her face in his curls. Vidar was right. She knew in her bones that his words weren't just those of a young warrior unable to imagine life with an injury like Gunnar's. His feelings were those shared by almost every man that she knew. An injury that left one lame was an injury that should result in death. Was she selfish to want Gunnar's recovery even if he himself didn't? She didn't know, but she did know that it wasn't in her power to grant him that alternative. He *would* recover. Despite her often confused and unfortunate feelings for him, she held no illusions about a future with him. She would heal him because the boy she had known deserved a second chance at life and Avalt deserved a chance to know his real father. She only needed to figure out if his father deserved him.

Chapter Six

Gunnar stayed awake the entire day. It was his first day of full consciousness and he despised it. His entire body throbbed in pain. He alternated between cursing every living Saxon male and vowing to get revenge, to lamenting the fact that the bloody horse hadn't killed him. Then he laughed at the thought. It wasn't a Saxon that had bested him at all, but his own horse. There were no tales about a noble warrior falling in battle because of his horse. And there would be no tales because it was ludicrous and pathetic. There was absolutely nothing to celebrate about it.

He was sure that his father had heard the details by now and he imagined the man laughing at the fact that his bastard couldn't even die in battle properly. It had been his one goal for Gunnar. All of his training, his entire life had been geared towards becoming a warrior. While Eirik had also been trained for battle, their father had made sure that the elder brother was trained in diplomacy and commerce—skills necessary for a jarl. But Gunnar was never meant for that life. He was meant to fight and die by the sword. And his death was meant to bring glory and pride to his father. Try as he might, Gunnar couldn't summon the energy to lament his father's loss.

Eirik's farm wasn't so far from his father's hall at a full day's ride. He wondered if his father might trouble himself to make the trip just to finish him off. But he couldn't stop the smile that came to his face when he imagined Kadlin meeting the man at the door. She wouldn't allow that to happen. And if it came down to a battle of wills between her and his father, Gunnar would bet every last piece of gold he owned that she would win.

The woman was magnificent. But thoughts of her brought with them an ache so intense that he tried to close off his mind to them. Except there was nothing to do but lie there and listen to the sounds of life going on in the house around him. Even if he wanted no part of it. There was no life for him and he didn't want it taunting him. He tried his best to close those sounds out, but occasionally they would reach his ears anyway. A chuckle he recognised as Vidar's or the low, soft voice he knew to be Kadlin's. That was the one sound he tried to eliminate above all others. He'd imagined her voice many times over the years, had made up entire conversations with her in his head, but now the sweet tones only made the pain in his heart unbearable. That voice and its soft words belonged to her husband now.

The mere thought of the man he barely remembered was enough to make Gunnar gnash his teeth against the pain that welled within him. It wasn't the pain of someone else loving her—he couldn't fault anyone for that—but it was that she loved someone else. Only love would have prompted her to marry. She had said as much herself when she had explained why she had refused Eirik. He wanted to understand that. Hoped that in understanding he could overcome his urge to kill the son of a bitch who had married her, but it was useless. The fact that she loved someone else, had given herself to him with the same sweetness she had given herself to Gunnar, was like an open wound festering inside him.

Now he was nothing but a burden to her, unceremoniously dumped at her door like an unwanted vagrant. He'd seen the wariness in her eyes, the perfunctory look on her face as she'd seen to his care. He was a burden she hadn't sought out or asked for. What woman would want to devote her time to caring for someone as grievously injured as himself? There was no real recovery for him, no real life to go back to. He wasn't a warrior, or even a man any more. He was nothing.

A child squealed as someone chased it across the room. Gunnar could hear its footfalls as it ran across the wooden floor, followed by heavier ones. Nay, perhaps that was the worst sound of all. Worse than Kadlin and her beloved voice. The child was a reminder of all that he had lost. His stolen childhood; the secret life with Kadlin that he'd only allowed himself to dream of on the coldest nights; their children around them in their hall as a fire blazed in the hearth and he told them stories from his battles. His eyes shot open when the scene became too vivid and painful. He'd almost forgotten those scenes.

The child squealed again and the girl—Ingrid, he'd heard her called—spoke to it and carried it outside. He wished she would keep her child at home, but perhaps she lived with Kadlin. With a gasp of pain, he swung his legs over the side of the bench and wobbled as nausea and dizziness warred for dominance within him. In the end, he was able to overcome both and braced his right foot on the ground to support his good leg as he leaned forward to grasp for the bucket he'd been reduced to using to relieve himself. When he was finished, he cast a disdainful glance at the large stick that had been left for his use. In his mind, he saw Harald wobbling around using a similar crutch for balance and recoiled at the thought of using it himself. But another need won out and made him grab it to hoist himself to his feet.

It was the need to flee. He wouldn't stay there with her. This wasn't his life. He wouldn't be a burden and he wouldn't submit himself to the life of the lame. He'd leave to find some hovel to die in.

But the moment he tried to push himself to his feet, the pain in the lame knee and shin be-came so intense that he fell to the bench and would have fallen to the floor if he hadn't braced the stick against the wall so that it caught his weight. He managed to bite back the howl of pain, smothering it to a grunt, but he couldn't stop the black spots that swam before his vision. A sweat had broken out on his brow as he fell back on the bench and his breath came in great, heaving gulps, causing sharp pain to stab into his ribs like a knife's blade. He'd try another day and keep trying until he could go.

'Why are you tormenting me?' Gunnar closed his eyes to the sight of Kadlin sitting at his bedside bearing food.

'Is it torment to bring you nourishment?' she asked, stiffening her spine against the cut of his words.

'Aye.' His voice was a raspy whisper.

It made the skin of her neck tingle in a way that might have been pleasant if she allowed herself to acknowledge such feelings for him. Those feelings had last sneaked in that morning just two days ago, when he had awakened to her bathing him. His tender gaze and words for her, before he'd realised his injury, had been wonderful.

For one brilliant moment, it had been like the years apart had never happened. That, perhaps, they had shared those years together and she was awakening him as she might if she had been his wife. Even knowing his pain, his roughened voice and nude body had awakened her own so that the urge to climb into bed and hold him had been almost too great to resist with the clarity of his gaze on her.

But just for a moment.

When she didn't immediately reply, he cracked an eyelid and glared from her to the platter of meat and broth in her hands and then back to her face. 'I don't want it. I have all I need right here.'

Her eyes widened at the sight of the laced mead tucked under his arm. Gunnar had requested all of his meals through Vidar and she had left the boy to the task, thinking to not force her presence on Gunnar and upset him while he was recovering. Vidar had always returned with empty bowls and platters, so she had assumed Gunnar's appetite had returned and all was going well. It wasn't a mistake that she'd repeat.

'That little worm!' Slamming the platter of food down on to the small table, she reached over

Gunnar, intent on grabbing the cask of mead. But he held tight and refused to relinquish it. They struggled for a moment, but his grasp on it was remarkably strong for someone so weak.

'Nay, I assure you, he's quite large. You should remember,' he mocked when she glared at him.

Both hands on the cask, her brow furrowed to see such a teasing grin curving his attractive mouth, his amber eyes half-lidded and lazy with the laced mead. His gaze held hers briefly, but then moved to where her torso was positioned across his hips, her breasts pressed to his groin. He nodded towards that part of his body when he spoke. 'I'm heartbroken you've forgotten his size, but if you allow me a few weeks more to recover myself, I'll be happy to refresh your memory.'

This was the Gunnar she remembered. Not the boy who would seek out her bed at night when he needed to escape his own home, but the man that boy had become. The one who was mocking and arrogant, and who used those talents to keep others at bay. The one who would stare at her from across the hall with eyes so deep and wrenching that they took her breath away, but in the next moment could wound her deeply by ignoring her for the rest of the evening. The one who kept himself aloof, just as he was trying to do now by making her believe their one night together could be relegated to a few words of banter.

Or perhaps he really felt that way. Perhaps she had just been another woman to him. The thought caused a knot to swell in her throat and it made her unreasonably angry, because she had dealt with her feelings for him. She had wrestled with them and caged them as any intelligent person would handle such wild things bent on doing nothing but harm.

She gave a harsh tug that made a grimace of pain cross his face when she took possession of the cask. She might have regretted the roughness had the pain not washed away the facade so that she saw a glimpse of the true Gunnar in his face. The one with the soulful eyes that spoke of heartbreaking sadness.

Regaining her footing, she rose to her full height and looked down at him. 'This isn't good for you, Gunnar. It makes you sleep and not eat. Your body can't be strong without food.'

'Leave me,' he grumbled and shifted on the bench, trying to find comfort.

Kadlin had expected his coldness, but expecting it didn't make it hurt any less. Though she told herself that it's what she preferred. It revealed his true intentions towards her and wasn't something he could cover up with his teasing words. She had thought their years apart had hardened her to him. His abandonment should have made her stop longing for him. It was easy to pretend that she had succeeded when he was off fighting in a world so vastly different from her own and she believed that he cared nothing for her. But seeing him now…she admitted that she was a failure and that nothing had changed for her. She despised his nature and his ability to affect her, but she loved him all the same. It was a weakness of her character that she could not overcome, but that didn't mean she had to give in to it. She could ignore her love. It was the only way to get through this.

Tossing the cask out of the alcove, she picked up the food and resumed her seat. But he only shook his head, refusing to eat.

'Why do you persist in prolonging this…this…'

he raised his hands to indicate their space in the alcove 'this recovery, this sham of an existence? That is the torment. My head aches constantly and my body isn't mine any more. I don't want this. I want my mead and to be left in peace.'

'Your head injury has healed. It's the longing for the mead that makes it ache now.'

'I don't care what makes it ache now, I only want it to stop.'

'I believe it will stop after you go a few days without the mead.'

'Drinking the mead makes it stop.' He stared at her with those heavy-lidded eyes that said he had already had too much of the stuff.

'To what end, Gunnar? Will you drink until death claims you? Do you suppose you'll find a place at Odin's table now if you expire from imbibing too much of your laced mead? What do you suppose waits for you now?'

'Nothing. Oblivion. It doesn't matter what happens to me. At least I won't be here.' He scowled and settled back against the straw pillows that propped him up, his eyes staring straight ahead.

'You're a bitter man, Gunnar,' she stated softly.

'I've lost everything, Kadlin.'

'What about those who might care for you?'

He laughed, a deep hollow sound that she could go the rest of her life without ever hearing again. 'Aye, and what of those people? Who might they be? Eirik, who sent me here half-dead... He's already said his piece. Vidar? The boy will recover quickly enough when he is given my treasure. Or do you mean Father? Do you think he'll lament the loss of a bastard he's never wanted? Especially one who has shamed him by getting injured instead of dying like a proper warrior should?' But then his eyes flicked to her briefly before looking forward again. 'Or do you mean yourself, Kadlin? Will you shed a tear for me when I die?'

His words left a heavy silence in their wake and the world seemed to stop to await her answer. How could he treat the love she had offered him so coldly? It was as if it had meant nothing to him. And what of Avalt? What about their child who was so much like his father? Shouldn't he know his father? But Gunnar didn't know about him yet and she felt strangely resistant to talk about him before she knew Gunnar's feelings. She couldn't bear it if Gunnar showed the same cold uninterest in their child as he showed her. Besides, he was hardly in the right frame of mind for such a discussion.

Instead of saying any of those things, she kept a tight rein on her emotions and offered truthfully, 'I don't want you to die, Gunnar.'

Then he looked at her with eyes she hardly recognised. They were so cold that she shivered. 'Go to your husband.'

Could a heart that held any love for her be able to conjure such ice? It didn't seem likely. She sat in stunned silence, surprised that he knew she had married and surprised that it filled him with such venom. There must have been talk among the men and that was how he'd found out. Surely he didn't expect that she would *not* have got married, not with the way he had left her that night. How could he fault her for that?

Incredulous, she stared at him, unable to move or think past his hateful words. Finally, she muttered the only thing that would come out coherently. 'You didn't want me.'

How horrible that day had been for her. She normally didn't think about the day of her marriage, because it had felt so wrong. The man had been wrong. He hadn't been Gunnar.

'Leave me and send Vidar with more mead.'

Shaking herself out of her morose thoughts, she straightened her spine and stood. 'Nay, no more mead. That's the last you'll get and I'll have Vidar's head for bringing it to you. I'm dumping it all.'

'Do not!'

The words were so strong and forceful that she was momentarily taken aback, but not deterred in her determination. 'Eirik entrusted your care to me, not Vidar. No more mead.' Turning on her heel, she left the alcove.

Gunnar called for her, but she ignored him and grabbed the cask, intent on dumping its contents outside before she went to find Vidar to box his ears.

Chapter Seven

A fortnight passed in slow agony for Gunnar. He was left to his bench in the alcove with nothing to do but listen to the sounds of the house around him. His body had begun to return to a normal pattern of sleep, so there wasn't even that welcome oblivion to take him away from it. Vidar had confirmed that Kadlin had made true on her promise to destroy the laced mead and she had gone a step further and even refused to send him ale.

At least the dreadful headache had begun to fade in the past days. He suspected that she had been right in that the mead had caused it, but going without it made him too aware of the world around him, too conscious of the fact that there was nothing for him in this life. He couldn't imagine Niflheim, a place that he was sure to see one day now that he would never battle again and earn a place at Odin's table, would be as awful.

The internment was all the more brutal because Kadlin was all around him: her voice, her smell, even the food sent to him had been prepared by her hand. It was the worst torment to be so near to her and not call her his, to not be able to reach out and touch her as he wanted. To know that she didn't want him. His only peace of mind was that her husband was still fighting and not there to claim her himself.

He couldn't even find solace in the only indulgence he'd allowed himself when he'd been away from her. Before, his dreams of her had been an escape to a place far better than his existence. While out of reach and unattainable, they had been a comfort. Now they were torture. They came every night that he closed his eyes; a vivid imagery of their night together, made all the more intense because he could match them with her scent, voice and even the way it felt to touch her. She was everywhere.

'Gunnar?' her voice was soft and hesitant, but she was smiling at him. A shy smile that he had never seen from her before. It tugged at some-

thing buried deep within him and made a rush of heat flare in his groin. Her hair lay around her in a glorious cloud of gold and silver, recently released from the braids by his own hands.

Caught by a subtle movement, his gaze fastened on her fingers, nimbly untying the nightdress that already rode low over the curves of her creamy shoulders. His mouth went dry as he watched her fingers work, waiting for that glorious moment when she would be revealed to him. His patience was rewarded when she slowly tugged the linen down, revealing her perfect breasts, tipped with pale, pink nipples. They begged for his mouth, but he knew if he touched her that he would lose control and she deserved so much more than that.

Instead, he wadded the fabric in his fists and pulled it down, revealing her body to him in slow degrees so that he could properly take in her perfection. The tautness of her belly, the swell of her hips, the pale hair at the juncture of her thighs, her long legs and shapely calves, the high arches of her feet. He placed a kiss on each one, causing her to giggle before he moved upwards, his lips brushing the silken skin of her legs. Try as he might, he couldn't tear his gaze from the sweet mound between her thighs. Just inches away, he raised up enough to urge in a whisper, 'Spread your legs for me.'

There was a sharp intake of breath, but she smiled a shy, teasing grin when she obeyed. Then it was his turn to catch his breath, because she was beautiful. His gaze moved down past the blonde curls to the pink lips that parted, revealing her sex, swollen and slick for him. When the sweet smell of her arousal met his nostrils, he couldn't help but touch her, wanting to taste her on his tongue. He traced around the engorged bud and then down to dip his fingertip into her wet heat. She was so tight and already so wet and ready for his possession that a surge of blood went to his groin, causing his erection to swell even more, almost painful in the confines of his trousers.

Gunnar awoke with a start and the dream disintegrated, but it stayed vivid in his mind because it wasn't just a dream. It was a memory from the night he'd spent with her. The jerk made pain shoot up his leg and brought back the reality of his surroundings with startling clarity. But there was something more this time, a discomfort that, combined with the pain of his wounds, would drive him to madness. His hand went to his erection, strong and throbbing beneath the blanket.

Throwing back the cover, he stared at the offending appendage through the firelight that snaked in around the edges of the curtain and then cursed as he fell back against the pillows. Not this, too! He'd half-entertained the notion that his wounds had unmanned him in all ways. He was crippled. What woman would want him now? Kadlin wouldn't and she was the only one who mattered to him. Now he was to be forced to be close to her with this.

He couldn't do it. It was bad enough lying there day after day, existing so close to her, but he couldn't do this. He couldn't lie there with the needs of a man, smelling her, having her so close, but so out of his reach. It was beyond what anyone could ask of him. He wouldn't—*couldn't*—do it.

Tossing the blanket to the floor, he pushed himself up, pleased that his arms were regaining their strength. There was less pain in his ribs now, so the movement was getting easier, though it still caused some discomfort in his middle. Swinging his right leg off the side of the bench, he grabbed Harald's hated stick to pull himself up. The lame leg was still wrapped tight and refused to give with the wood bound around it, so he grabbed it and pulled it until it joined his right. But instead of bending, it laid in a rigid, useless line from the bench to the floor. Pain shot through his shin to his knee and he grimaced, gritting his teeth against it, but he managed to not make a sound. At least there was no dizziness or nausea now.

When the waves of pain receded, he opened his eyes and listened to the sounds of the house. He'd drifted off to sleep with the murmuring of voices around the fire, but they must have gone to bed because all was quiet except for the occasional crackle of the fire and the gentle rain outside.

The day before, he had demanded a pair of trousers and Vidar had provided him with a pair of his. They had been clean and fresh-smelling, making him wonder if Kadlin had washed them herself or relegated the duty to the girl, Ingrid. But when the domestic image of Kadlin performing the intimacy had come to mind, he'd banished it instantly and brutally tore the bottom half of the left leg away. Keeping his jaw clenched, he worked them gingerly over his injured leg before putting his right leg in. Happy to see that the pain and strain of dressing had taken care of his erection, he awkwardly pulled them up his hips. But the muscles of his thighs strained the fabric and tore the seam. They weren't an ideal fit, but they would have to do. Fastening them awkwardly, he reached for the simple linen shirt Vidar had left him and shrugged it on over his head before hefting himself to his feet with the stick.

By no means did he feel able to walk any great distance, but he knew Eirik's farm well because they had played there often as boys, so he knew how far the forest was across the field. He would go there to hide. With luck no one would find him and then he'd travel on to a washout he knew of in a dried-up stream bed. It was hidden behind tree roots and brush, or it had been the last time he'd seen it. It wasn't very far from the house, but far enough that he could disappear into it and not be found. He could hide there until…well, just until. Anything to be away from her.

He'd walked a bit every day since Kadlin had taken the mead away. Hidden in the sanctuary of his curtained alcove, pacing back and forth and building up strength. The thought made him smile because his strength was that of a boy. Perhaps endurance would be a better choice. He'd built up his endurance, because every wobbly step had caused him pain and disappointment. If not for the cursed sapling, he would not have even made it one turn of the alcove. But because he had it for support, he'd been able to make a few turns, increasing each day until he felt he could take enough steps to make it to the forest.

Kadlin had not come to see him since that last time when he had told her to go to her husband. Guilt ate at him for saying it, for causing the pain that had filled her eyes just after he had spoken those words. None of this was her fault and he was a true bastard to make her feel pain. She was simply trying to do something that only she would do—care for him. It had been his hope that keeping distance between them would make the inevitable easier on her.

Ha! That was a lie. He was selfish and simply couldn't stand to be in her presence if he couldn't claim her. That was the only truth in his gesture and it hadn't changed in all the years he had known her. Being in her company and not being able to have her was too heart-wrenching for him to bear. It always had been.

Setting the crutch beneath his arm, he limped across the narrow space to the curtain and peeked out. It was the dead of night and quiet. A low fire flickered in the hearth, but the front room appeared to be empty, just as he'd suspected. Already, sweat beaded his brow, but he gritted his teeth and stared at the front door, determined to make it outside without waking anyone. Taking a deep breath, he reached back for the light blanket and balanced awkwardly against the wall as he brought it around his shoulders and tied the ends under his chin.

Putting the crutch under his arm again, he pushed the curtain back and made his way into the room, not bothering to stop for food or water. He'd be unable to carry them and it didn't matter if he had them to sustain him, anyway. Once he reached the door, he turned briefly to look down the short passageway. She must sleep in one of the small chambers there. If he could have made the walk without risking discovery, he would have gone to see her again. To sear her face into his memory, to steal that one last vision of her beauty for his own selfish enjoyment, but he wouldn't risk the chance of discovery. Her goodness would demand that he stay and he wouldn't hurt her again by refusing. It was best that he simply disappear.

He un-notched the latch and gently pushed the door open. Once he was assured that he had made no sound, he made his way out through the opening. It wasn't an easy task with the sapling and his unbending left leg, but he managed to make it and bring the door closed behind him. He paused, then, to rest briefly against the door, taking a few deep breaths. His limbs were already beginning to shake from the exertion and beads of sweat rolled down his back.

From the light of the three-quarter moon, he could see that the treeline loomed in the distance. It seemed impossible. But there was no other choice; he couldn't continue to be so near to her. If he could just make it to the trees, he could rest for an hour or so before moving on. Hanging his head for a moment to gather his strength, he secured the stick under his arm and moved forward. Each step was jarring, painful and awkwardly pathetic, but he didn't stop to think about it. He simply kept moving forward until he had put some distance between him and the house.

Sweat beaded with the rain and rolled down his face. He moved in short, measured steps because the sod was uneven and soggy, so he had to carefully scan the ground before finding a stable footing for the crutch to move forward. His arm ached from the exertion and he found himself wondering how Harald managed so well on his own crutch. His leg felt like it was simultaneously on fire while being stabbed with needles. He cursed with each painfully slow step.

About halfway to the forest, he stopped to rest when he heard a sound that was suspiciously like that of wood knocking on wood. His first thought was that it was the door, but when he glanced back over his shoulder he didn't see anything, although the angle of the moonlight along with the wooden overhang at the front door created a shadow. He paused long enough to watch for movement, but when he didn't see anything he looked towards the trees again and stepped forward. With his momentum broken, the first step was particularly jarring, causing pain to explode throughout his entire injured leg. He gasped and stumbled, forgetting to watch where the stick was placed, so the end disappeared into a muddy hole which knocked him off balance.

As he fell to the ground, he couldn't contain the groan of pain that escaped him. His leg was on fire. Spots danced before his eyes and his fingers clenched in the mud as he tried to combat the simultaneous waves of pain and nausea that had overcome him. They caused a roaring in his ears that blocked out all sound until he heard her calling his name. At first he thought he'd only imagined it, but then it came again followed by the sounds of her feet slapping against the wet ground as she ran towards him.

'Nay!' he yelled and pushed himself up on to his one good knee. He scrambled for the crutch, but finding the useless thing broken in two, he set his sights on the edge of the forest and began to claw his way there, half crawling with his good leg, half pulling with his meagre upper body strength. Every inch of progress made his entire body vibrate with pain, but he couldn't stop. He had to get away.

'Gunnar!' She had come close enough to stand above him.

'Go away! Go home!' he ordered and didn't dare stop to look up at her.

'What are you doing?' When he didn't answer, she rushed to him and put her hand on his shoulder. 'Gunnar?'

He jerked away, jarring his leg again, tightening his jaw against the excruciating pain. He stopped then and held up his hand to warn her off.

'Gunnar, you're going to hurt yourself. Let me help you.' The pity in her face was exactly what he couldn't bear to see from her.

'Just go, Kadlin. I don't want help. I want to be left alone.' But he fell heavily to the ground, his entire body betraying him as his strength seemed to seep out from his fingers and disappear into the mud. The rain poured down around him, soaking him through, and he didn't care. Perhaps it would wash him away. The only person he had ever cared about was standing above him, watching him fall apart, seeing all of his weakness exposed. He slammed his hand down against the wet earth, wanting it to open up and swallow him whole.

But she wouldn't leave. She stood there, staring down at him. There were so many reasons that he didn't deserve this woman. He didn't dare count them all. By the gods, couldn't the woman ever do what he wanted? Then he remembered his dream when she had done exactly what he'd wanted, how she had so sweetly parted her legs for him and groaned when his manhood twitched to life. This was madness. His body was alive with anguish and he still wanted her!

The knowledge filled him with such rage at the uselessness of his body that it gave him new strength. When she finally knelt down at his side to run a gentle hand down his back, he lost control. With a cry of rage that the rain didn't quite succeed in drowning out, he leapt for her, knocking her on to her back and ignoring the pain in his body to move on top of her and pin her beneath him.

'Why can't you leave me alone?' His eyes were furious as they bored into her.

'I'm trying to help you,' she snapped.

'I don't want your help. Can't you see that?'

'What I see is a warrior who would rather submit to his wounds than to fight them. A warrior who would choose death over life, even if it means that death isn't a glorious one in battle.'

A wave of fury came over him; she didn't know what it was like to be injured so badly that the only life he had known was taken from him. What was left for him now but the life of an invalid? But then almost as quickly as the thoughts crossed his mind, they left him in a rush and his forehead dropped to rest against her shoulder. It wasn't her fault that this had happened. She didn't deserve his anger. She was only helping him. Bastard that he was, he might have deserved his injury, but she certainly didn't deserve the burden of his care. 'This isn't my life, Kadlin. I *was* supposed to die. It was all supposed to be over so that this pain could finally stop.'

She stiffened beneath him and he realised that his weight might be hurting her, but he was too bloody weak to push himself off her just then. 'So that *what* pain can finally stop?'

Nay, that was one question he could not answer. His body was already riddled with pain; he couldn't expose his heart to her, as well. It already ached so badly that each breath was a challenge. The pain of leaving her that night years ago had threatened to end him—to admit to that pain after she'd chosen someone else would certainly finish the task. It was why he needed to be away from her.

When he raised his head to tell her just that, he couldn't form the words. She stared up at him with those startling blue eyes that always seemed to see right through him, as if she and she alone could see who he wanted to be. Except that no matter how he tried, he always failed her somehow and never quite became that man. A stray shaft of moonlight caught the pale locks of her hair and turned them that ethereal silver that he loved so much, and he realised that he had somehow lost the strand that he always carried with him. It was fitting, he supposed. He wasn't ever meant to have any part of her.

His gaze fell to her perfect lips, parted as she awaited his answer. He wanted to kiss them, even with pain vibrating throughout his entire body, he wanted to taste her one more time, but he knew that if he did he'd lose everything to her again. 'It doesn't matter. Nothing matters.'

Chapter Eight

Before Kadlin could stop herself, she pushed hard with both hands and flipped him on to his back on the wet ground. If she wasn't so angry, she would have stopped to think of how badly the movement could injure him, but she was too furious to care.

'How can you say that to me? How can you be so cruel?'

Stunned, he stared up at her. 'I'm not cruel, Kadlin. Not to you. Not now.' And his hand moved to touch her cheek, but she jerked away.

'But to suggest that your pain doesn't matter to me? That it doesn't cause me pain, as well? Do you not know me, Gunnar? Do you not remember anything about our days together?'

'I do know you and I know well that I cause you more pain than any other. It's why I should go.'

Without bothering to reply, she pushed away from him and rose to her feet, angrily shaking the mud free from her nightdress. Not that it mattered; she was covered with it and the rain had soaked her through to the bone. For one heart-stopping moment, she had believed that the pain he spoke of was the pain of losing her, of being away from her. Fool that she was, she believed that he might harbour some regret for the way things had ended with them; that he might miss her and wonder what would have happened if he had returned to marry her. But then he showed her again how her feelings meant so little to him.

When would she learn that he wasn't good for her? Her father had tried to tell her that, but she hadn't understood. Gunnar himself had wounded her badly when he left, but apparently even that hadn't been enough to sever her feelings for him. She should let him leave if that's what he wanted and scrub him from her heart for ever.

Turning on her heel, she began to walk towards the small sod house, her fists clenched at her sides. But her fury hadn't expended itself yet, so she turned back to leave him with a few more words. 'Perhaps the injury wasn't supposed to happen to you, but it did. It happened and there is nothing you can do about it now. You can but fight to get better. There is no other choice.'

'Nay.' The surprise had left his strikingly handsome features a cold mask. The rain had turned his hair a deep, dark red and his beard was growing back so raindrops glistened in the stubble. His eyes were golden but still fierce, appearing to reflect the moonlight as he stared up at her. Once, she would have said that fierceness was one of the reasons she loved him, but she didn't love him any more. *She didn't.* 'There is no fight, only acceptance that I'm lame and have no place here, except as a burden.'

Just that fast, her own anger receded. It still existed. There was no way she could vanquish her anger that she had loved him and he had abandoned her. That anger would probably always exist, but now wasn't the time to vent it. Not now when he was in such anguish. 'Is that your worry, that you're a burden to me?'

'I won't be a burden to you, Kadlin. It was Eirik's choice to send me back, but it was unfair of him.'

She took a few steps towards him and his

eyes followed her as she knelt beside him again. 'Be assured, Gunnar, if I didn't want you here I wouldn't have allowed them to bring you in from that cart. You need somewhere to rest and recover, and I could never deny you that. No matter what you've done to me.'

He flinched from her words. When he dropped his gaze, it lingered briefly at the neckline of her nightdress, but he looked away towards the forest before she could read his expression. There was something more than his not wanting to be a burden, but she wasn't sure what it was. She waited patiently until he finally shook his head.

'I cannot.'

If he had taken a knife to her heart, his rejection couldn't have hurt any worse. 'Then do as you wish, but don't fool yourself into thinking that you do it for me. You do it only for yourself. Goodbye, Gunnar.' He didn't want her or anything to do with her. His bitter words after their tender night had told her as much, but she had to keep giving him opportunities to reject her.

'Kadlin.'

She ignored him and kept walking. She wouldn't do it any more. She was finished. If he wanted to leave her again, then she couldn't stop him.

'Wait, Kadlin!'

But she stayed strong and kept walking. If he wanted her help, he wouldn't have pushed her away so many times.

'By the gods, woman, stop and face me!'

It was the challenge mixed with the command that brought her up short. It was a glimpse of the old Gunnar, the one filled with fire and longing. The Gunnar she had given herself to. Fighting past the ache in her throat that warned of tears, she slowly turned and saw that he had raised himself up on his good knee. His injured leg stuck out awkwardly in front of him. Lines of pain held his mouth firm, but his eyes held fast to hers.

'I cannot stay and continue along as we have been. Despite my leg, I won't be an invalid. I'll take a chamber of my own and you'll leave my meals at the door. There will not be—' He broke off and looked away briefly before meeting her gaze again with renewed determination firming his jaw. 'There *cannot* be any other contact between us.'

'You would make us strangers?'

'I will reward you for your assistance once I'm well again.'

A reward, as if she was nothing to him but some well-meaning acquaintance who might not have bothered otherwise. A reward, as if he could buy himself away from what lingered between them. She swallowed repeatedly past the lump in her throat that threatened to choke her. He was already looking at her with the eyes of a passing acquaintance, relegating himself to someone she barely knew. She was wrong to think that he couldn't hurt her any worse than he already had. Now she realised that if he stayed, he could completely destroy her. 'I don't want your reward.' She made her voice as cold as she possibly could.

He stared at her, stubborn and wilful, but he must have seen something in her eyes that changed his mind. After a moment, he gave her a barely perceptible nod. 'Then I'll accept your kindness, provided I have my own space.'

Closing her eyes, she allowed herself a moment of weakness, before nodding her assent. He was right. Distance was the only way to make it through. If he could distance himself, then so could she. She had to.

'Then let me help you back inside.' Her voice was surprisingly strong.

Taking a deep breath, he nodded and held out his hand to her. Understanding the courage and humility the request had taken, she wrapped her hand around his without comment. He grunted as she slipped her shoulders beneath his and helped him stand. Fitting herself beneath his arm, she wrapped an arm around his waist and helped him take a step forward. She refused to acknowledge her surprise at how solid he felt beneath her hands. It didn't matter. Neither did it matter that something fluttered in her belly when his hand closed over her shoulder. Their progress was slow, but eventually they made it to the door where they stopped to take a rest.

His breath was more laboured than hers and, perhaps because it was dark and he was so close to her ear, it brought to mind how he had fallen on top of her that night, his face pressed to her neck in the aftermath of what they had done. He'd been shaking, *shaking*, with the intensity of what had happened between them. Her entire body flamed with the memory and she forced herself to wipe it from her mind. When she wrapped her arm around his waist to urge him forward again, he caught her chin and gently lifted her face to look at him.

'Thank you.' The dark red of his hair caught a shaft of moonlight and rain ran down his face in rivulets. She had to blink to rid herself of the spell his eyes cast on her. They looked so earnest and deep.

Instead of replying, she simply nodded and pressed him forward.

Gunnar bit back a groan as he half fell to the bench nearest the fire. The rain might have turned the night cold, but he didn't know. The exertion and pain of moving himself had left him overheated and exhausted. He wanted to sink down and allow his eyes to close, except that he couldn't take them from the woman adding wood to the fire. With every beat of his heart, fresh agony pulsed through his leg, but focusing on Kadlin helped to keep it from overtaking him. Her movements were infused with the grace and dignity that was so much a part of her. He hadn't allowed himself to really see her since he'd returned. He'd been too angry, too focused on things that he'd lost, things that had never been his, to see what was in front of him. But the pain in her eyes when she thought he was rejecting her had woken him from his self-absorbed stupor. This was Kadlin, the woman he'd spent his entire life wanting. He was a fool to let this opportunity to be near her pass him by. He was a fool to request distance when all he wanted was to be in her presence.

She had become a woman in the years he'd been gone. His gaze caressed the long, graceful line of her back as she moved to shelves set against the wall and began fumbling through the linens folded there. Her hips seemed fuller, more womanly than the willowy curves he remembered. Thanks to the rain, the wet nightdress clung to those curves as she moved and he couldn't tear his gaze away. But he wasn't prepared to see that the front of the gown was as soaked as the back. When she turned around, her full breasts were on clear display, the pink nipples dark, darker than he remembered, pressed against the sheer fabric. She'd grown fuller. His mouth went dry as he recalled tasting them.

He lowered his face to the valley between her

breasts and breathed her in, wanting to remember for ever the way she smelled of sunshine. When her fingers delved into the hair at his nape, he couldn't stop his hips from instinctively pressing against her centre, which was open to him, her legs draped around him. His erection pressed against her through the soft leather of his trousers and when she gasped he knew that her delicate flesh would be swollen and ready for him.

His hand cupped the firm globe of her breast as he raised up to look at her. He'd dreamed about her body many times, but he hadn't seen her nude since they were children. The pale pink of her nipple was the exact shade of her lips. He couldn't resist finally sampling it as he'd tasted those lips just moments ago. She gasped the moment his tongue touched her, so he took the entire tip into his mouth, sucking deep until she moaned.

Gunnar looked away to rid himself of the dangerous memory, but it didn't help because when he looked back she stood before him. Those beautiful nipples were at eye level. 'Kadlin...' he whispered.

'Raise your arms.' She prodded and gripped his shirt.

But he pulled back and gritted his teeth against his longing for her as he pulled the shirt over his head. The blanket he'd tied on earlier had been lost outside during their struggle. He closed his eyes when she touched him to untie the soaked binding around his ribs. Even though he knew that she only touched him to tend to his wounds, his body wanted to make it mean something else. Her every touch moved through him like a caress. She unwound the binding and then rubbed her palm gently across the area that had been so bruised when he first came here. The bruises were fading now, but were still a bit tender.

'I think your ribs are almost healed.' She spared him a glance. 'How do they feel?'

'Better.' He gave her a small nod of thanks. That seemed to placate her, because she grabbed a length of linen to dry his hair, but he took it before she could linger and finished the job himself. Then he dried his torso, unwilling to torture himself further by letting her do it. But no matter how he tried, he couldn't stop his eyes from going back to the taut points of her breasts, outlined so clearly in her wet nightdress. 'Go change your clothing. You must be cold.' His voice was rough, so he cleared his throat and forced his gaze away.

She watched him absently as she used a length of cloth to dry her own hair. 'I'm not cold. It's unseasonably warm tonight. Besides, we should change your wrappings so you can go back to bed and rest.'

He almost laughed. There would be no rest for him this night, not with his carnal thoughts of her coupled with the pain of his leg to keep him awake. 'I doubt I'll find any rest tonight.'

She draped the linen around her shoulders, mercifully obscuring most of her beauty from him, and walked to a table set on the opposite side of the fire. It was filled with what looked to be cooking implements with various pots and baskets set on a shelf above it. Instead of watching her as he longed to do, he leaned his head back against the wall behind him. It allowed him to clear his mind and calmly acknowledge all that had happened that night. For the first time, he allowed himself to enjoy the familiarity of her presence. It was soothing to listen to her movements, to know that she was so close, even if she wasn't his to claim. He'd been in anguish for so long because he couldn't have her that he'd never really learned how to enjoy just being near her.

'Gunnar?'

This time when he opened his eyes to see her before him, he allowed his mouth to tip up in a smile.

She pressed a cup into his hand. 'Drink this.'

Without even questioning her, he brought it to his lips and took a drink. It was a pale broth, but had a bitter taste. He wouldn't refuse it, though. 'How is it that you're even more beautiful than you were when I left?'

A flush tinged her cheeks, but he wasn't sure if it was from his words or the rain. 'I'm not sure I would agree.'

'That's only because you don't see yourself as I do.' He took another drink and watched as she knelt at his feet. The position made his mind jump to a dangerous place so he was quick to close that door. Instead, he took another sip and simply watched as she took off his boot. Her brow furrowed in concentration as she worked. The beauty of her features never failed to make his breath hitch. Though he was careful to skim across the curve of her breasts, his gaze went to her gracefully long fingers. For the first time he noticed that her fingernails were shortened down to the quick and her knuckles were reddened. From the cold? Nay, she'd claimed to not be cold. From work, then? Didn't Harald and the girl, Ingrid, do much of the work around here? Then he realised something he should have noticed all along: there were not any servants about to help her with the running of the house. It wasn't a large house, but she'd still have need of clean clothing, soaps, storing food for the winter, wood, and all the other things needed for survival.

'Where are your servants, Kadlin?'

She glanced at him quickly, as if startled, but paused only briefly before going back to his boot to tug it off. She was quiet until she'd divested him of his wool sock. 'I have Harald and his children. Ingrid, in particular, is a big help to me. I'm sure you've heard her around.' She stood and walked to drape the sock near the fire to dry with his shirt before coming back to take off the other sock. He hadn't been able to get his boot on that leg.

'Aye, I've heard her. Why don't you have other servants?' Then he asked what he'd wondered all along. 'Why are you here, in Eirik's house?' He had the feeling she was avoiding him, as she took off the sock and walked to put it with the other one.

'I sent him word that I'm here.'

'But why are you here instead of your husband's home?'

'Drink your broth.' She turned back to him only after he'd taken a long drink to drain the cup.

Almost immediately he realised that her face had become a bit fuzzy around the edges and his limbs were heavy. 'You've given me the Saxon's potion,' he accused.

She smiled. 'I've my own sorcery. You need rest and you've jarred your leg so much tonight, I'm afraid you've worsened the damage.'

That did make him laugh. 'It can't get any worse. It's useless already.' But he cooperated when she moved a stool over and helped him prop the injured leg up on it. Except when her hands found the fastenings of his trousers, he grabbed them with his own. 'Why do I feel as if you're always trying to undress me?'

She grinned at his words, but only to hide the way her heart leapt from the way he held her hands. His palms were warm and callused, and felt so right against her own. He probably didn't even realise the way his thumb caressed her knuckles. It was ridiculous to react this way; she wasn't a girl, and he'd all but said that he wanted their relationship to be that of strangers. Yet, he'd completely belied those words with his questions about her life. The man was infuriating in his inconsistency.

Taking a deep breath, she pulled her hands free of his and smoothed them down her hips. He watched the motion intently, making the butterflies in her belly even worse, because she knew that more of her body was revealed to him than was appropriate. He'd watched her before, though he'd had the grace to look away, but now with the poppy in him, he did no such thing. His hot gaze seared her from her hips to her breasts.

'Did I tell you how beautiful you are?' His voice was husky and low, a timbre that hit something deep down inside her. His damp red hair was mussed, reminding her of how it had looked after her fingers had run through it. Thinking of that made her remember where his mouth had been when she'd tangled her fingers in his hair and a strange pulse of anticipation settled between her thighs. Nay, not anticipation, because nothing would happen.

Ignoring his question, she once again reached for his trousers.

'Nay.' He held her off again.

'We need to get your trousers off. They're drenched and they'll soak your bedding. I'll not have you catching your death tonight.'

'Don't you understand what you do to me?' He grinned up at her.

If his heart was pounding anywhere near as hard as her own, then she had a fairly good idea. But it wasn't enough for her to assume. Some deep, dark longing made her look down to see the hardness straining against his trousers. For a moment there was nothing but the sound of their breathing filling the silence as she stared.

A sweet warmth filled her limbs, making her fingers tremble as her blood became heavy with it. She recognised it immediately as arousal and knew that she had to stop it before she couldn't think any more. What sort of person was she, lusting after the man who had abandoned her? Worse, he'd left her with child without so much as an enquiry. She hated herself for what he had done to her.

Straightening, she took the linen from around her shoulders and draped it over his lap. 'There. Now help me take them off. I still need to bind your ribs and change the binding on your leg.'

Jaw clenched tight, he fumbled with the fastenings beneath the linen and she averted her eyes until he had managed to push them down to his knees. Kneeling, she worked them down past his injured left knee and shin and then worked them free of the right. Despite his lack of activity, his legs were still muscular and powerful in the way of men who fought and laboured for a living. She dared not let her fingertips linger and tried extra hard not to look at his now-bare chest and rippled stomach. Though he'd lost weight, his torso was still tight with muscle.

Hanging the garment to dry near the fire, she

retrieved strips of linen she'd prepared days ago, before going back to him.

He lounged back on the bench, as lazy and sure as a king watching her with his half-lidded gaze. The strip of linen across his lap was his only modesty, so she knelt again. His leg was safer territory. Binding his ribs now would take her too close to him and what she knew was under that cloth.

'You work too hard. Your husband doesn't take care of you like he should.'

When she glanced up, he was watching her hands. She self-consciously rubbed them together, silently acknowledging that they looked like hands that washed the laundry and the dishes. Anger welled up inside her that he would dare to find her lacking, but she beat it down. It was the poppy talking. 'I do what is needed.' Untying the knot holding the wet binding together, she gently began to unwrap it from the wood braces.

After a moment, he absently picked up a lock of her hair and wrapped it around his finger. 'If you were mine, you wouldn't be forced to work.'

She jerked back as if he had struck her. 'Don't

speak to me of what could be. You made your choice.'

'You're angry that I left.' His gaze traced her face.

'I'm angry that you abandoned me and didn't come back,' she clarified and went back to his leg.

'I presumed your husband wouldn't welcome me.' His acerbic tone caught her off guard.

Kadlin stared up at him, a bitter seed taking root. Then he stroked her cheek with a tenderness that belied his tone and his expression turned almost wistful. It was the herb, she knew that, but it didn't stop her heart from flip-flopping in her chest to have such tenderness aimed at her. 'I always imagined that you'd belong to me, that I'd give you children.'

The air froze in her lungs, or maybe it was sucked from the entire room. Nothing moved and there was no sound save the pounding in her ears of her own heartbeat. How was it that his wishes had so clearly aligned with her own and yet here they were, physically close but so far apart in all the ways it mattered that he might as well be back in the Saxon lands? That look in his eyes made her want to say it, to tell him about their son and watch his face change. Would it be happiness, heartbreak, bitterness? She even parted her lips and whispered the words, 'My son…' before she could stop herself.

His brow furrowed before smoothing again as realisation dawned. A brief flash of pain crossed his features, but then it was gone. 'Ah, so the child that I hear is yours. I made myself believe that it belonged to Ingrid.'

She sucked in a breath to say…she didn't know what…to say *something*. But he surprised her yet again with a strength she hadn't known he possessed, when he grabbed her shoulders to pull her towards him and his mouth claimed hers. It was a clumsy and sloppy brushing of lips, made all the more potent for its awkwardness. She was sure that he hadn't planned it any more than she had. It was just there between them, alive and smouldering. A moan caught in the back of her throat when his tongue darted out to stroke her bottom lip and it was like liquid flame heating her where it touched. But just as she leaned in for more, he pulled back, his hands falling to his sides and his head falling back to thump against the wall.

Fingers on her lips, she rose on shaking legs and made her way around the fire to the table and leaned heavily against it. One thought pounded through her skull, obliterating everything in its path. She wouldn't survive this. Her heart still belonged to the warrior across the fire and no matter how she'd tried to kill that longing for him, it still lived and thrived.

Would he suspect that her son was his? She had to keep Avalt from him. At least for now, until Gunnar was improved enough to leave. If he found out the truth now while they were in this forced proximity, he'd whisper empty words that would make her foolish heart forgive him for his abandonment and start to imagine a life with him and their son as a family.

Or perhaps even worse. He'd whisper bitter words that would hurt her all over again.

Chapter Nine

Gunnar awoke the next day in his new bed. Though the usual pain was present as a dull ache throughout his leg, his head was strangely clear with no headache. Memories of the previous night came to him. First of himself, hobbling towards the forest in the rain, and then Kadlin helping him back inside. He'd been so foolish trying to leave; so willing to give up his time with Kadlin to indulge himself in self-pity. It was true that the injury had irrevocably changed his life and that there would be no future as a leader for him, but then, that wasn't so much of a change. He'd already refused every command post he'd been offered. His only goal had been death by battle.

If he hadn't been so self-absorbed with his injury, he would have realised the gift he'd been given. To see her again was all that he'd wanted and here he was wasting his opportunity because of a bloody leg that wouldn't ever work properly again. All it had taken to make him realise that was her standing outside in the pouring rain yelling at him. She'd been magnificent. The girl he remembered had become a woman so fierce and tender at the same time that she stole his breath as he watched her.

He smiled as her voice came to him through the door, though he couldn't distinguish the words meant for someone else. An actual door because she'd honoured his demand to be relocated. Only brief snatches of memory about moving teased the edges of his mind. Vidar had been summoned to help and had draped his arm across his shoulders while Kadlin had helped on his other side, because she had laced his broth with something potent.

Opening his eyes, he glanced around the small windowless chamber that was to be his new home. Though it was furnished scarcely like his alcove had been, it was bigger, giving him enough room to make a few circles to strengthen his leg. There was no hearth, so it was quite cool, but he'd been hot ever since he'd awoken from the haze the Saxon witch's potion had plunged him into. There had been many nights he'd awoken sweating and uncomfortable in the alcove so near the fire. The cool was a welcome respite.

His request for space hadn't been in the manner in which Kadlin had taken it. She thought he was rejecting her and her help. The truth was that he needed space away from her to recover in private, to become the warrior that he had been, without her hovering over him. There would be many falls on his path to recovery and he couldn't bear having them all play out before her. He'd spent his entire life trying and failing to be something more than a disappointment to the people in his life. He couldn't bear to see that same disappointment reflected in Kadlin's eyes.

He wouldn't become less of a man in her eyes. If she ever looked at him with pity or anything close to it, he feared what he would do, what he would become. In all his life, she had been the only one who had seen more than condemnation and disappointment in him. She had always seen more and she made him want to find more to give her, at least for the little while they would be here together. He owed her that much.

Raising himself on his elbows, he grimaced as he jarred his leg, setting it to throbbing again, as he moved the pillows so he could lie back on them. The smile returned, though, as he remembered how the wet nightdress had revealed the globes of her breasts with their pink nipples and the soft curves of her hips. She had changed so much in the time they had been apart, with little of the girl left in the woman's body. He wasn't married and he wasn't one of the Christian monks forced to be celibate. She was married, but her husband wasn't there and Gunnar had never claimed to be honourable. And she wanted him. Her blush when she'd caught him looking at her had told him as much.

She wanted him and he meant to have her again.

There was some other memory tugging at the edge of his awareness. It must have been something that had happened after she'd given him the broth. Settling back, he closed his eyes and tried to remember everything that had happened the previous night. Had he kissed her? Nay, probably not, but he'd wanted to and perhaps he would soon. Her voice came to him again, singing. The soft sound filled the front room of the house with a melodious timbre and drifted back down the passageway to reach him through the door. He remembered her singing when he'd awakened to her bathing him and wondered if he could convince her that another bath was in order.

A child's squeal broke through his reverie. *Her child!* Just that quickly, the memory he'd conveniently tucked away came back to him. For a moment, he was gripped by a shard of pain in his chest so sharp that he had to suck in a breath to fight it. Then, quicker than he'd ever imagined it could happen, all of the despair came back. The life he'd wanted with her savagely mocked as some other man's child called her mother. All of the crimes of his past had come back to seek vengeance on him, gaining retribution with a force he didn't know he could withstand.

Another man called her wife, another man's seed had taken root in her body, another man's child suckled at her breast. He raked his hands through his hair, holding them there so his palms covered his ears, muffling the sound of the boy.

My son, she'd said. A boy. Not the son that he'd imagined them creating, teaching to become a warrior; not the daughter he'd longed to watch grow up to have the grace of her mother; not a child who would ever call him Father. Nay, this was that other man's child.

'Gunnar, are you awake?' There was a brief rap on the door before she pushed it open and poked her head inside.

He opened his eyes, but couldn't hide the pain he was sure shone on his face. A strange smile curved her lips, but it faltered when she saw him.

'What do you want?' He hadn't meant for his tone to be so harsh, but neither could he soften it. Whether it was right or not, the sharp stab of betrayal moved through him, leaving a jagged wound in its wake. She had married someone else as if whatever was between them hadn't existed. The rational part of himself reasoned that he himself had never promised her anything. He'd never spoken words to bind her to him and had left her rather harshly. But it didn't matter to the part of him that wanted her to be his, the part that knew she was his. That part was past reasoning.

'Is your leg worse?' Her brow furrowed, puzzled by his mood and hurt by his tone. A pang of guilt needled at him, but he pushed it aside.

'Worse than useless, you mean?'

'I've asked Harald to come look at it.'

'Does Harald possess some magic that he's been hiding from me all this time? If so, then he should have already fixed it. If not, then I fail to see the point.'

Her lips parted to speak, but then she just shook her head and stepped back. The guilt for causing the pained look on her face tore at him and his eyes fell closed as he summoned the energy to confront her.

'Kadlin, wait.' Her face came back around the door, but it was shielded now, as it should be. His jealousy was intent on hurting her, but it wasn't right. The truth was that he wanted to hold her, despite everything that had passed between them, he wanted to call her over and have her crawl into bed with him. He wanted to bury his face in her hair and pretend that none of this had happened, that he'd never stopped visiting her bed as a child. Perhaps he even wished that he'd violated her father's order to stay away from her and made her his years ago. They could have married then no matter the consequences. But even as the scenario played out in his head, he knew that he had made the right choice for her. He would only have failed her.

'Send Harald back when he comes. I'd also like food if it's not too much trouble, without the potion.'

She only stared at him with those deep blue eyes that made him feel as if he could see to her heart. They never failed to make him want to seek solace inside them, inside her. Only she had the ability to give it to him and the knowledge rankled more than it soothed.

'I'll have Vidar bring you something.' She turned, but something compelled him to call her back.

'And, Kadlin...?'

She turned back to him and arched an eyebrow. He raised a hand to the stubble on his chin and raked his fingertips across it. 'I'd like a shave when you have time. The itching is infuriating.'

An hour later, after she'd seen Avalt off with Ingrid and safely away from Gunnar, Kadlin found herself scraping the beard from his chiselled jaw.

The first time she had done it, he'd been unconscious and manageable, while she'd been distraught and worried. This time his gaze pierced her as she worked, watching her with an intensity she couldn't ignore. What did he want from her? She'd thought he would relish being away from her after his demand for his own chamber, so the request for a shave was a surprise. To be honest, she wasn't up for the contact.

After their confrontation last night, she'd barely managed to get any sleep because she'd stayed awake thinking about his revelation, but she was no closer to a resolution now than she had been last night. Did he really not suspect that Avalt was his son? It seemed so unbelievable that she couldn't credit the idea, except that his mind had been addled by the poppy. He couldn't lie so easily and fake innocence so well under its influence, could he? Also, he hadn't once asked about their child since he'd returned. True, he had been gravely injured and was still in the early stages of recovery, but if Gunnar had suspected, he'd have asked at some point, surely. Of course, he said he thought the child was Ingrid's.

Sucking in a deep breath, she pulled back and

wiped the blade on the damp strip of linen in her lap. The small bits of red hair stood out in stark contrast to the cloth. Her heart clenched as she studied them. Sometimes the fact that he was home would catch her at strange moments, splintering everything else so that point was brought to light. It was such a strange shade, she'd never thought to see it again, except for on her son. Yet here she was scraping it from his jaw. He was *here* and she could touch him.

Placing a fingertip on his chin, she raised his face to better reach his neck. She almost sighed in relief to have his gaze removed from her, however briefly. His firm skin gave only slightly under the blade as it ran up his neck. The heat of him warmed her fingers, but she tried not to notice.

Last night was too fresh in her memory and left her twisted inside. One kiss from him had taken her right back to the life she had imagined for them. The one where he slept next to her every night and they worked together during the day creating a home for their family. Except there was no future with him. He had abandoned her—them. He had abandoned her and their child the moment he had walked out of her life. He had taken a night that was so special to her and turned it into something horrible and painful. Worse than that, he had made it so that she could never trust him. What sort of man took a heart so innocently offered and severed it in two?

Even last night he'd been intent on leaving her again. Nothing had changed. He was staying, but perhaps that was only until he recovered enough to attempt to leave again. If he tried again, she would let him. She couldn't allow herself to get close to him and face his rejection again.

This time when she drew back to wipe the blade, he lowered his chin just enough so that he could look at her. 'Are you all right? You don't seem yourself.'

The deep rumble of his voice hit her low in her belly, making her acutely aware of the fact that he wasn't wearing a shirt. It shouldn't matter. She had too many other concerns to care about his bare chest, or his rough voice, but it didn't seem to matter. Her heart shuddered regardless. Instead of answering, she shook her head and gently pushed his chin back into position, except that he refused to budge.

Her gaze locked with his, prompting him to

murmur, 'You've changed in so many ways, except your eyes. They're still the same as they were when we were children.'

Despite herself, she asked, 'How do you mean?'

One corner of his mouth tipped up in a smile. 'The way they look at me, as if they can see all the way through me. Can you see straight through me?'

'There was a time when I thought I could…but now I'm not so sure.' Left unsaid was the way he had left her. The fact that she had poured her heart out to him that night only to have him tear it in two and throw it away.

'You're the only one who's ever seen me, Kadlin. Everyone else saw only what they wanted. What they expected.'

'Then I suppose that makes me the fool.'

His display of temper this morning hadn't left her feeling reassured at all with where she stood with him. His behaviour in the front room last night had been completely opposite from the man she'd met this morning. He blew hot and cold. Last night she'd been sure that he would've ripped the nightdress from her had he been in possession of his faculties—and such was her weakness for him that she might have let him—but this morning he'd treated her like a stranger.

Nay, not a stranger. A stranger he would have met with cool detachment. There had been venom beneath the words he spoke to her. Perhaps he was angry at her. Perhaps he imagined that she had moved on and fallen in love with someone else. Kadlin could only imagine the pain that might cause if he felt half as much for her as she did for him. Even imagining the women that he must have spent nights with over the past two years was enough to twist her insides. Had he actually taken one to wife, she didn't know that she could bear it.

Yet he was the one who had ended everything. And now, now he spoke soft words that made her remember how he'd talk to her all those nights he came to her in her bed. Nay. It didn't bear thinking about. She shook her head and forced a deep breath. Only Gunnar could have her so torn up inside that she couldn't think straight. She despised how he had used her and then left. Why did her weak heart insist on making something more out of him than he had proven himself to be?

The first step was getting him better. She'd have to deal with him carefully until then. It might even be best to keep Avalt out of his sight. If Vidar had known that Avalt was Gunnar's son without being told, then Gunnar would probably figure it out, as well. She needed to be fully prepared for his response to the news before she faced that.

He didn't reply, leaving her to finish shaving him in peace, but the direction of his gaze changed from her face to her breasts. More than once she saw him looking at them and felt them tighten in response. It hardened her resolve to finish with haste and leave him alone. Once she had, she gathered her things and left without a word, going to the front room and depositing her burden on the table and then leaning heavily against it to regain her composure.

Her husband had been killed over a year ago in battle. She'd spent the time since avoiding her father and his pleas that she find another to marry. Though she had tried to deny it, part of her hesitance had been because she still imagined that husband to be Gunnar. Those thoughts were not good for her and had often left her angry, and as the year passed she had begun to come to terms with the idea that Avalt needed a male guardian. There was no question that she would marry eventually. Now that Gunnar had returned, perhaps it was better that marriage happen sooner rather than later. Something needed to save her from her own madness.

Chapter Ten

Days passed and Gunnar was no closer to resolving his feelings for Kadlin. The woman was in his blood and only death could cure him of her. But death wasn't an option any more, not now. It appeared his lame leg wasn't going to kill him. There was still no certain future for him so he didn't even allow himself to think ahead. Every day was simply waking up and working to make the leg better, or at least somewhat serviceable. There were plenty of days ahead of him to figure out what it would mean when the leg could support him.

But it was doing a bad job of that at present.

Tightening his grip on the sapling Harald had replaced for him, Gunnar stared down at his useless appendage, silently willing it to work. It did nothing except refuse to support the weight he demanded that it accept. Instead of behaving properly, a splitting pain moved through the limb every time he let go of the wall to give it his weight. He clenched his jaw and breathed through his teeth as he took his palm from the sod wall and let his weight rest on his left leg, but eventually the muscle gave and he had to grab the wall again to keep himself from toppling over.

With a loud curse, he threw the sapling, causing it to sail through the air to land with a satisfying thud on the ground several yards away from him. Though it would be difficult to retrieve without crawling on the dirt like an invalid, he smiled just the same to see it lying there. He hadn't even been trying that hard and had landed an impressive throw. His leg might be rubbish but at least some of the strength in his upper body was returning.

Grasping his still-sore ribs, he stifled a groan as he dropped to his bottom on the bench. He had taken to coming outside when everyone left in the morning to go to the river. It was an outing they took without fail when the weather permitted and he'd learned to cherish the solitude. He wasn't ready to be around people now and he knew it. Best for all if he kept to himself, but the chamber Kadlin had assigned him seemed to grow smaller by the day. There were only so many times a man could walk a circle around that room without going mad. Somehow Kadlin had guessed what he was up to, because one day a bench had appeared outside. He tried not to dwell much on the fact that he couldn't have dragged it out himself had he tried.

A mild sweat had broken out on his forehead, so he swiped his hand across it, rubbing the moisture on his trousers. He hadn't bothered with a shirt, knowing the exertion would make him break into a sweat. Any exertion seemed to do that and he was growing impatient waiting for it to get any easier.

Just as he was catching his breath, the whinny and accompanying hoof beats of horses caught his attention. Battle-hardened and honed for danger, his first thought was that of a threat. Though the farm should have been safe, nestled as it was on his father's lands, safety could never be taken for granted. It was then that he realised he hadn't brought a weapon with him and the bloody stick was too far away. That just went to show how too much rest could make a warrior soft. He was just pushing to an awkward stand, with his weight shifted to the right to alleviate pressure from his left leg, when he caught sight of his father, Hegard, riding out from the forest followed by two men. As they came closer, Gunnar recognised them as men who had sailed with Eirik, but who had declined to make the trip to the Saxon lands.

He waited, a knot settling like a solid weight in the pit of his stomach. His father sat his horse like a king, just as broad and powerful as his oldest sons. Eirik had his golden hair, while Gunnar had inherited the red locks of his mother. A trait that Gunnar suspected had attracted the man to his mother, but repulsed him in his bastard son, though Gunnar had inherited his father's intense amber eyes. They were rare and, Gunnar suspected, the only reason his father had laid claim to him. Although his mother was the younger sister of the man's true wife and had been too young to have been promiscuous, so he'd had little choice in the matter of claiming him.

When they were close enough, he raised his hand in greeting, his voice solemn as he greeted each man by name and then turned his attention to his father. The man had aged a great deal in the two years since Gunnar had seen him. His blond hair was streaked with more white at the temples and he'd added at least a stone in weight. He didn't look well, but Gunnar had trouble summoning sympathy for him.

'Father.'

He dismounted before giving his bastard son the solid force of his attention. His manner was stiff and sombre, that of a leader set to performing some unsavoury task. Gunnar assumed he fit that unsavoury category in his father's eyes. He wasn't even surprised that it had taken so long for his father to make the ride to see him, despite that fact that he must have known Gunnar had returned the moment their ship struck land. His father had made no secret of his feelings for him during their last conversation. Gathering himself for the confrontation sure to come, Gunnar squared his shoulders.

'This yours?' Hegard gave the sapling a critical look before deigning to pick it up. Turning it in his hand, he took the few steps needed to reach Gunnar and held it out to him.

Of course, his father couldn't have simply ignored the fact that it was there. He wasn't picking it up out of some long-buried goodness lurking inside him. Nay, he needed to bring it over, to rub it in Gunnar's face exactly how useless he was now. The flare of triumph that sparked in his eyes when Gunnar reached out to take it proved as much. A bitter tang filled Gunnar's mouth, but he refused to give way to the bitter words that accompanied it, and instead quietly leaned the sapling against the wall of the house.

'I'd heard rumours that you were back. I had to come see for myself if they were true. Word is that you're half-dead.' He looked Gunnar over from head to foot before grinning. 'It appears the rumours exaggerated your condition. Though the "half" seems accurate.'

Gunnar looked over the man who had ruled his life and wondered why he'd ever really cared whether he'd had his approval. 'I'm alive,' was all that he offered.

Hegard watched him appraisingly, the exact same golden eyes that Gunnar possessed staring back at him. They were fierce and alive with cunning, as if sizing up an opponent and finding something there that he hadn't expected. Gunnar didn't know the real reason for his visit, but there was one.

'Aye, that you are.' He made a show of looking around, his gaze darting from the house to the green fields on either side. There was nothing there except the sheep grazing in the distance. Even Harald's house couldn't be seen as it sat over the rise in the distance. 'I couldn't help but notice that you didn't bring Eirik back with you. I believe when last we spoke I expressed to you the importance of not returning without him.'

'It wasn't my intention to return at all. But Eirik does as he wants, I'm not his keeper.'

'I also hear that Eirik married his Saxon slave. He knew that it meant giving up his place here.' The jarl shook his head and barely controlled the disgust in his voice. His father couldn't comprehend how one would choose love over glory. Gunnar might have understood his frustration if he'd never met Kadlin. But since he had, he felt the need to come to Eirik's defence.

'He loves her.'

'Bah! Love is a sentiment best left for girls and widows. Men don't allow for such weakness. It won't go well for him to bind himself to a slave. Not in the long run.'

There was no use in arguing the point. The bitter man would never understand Eirik any more than Eirik would understand him. Gunnar shrugged. 'If that's true, it's a lesson he'll learn eventually.'

'You know it's true. You, Gunnar—' he pointed at him for emphasis '—out of all of my children, true born and bastard, you are the most like me. I've long known that to be true. You know what must be done and you accept the sacrifices that come with that duty.'

Stunned, Gunnar didn't know how to respond to that. His father had never acknowledged him in that way before.

'You understand first-hand that duty and honour outweigh what we might want personally.' His father slanted a knowing look at him before glancing to the open door of the sod house as if looking for someone. He must know that Kadlin lived there. Gunnar wondered just how much the man had guessed about his feelings for her, how much he had known all along. Though his father had never said, Kadlin's father, Jarl Leif, must have notified him of Gunnar's nightly visits to her as a child. He must have also told him of the night he'd told Gunnar not to return.

Gunnar took a deep breath and held it. Duty and his consideration for Kadlin's happiness were the only reasons he hadn't run away with her, despite Jarl Leif's wishes. Aye, his father must have known that.

When the jarl fell silent, awaiting his response, Gunnar offered, 'I do understand.' But he was wary of what the man was leading up to.

'We have to be leaders. We have a special role.' He held his hands wide apart to emphasise the length of the land around them. 'We must do what is right for our men, for our people. What we want has to be for them.'

'Aye.' Gunnar's voice was strong, but his stomach soured because he knew what the jarl was going to say. Somehow he knew that it had been coming to this. His leg throbbed and his ribs ached with the pounding of his heart.

'Eirik is not like you and I. He is nobler, more controlled, temperate. He is slow to anger and calculated in his actions. It's why I'm so surprised by his choice of that woman.' Jarl Hegard shook his head, for once looking unsure and almost flustered. Then his eyes sharpened and he shook his head. 'But you and I, we go to battle with fire in our eyes and blood in our hearts. I remember well how it felt and I've seen that same look on your face when you've wielded a sword. *We* are the true warriors. We lead our men to battle and win every one. But Eirik is better because he is a warrior and a leader. A true jarl. He doesn't have to work as hard at it as we do. A rare combination in a jarl. He'll be a better one than I.' He paused and let those words sink in before dealing the final blow. 'And better than you.'

Gunnar wanted to deny his words, to explain how he had led his men to many victories over the past years, how each of them had earned a fortune beneath him. But he wouldn't offer up the words. They would be seen as weakness and used against him. His father had not come to debate the finer points of leadership with him. The man hadn't come to have a conversation with him at all. The jarl had come to deliver a message. Gunnar wouldn't stoop to begging for his place before that message was delivered. Whatever his father might think of him, Gunnar knew who he was and knew what he wasn't. He was a fine warrior who had more than earned his place in the world; he wasn't the weak bastard the man had intended him to be.

His father's gaze pierced him as he took the few steps necessary to breach the distance between them, and even with his injury they were of the same height. Gunnar forced himself not to flinch when the older man put his hand on his shoulder. 'I have made many mistakes and I see those same mistakes in you. We are not meant for this. If you truly wanted to do your duty, then you would have made sure that Eirik returned here to resume his rightful place as jarl. Instead, he rules in a land far away with his Saxon whore. Tell me, Gunnar, did you plan to have him stay there so that you could return here to claim what you think is rightfully yours?'

Gunnar met his father's gaze head-on. 'My brother chose to stay because he wanted her more than he wanted his place here as jarl. As I mentioned, I had no intentions of returning.'

'Ah.' The jarl moved back as if his curiosity had been assuaged and walked the few steps back to pick up his reins. 'Then he is a fool and so are you for missing an opportunity. But the fact is you failed to bring him back; you have no place here any more. You knew the consequences.' He mounted and jerked the lead to turn his horse, but instead of moving forward, he turned to give Gunnar one last look.

'Have I ever told you how much you remind me of your mother? It's your colouring, your expressions, but something more. That damnable sadness that always lingers there in your eyes. It's just like her. She never learned to hide it, but you…you don't even try to hide it. It's never sat right with me.' Gunnar met his gaze without wavering and held it until the jarl sighed and clucked his tongue to get the horse moving. 'Take the time you need to heal and then I want you gone. Back across the sea or to some other ends of the earth. Somewhere away from here.' With those words he kicked the horse into a gallop back the way he had come.

Gunnar fell back against the wall, gradually sliding to the bench, his muscles fatigued from holding himself up for so long. They shook from the effort as he slumped down. For one heart-stopping moment, there was no sound other than the roaring that filled his ears. Everything that he had done up until he'd left for the Saxon lands to gain his father's confidence, his trust, had been for nothing. Gunnar had never been good enough to be jarl in his father's eyes. This wasn't a new revelation by any means; his father had made it clear two years ago when he'd told Gunnar not to return without Eirik, but the words stung none-theless.

Impotent rage coursed through his body as he glanced up to watch his father disappear down the forest trail. He'd known that there would be no homecoming for him, particularly now with his lame leg. There had never been any chance that his father would welcome him back, so the man's words shouldn't have been a surprise, shouldn't have held any power to hurt him. But the ever-present pain in his chest had become unbearable.

Nothing had changed at all. Even now, with Kadlin so near, he couldn't claim her. He'd failed Eirik so long ago when they were children, leaving him to the abuse of his attackers; he'd failed his father by not earning his approval; he'd even failed his mother who had seen fit to abandon him. He had absolutely nothing to offer her, not even himself as a whole man. How was he to live in such torment?

Chapter Eleven

Kadlin waited until the jarl had disappeared into the forest before approaching Gunnar.

The nearly overgrown trail that led to Jarl Hegard's hall passed very near the river at one point before heading around to a narrower spot for crossing. She had recognised him the moment she had seen him and knew that he was coming for his son. The truth was that she had expected him much earlier. If the men who were sure to have made the crossing on the ship with Gunnar hadn't reported to their jarl that his son had returned, the two men who had accompanied Vidar to see him to the farm certainly would have. The jarl would have known about Gunnar's presence for weeks now. Long enough to have made the day's journey to visit.

Her heart had leapt into her throat the moment

she had seen the man. Her only thought was that he had come to take Gunnar away from her. Nothing had been resolved between them and Gunnar was going to leave her…again. Surely his father would want him at home to finish his convalescence. The fear had made her run the entire way back to the sod house, so that she had reached it just seconds before the jarl and his party had come into sight. But it had seemed ill mannered of her to involve herself in their private moment, or perhaps some foreboding had stilled her feet and made her hide herself behind the house. Whichever it was, she'd stayed there, hidden, every word from his father making her angry until it had taken every ounce of willpower to keep herself away from Gunnar. Neither would appreciate her involvement and she knew Jarl Hegard well enough to understand that a woman's interference would only make him harsher, angrier. So she'd stayed her feet, eyes closed with impotent anger as she'd listened to them until the hateful man had left.

Wiping a tear from her cheek and composing herself, she stepped around to the front of the house, her gaze finding Gunnar immediately on

the bench she had left for him. He stared at the
point where his father had disappeared so intently
that he didn't even notice her approach until she
was upon him. Or perhaps he'd known she was
there, because he didn't seem startled at all by her
presence. His fierce gaze shifted the slightest bit
to settle on her. The weight of it held her silent for
only a moment before she couldn't take the pain
that she knew was hiding inside it, somewhere
so deep that he would never let it out.

'He's wrong, Gunnar.'

He did flinch then, as if just noticing her presence. Removing his gaze from her and looking out away from the direction his father had
gone, he laughed. A short raspy breath, devoid
of humour and filled with all the darkness that
had been building inside him. 'Is he wrong? He
seemed fairly certain of himself and my inabil-
ity to be jarl. You know the old son of a bitch is
never wrong as well as I do.'

Annoyed by his flippant response, she hurried
to his side to sit on the bench beside him to make
him pay attention to her. The flippancy was his
usual response to his father. She realised now
that he used it as a weapon to help deflect the

pain so it wouldn't cut as deep. 'That's not what I meant, but even that's not true.' She took his face between her hands and made him look at her. When his eyes fastened to hers, she refused to let go. 'You have all the qualities of a jarl, Gunnar. You have led many men and sacrificed yourself for them again and again. If the stories that I've heard around my father's fire are true, then you already are a jarl in many ways, except for land.' Surprise flashed in his gaze, so she elaborated. 'Aye, the stories of your bravery and courage have made it all the way across the sea to my father. When I have visited him, there is always a story recited by a storyteller about the courageous, red warrior who fights with honour. Vidar has even confirmed them and told me more. I know that you are brave and loyal and worthy of so much more than your father can ever understand. Don't let him make you think that you are any less than you are.'

'But I am less than I was.' He indicated the leg wrapped in bindings and raised a sardonic brow, challenging her to deny it.

It broke her heart that he actually believed it. 'Do you truly believe that the men you have commanded all this time, the men you have made wealthier and stronger for being in your service, will turn their backs on you?'

He smiled again, a brief upturn of his lips that faded as quickly as it had begun, making her think he was laughing at himself more than anything she had said. 'I will never lead them into battle again, Kadlin. I may eventually be able to sit on a horse, but the first blow would knock me down. A true warrior fights on the ground anyway, with his sword, his axe, his fists and any other bloody thing he can get his hands on.'

'Aye, that may be true, Gunnar, but have you considered that your father rules quite well from his perch on his dais and hasn't battled in years? You would simply command in a different way.'

His heavy gaze touched every part of her face, sweeping across her brow before settling along her lips. Its weight brushed her like an actual caress, but he wouldn't touch her. Except for the morning when he'd awoken to her bathing him when he'd grasped her hand, and then again when his senses had been dulled from the laced broth and he'd kissed her so clumsily, he'd held himself back from her. Even when she'd nestled herself under his arm to help him walk, he'd been careful to only touch her in a perfunctory manner. But his eyes were doing everything that she knew he wanted to do to her and it left her momentarily breathless. A curl of warmth unfurled deep in her belly and spread outward. Why? Why could he always do this to her?

Finally, something snapped in his eyes and they were shuttered against her. He even pulled back just slightly so that her hands fell to fists in her lap. 'I gave up on caring what my father thought long ago.' With a shake of his head, he reached for his sapling and pushed himself to his feet. She would have helped, but she didn't think he would appreciate the gesture and she was still reeling from the sting of his rejection and how fast he had directed the subject away from her question.

Turning to go back inside, he paused and slanted a glance at her. 'He told me when I left two years ago not to come back unless I could bring Eirik home to claim his rightful place as jarl. It's why I was delivered to your doorstep instead of my father's. Nothing he said to me today is anything that I didn't already know.'

Stunned by the admission, Kadlin sucked in

a deep breath. She wanted to ask if that's why he had abandoned her, but she couldn't get the words past her throat. She wanted to ask if he'd even thought about coming back to her, but this wasn't the time and if his rejecting her touch stung so badly, she could only imagine how hearing her worst fears confirmed would feel. If he confirmed that he'd only used her that night with no intention of ever seeing her again, then the pain would be too much to bear.

Swallowing past the lump of pain lodged in her throat, she asked, 'Then why didn't you bring him back?'

'I thought about it. When I stood there on that beach and watched him pledge himself to Merewyn, I knew that any hope I had of being in my father's good graces had gone. I knew that I'd never be welcomed back, would never see home again. That's when I realised that it had never really been my home. If not Eirik's Saxon, there would have been something else. My father never wanted me, except to use as a weapon against Eirik. I saw that clearly then. That's the moment I realised it didn't matter what he thought.'

What was there to say to that? *I'm sorry* seemed

paltry and inadequate to express the sorrow she felt on his behalf and the anger that she felt towards his father. She realised that her childhood had been sheltered. With a mother and father who loved and cherished her, she'd never been able to completely understand what life had been like for Gunnar. Though he'd sought her out often enough in his childhood, she'd only welcomed his attention without really understanding what drove him to dole it out to her. He'd needed someone to love; someone to hold on to when his world became too harsh for him to bear; someone to love him back when no one else would. She'd never completely understood until that moment how much his own father had stood in the way of Gunnar's happiness. Her happiness, as well, because if he'd been half the father her own father had been, then he would have looked for ways to help Gunnar become a man with a high station in life, regardless of his plans for Eirik. Nothing would have stood in the way of their eventual marriage.

'Help me inside.' Gunnar's voice broke her reverie and she realised that he held his hand out to her. Though his words were spoken as a command, the request was in his eyes.

Fitting herself beneath his shoulder, she closed her eyes briefly when the warmth of his arm stole around her. He wasn't wearing a shirt, so there was nothing to hinder the heat of his skin from reaching hers. She had to fight the temptation to bury her face against his shoulder, to breathe in his scent that was distinctly male and as potent as it had been the night he'd come to her. When his fingers gripped her waist, it was as if she had become more aware of him, and hums of pleasure moved throughout her body from that contact point.

They moved slowly through the front room. His strength had already improved immensely from the night he'd tried to leave and he'd already put on considerable weight from when he'd arrived so thin and broken. He had been moving better on his own, but the strain of standing for so long had drained him because he leaned on her heavily. Kadlin was happy to see the improvements, even though it meant that he would leave her soon. She knew that despite his current feelings, he would find a way to command his men again and she honestly didn't know if he would want his future to include her. Even more, she didn't think that she could forgive him for leaving her.

Once they reached the door of his chamber, he stopped and pulled his arm from around her. 'Thank you.'

The words were whispered in that raspy voice that somehow managed to crawl its way through her. She nodded and pretended that it hadn't, because she had become very good at pretending. 'I have to get back to...' She had almost said Avalt, whom she had left playing in the sandy banks of the river with Ingrid and her siblings watching over him, when she'd come running to Gunnar's side. But she'd carefully avoided all mention of her son, afraid that she might say too much without even realising it. There was nothing she wanted to say on the subject now. 'I'm needed at the river,' she clarified.

His eyes had gone hooded, though, and he watched her as intently as if she were the only person in the world. It made her acutely aware that he was a strong, attractive male and they were alone in the house for the first time since he'd recovered enough to stand upright. The warmth from earlier returned to unfurl in her belly and curl its tendrils outward to weigh heavy in her limbs. When he focused on her mouth, she parted her lips almost as if he'd commanded her to and took a shuddering breath, while her nipples beaded beneath her dress. Before she realised what she had done, she licked her tongue across her bottom lip, not as any sort of enticement but because it felt as if every bit of moisture had moved to other parts of her body. But that's how he saw it and a flash of heat danced in his amber eyes, lighting them from within. It took every ounce of self-control to turn away from him, but she did it because though he'd taken everything else from her, he'd only made her sense of self-preservation stronger. If she hoped to retain any part of herself, she needed to get away.

'Kadlin.' The word chipped away at her, making her pause long enough that he continued. 'What did you mean?'

'What?' She'd clearly lost all ability for rational thought because she had no idea what he meant. Without thinking of the consequences, without realising that she was walking back into his trap, she turned back to face him.

'Outside, you said that my father was wrong,

but you didn't mean about becoming jarl. What did you mean?'

'I meant that he was wrong when he said that you are like him. You are nothing like him. At all. He is weak and must compensate for that with his anger and brute strength. I've never understood why my father counted him as such a good friend.' She shook her head and stepped towards him, wanting to take his arm, but unwilling to break across the barrier between them. 'You are not weak. You have within you the power to do great things, things that he never could do. He's only jealous of you. He sees that in you and views it as a threat. I pity him.'

The shuttered facade that almost constantly shielded his eyes wavered, then the entire aloof demeanour that he wore as a second skin cracked across his face. It fell away with the furrowing of his brow, the grimace that curled the corners of his lips upward in a shudder of pain he tried but failed to completely suppress. His eyes fell closed to fight it back, but when they opened she was staring into the eyes of the boy she loved. He stared back at her and though his hand had come up to cup her cheek and his thumb traced her lips, he was looking deep into her eyes. He was seeing *her*. For one brief, extraordinary moment, she was seeing *him* and there was nothing between them. The years between them didn't matter.

'I have done bad things,' he whispered.

'You have let anger guide you, but it's not who you are.'

He took in another shuddering breath, as if barely able to accept her words. Then he moved closer, crowding her against the wall, but she couldn't move to push him away. 'How do you see things in me that I don't even see in myself? How is it that you make me want to be the man that you see?' He was so close now that he looked down at her, his breath hot where it fanned across her cheek.

'Because you are that man, Gunnar.' Her voice had lowered to a whisper. 'I know you, I've always known you. It's you who is hiding.'

His eyes finally released hers when they moved to her mouth and his hand moved to cup the nape of her neck, his fingers disappearing into her hair. That was her only warning before his lips crashed down on hers. His grip tightened in her hair and he angled her head back to give himself better access to her. Her lips parted under the assault, greedy for more of him, and he gave it to her when he pushed his tongue between them to brush against hers. The wet, hot friction was so delicious she moaned in the back of her throat and mimicked the movement back to him. It was not a gentle kiss. It was too filled with desire, longing and pain to be gentle. But it quickly grew out of control, consuming them with its heat and demanding more.

His grip on her hair tightened painfully, but even that only heightened her awareness of him, her need to be possessed by him. When he pulled her against him, her body sought to press its softness against the hard muscle of his, as if that alone could assuage the ache inside her. It only made it worse, and made her more restless to feel him, all while knowing that nothing less than the heat of his skin against her own would do.

Then he abruptly pulled back and pressed his forehead against hers. His eyes were closed so tightly that it looked like he was fighting pain and she thought she'd inadvertently hurt his leg, until he opened them to look at her. 'Ah, love, how do you consume me so?'

Just that quickly, she realised how close she'd come to giving in to him. His words so clearly echoed her own confusion. She had no right to want him as she did, knowing how deeply he had hurt her. It was a betrayal to herself that she let him consume her. Unable to speak, she pushed him back, pulling herself from his grasp and running out of the house. No matter what he said or did, he was not the boy she longed for. Too much had happened for her to ever risk forgetting that.

Chapter Twelve

Kadlin gently ran her fingertips through her son's baby-fine hair as he slept at her side. The movement roused him and he latched on to her breast again, unwilling to give it up just yet. The dark clouds threatening rain had kept them from their usual morning outing to the river, so he'd settled down to an early nap. Avalt was almost a year and a half now, so he generally only took milk in the morning and evening, but he'd asked and she hadn't been able to refuse him. She really didn't mind, though. Being with him soothed her and she'd needed more of that since her encounter with Gunnar…his father.

His father.

Those words had been appearing more and more in her thoughts lately. Avalt was so like Gunnar in his appearance that it had never been far from her mind, but always in a way that was distant. She would wonder if perhaps one day he would meet his father; or if he would grow up to look as much like his father as he did now. Those thoughts had always been of one day in the future. Not now. Yet his father was here now, so near yet still without any knowledge of his son.

She closed her eyes and let her head drop to the bed. The guilt of keeping Avalt from him was eating away at her. In the beginning it had been easy to justify. Gunnar had been, understandably, too absorbed with his injury to handle anything else. It had been the reasonable thing to do to keep that information to herself. Fair and kind, even. But now Gunnar wasn't confined to his bed any more. He arose every morning when they left for the river. He even came out sometimes in the afternoon when Avalt had his nap. He was improving every week, though it hadn't escaped her notice that he only roused when Avalt was away. It saddened her that he had shown her child no interest, even as it played into her plan to keep the truth from Gunnar.

Now the idea of not telling him about his son only seemed cruel and more than a little selfish, which made her even more angry with herself, leaving her in a foul mood.

That mood could partially be blamed on the visit from Jarl Hegard, or what had come after the visit—her talk with Gunnar. More specifically, the way he had kissed her. That kiss! She despised how readily she had capitulated to his kiss. Nay, it wasn't even that. It was those eyes and how they had looked at her, broken her with their intensity. Making her feel things, see things, that she knew didn't exist. He was no more the boy she had loved than she was that same girl, but she'd responded to him just as if he were. She'd opened to his kiss as easily as she'd invited him into her bed that night.

Why did he get to have this hold over her? How did he get to make her want him when it was the worst thing she could possibly do? By the gods, she wanted that man and she despised the weakness he caused within her. It had been that way for as long as she could remember. There had never been another man she had wanted. She'd known it since she'd been old enough to realise what happened between men and women. Even when he'd first pressed his lips to hers all those years ago when they had been children and she hadn't even known what that strange longing had been, she had wanted him. She had kissed other men, hoping that one of them would make her forget about this infuriating one, but none of them ever had. None of them had ever wielded the power over her that he did. With one look from across a crowded room he could reach inside her to places no one else had ever been able to breach with a kiss.

Not even her own husband. A dear friend, one who had given her so much so that her child would have a name, but she couldn't even fathom kissing him. Not that he hadn't tried. Dagan had agreed readily to the idea of marriage when she'd explained her situation to him and broached the idea of marriage. He'd known that he'd only be getting gold and a better station for himself out of the agreement. Not her, at least in the beginning. Yet, even on their wedding night when they'd been secluded in her chamber, he had kissed her. She'd allowed it because she felt that it was so little to ask and refused to let it go any further. However, she'd felt nothing, except guilt because the kiss was unfaithful to Gunnar. Unfaithful. It was a word that meant nothing because Gunnar had left her and she had been a fool for even feeling it.

But even that wasn't the complete source of her anger. It was the man himself. The fact that he'd reverted to his grouchy countenance and avoided her as much as he was able in the days since the kiss. When she'd left their encounter, albeit running, she had left thinking that they had reached some new understanding between them. She'd seen past his harsh front and into his heart, yet it hadn't lasted. Or maybe he was spiteful that she had seen the other side to him and was doing his best to reconstruct that front. She had half a mind to go to his chamber and make him stop hiding from her. If she could shake him, perhaps he would understand that he didn't need to hide from her. In the end it didn't really matter. He wasn't the boy she had loved and despite her desire for him…desire wasn't love. She was older now and wise enough to know that it was foolish to get the two confused.

Avalt's small hand grasped her finger and she brought it to her lips for a kiss, before gently moving away. Catching her gaze on the fur he laid upon, she paused and fought past the sudden catch in her chest. Gunnar had made no enquiries about a possible child. He'd made the choice to remove himself from her life. That night when he'd come to her, he'd come to tell her goodbye. Shaking her head, she rose to her feet and adjusted her clothing, repinning the strap of her apron dress in place.

She realised now that it had been her own girlish wishes that had possessed her to pull him into her bed. Her need to hold on to him, when he'd never given her any indication that he'd returned her feelings. At the time, she had thought she was being so bold, stripping his barriers away so that he had no reason, no excuse to hide from her. And here she was again, contemplating the same thing. If only his father had been different, if only she could make Gunnar admit that he needed her in his life, if only… She smiled and gave a small, sad shake of her head. All of the *if onlys* in the world couldn't make him hers if he didn't want to be.

A horse's whinny made her heart leap to her throat. Kadlin moved into the passageway, bringing the door to her chamber shut quietly behind her.

'Kadlin.'

Taking a fortifying breath, she walked the few steps to Gunnar's door and saw that he was already manoeuvring himself so that he could get to his feet.

'Stay in your chamber. I'll go to the door.'

His command startled her, because it had been almost exactly what she'd been about to say to him. He'd taken to wearing the trousers she had altered for him with no shirt. She hated that her gaze roved over the broad expanse of his chest before meeting his.

'Nay, I'll go see who it is. You stay.'

She was already turning to walk down the passageway when he called to her again. 'Do not. You don't know who it could be. There are men about who wouldn't care that you're a jarl's daughter.'

'Aye, but this is Eirik's land…' But she paused because that wasn't entirely true now. 'Jarl Hegard's land. Not many would risk the ire of two jarls for the measly supplies we have on hand. Stay.'

She didn't give him a choice and smiled when he cursed. Let him deal with someone as infuriating as himself for once. She was still smiling when she opened the door to see Baldr approaching. He was alone, his usual retinue of warriors suspiciously absent. Swallowing her disappointment, she forced her smile to stay in place and offered a greeting, making sure that Gunnar could hear her.

'Hello, Baldr.' The movement coming from his chamber stopped as she'd known it would. Gunnar would know her father's warrior.

In the two years since her confrontation with Baldr, he'd surprised her immensely with his behaviour. He'd accepted her marriage with surprising grace, going so far as to wish her well. Even after learning of her husband's death at the hands of the Saxons, he had not pressed his suit. Instead, he'd sat quietly while it had been her father who had pressed for her to consider marriage again. In the year since she'd moved to Eirik's farm, he frequently stopped by to check on her during his many trips between her father's and Jarl Hegard's home. Sometimes he'd even bring supplies. This time he had a cask of mead strapped to the horse that walked beside him.

'A gift from my father?' she asked, raising a brow.

'Aye, though I suspect that it's more a bribe

than a gift.' Baldr smiled as he dismounted and then moved to untie the cask from the packhorse. 'He misses you, Kadlin, and wants you to come home.'

'I miss him, too, and my mother. However, he knows his constant pressure to marry forced me to leave him. Remind him that I'm perfectly content here on my own, with no need for a husband.' Only that wasn't true any more. It was simply best to allow Baldr to believe that so he wouldn't offer himself as a candidate.

His mouth tightened, but it was the only indication he gave that he might have taken her words personally. 'I will tell him…again.'

She nodded and waved him inside. 'I'm afraid I don't have much to offer you. Some stew, if you want to stay.'

Setting down the cask next to the other cooking supplies on the far side of the front room, Baldr glanced back over the empty benches. 'It's quiet here this morning. Where are all the brats from across the field? I don't think I've ever been here without them underfoot.'

'They're at Harald's, slaughtering a pig today. We've grown tired of fish and mutton and wanted fresh meat before it gets too warm.' The words had come naturally, too quickly for her to remember that although Baldr had been kind, she didn't completely trust him. It wouldn't do to let him believe that they were all alone. Though she knew that Gunnar wouldn't allow him to harm her and perhaps that knowledge had made her tongue so loose. She might not be able to trust Gunnar in other things, but she knew that he would keep her safe. She refused to acknowledge the sudden warmth that stole through her chest at the thought, or to contemplate its meaning.

Giving herself a mental shake, she grabbed a bowl and went to the hearth to fill it with stew. 'Please have some—I was just about sit down to eat. They'll be back any moment and I'll be busy preparing the pork. I'll make another stew, but there will be so much I'll have to salt it.'

'Many thanks.' He smiled and took the bowl from her as he sat on an empty bench. 'Is your son about?'

She nodded. 'Sleeping.' Then she quickly changed the subject, asking about her brothers and sisters back home. They talked of them for a while before moving on to other people from home.

After it had become apparent that Baldr didn't

know, or was intentionally not mentioning Gunnar's presence in her home, she had meant to make him aware of the fact at least a dozen times in the conversation. Yet something held her tongue. Though it made no sense because Baldr would have no reason to harm him, she didn't want to make him aware of Gunnar. Not until Gunnar had recovered his strength, should he need it.

But he wouldn't need it today; she was being ridiculous.

'Kadlin.' Baldr was just leaving, his hand on the door, when he turned back to face her. His unnerving gaze raked over her face before he spoke. 'I have kept my distance and not pressed you all this time.'

Immediately, her stomach began to churn in anticipation of his next words. She held up her hand to ward them off. 'Nay, Baldr, not now. I hear enough of this from my father.'

Pushing the door closed, he grabbed her wrist and held it. It was a gentle hold that didn't hurt at all, but she tried to tug it away just the same. Only he wouldn't let go.

'Hear me out.'

The hard look that crossed his face made her realise that her best option might be to at least pretend to listen to him than refuse him outright. She nodded.

'You've played house for over a year now, but it'll be over soon. Jarl Leif has been generous, but he hasn't been able to give me what I really want.' The way his gaze pierced her made it perfectly clear what that was: her. Or more accurately, the station in life that marrying her would give him. He pulled on her wrist to bring her closer, close enough that his breath brushed across her temple as he spoke. It repulsed her, so she leaned back and wondered if she should have armed herself with her kitchen knife. 'Jarl Hegard has made me a proposition, one that I'm finding difficult to refuse.'

Dread settled like a weight in her belly. There was only one thing that could be, one thing that would make Baldr so bold after biding his time for so long. 'This farm.' The jarl was even worse than she had thought. He could have given it to Gunnar, but he'd had to do the one thing sure to twist the knife deeper. He had to give it away.

'Aye, perhaps more.' Baldr smiled, the first true smile she had seen from him in ages. It lacked the polite veneer of the ones she had become accustomed to seeing. This one lit up his face and brought that hint of cruelty that he tried so hard to hide back to his eyes. Those eyes gleamed with approval, but not in a way that made her feel valued. He made her feel degraded. 'You're smart, girl. Believe it or not, I actually like that in a woman. Sweetens the challenge.'

'I believe it. It must make the spirit-crushing that much more satisfying.'

Before she had a chance to even realise what he was going to do, he released her wrist and grabbed her braid, twisting it around his fist and reeling her in closer. Her hands immediately went to his chest to push him away. 'I'd never crush your spirit, Kadlin. I like your fire. I like it so much I plan to marry you. You could stay here in your home, our home, with your bastard. I'd let you keep him as long as you give me sons of my own.'

The very idea of bedding him made bile threaten to rise up her throat. 'Don't do this,

Baldr.' But even as she said it, his other arm went around her waist, pulling her against him.

'I'm not doing anything, yet. I'll give you time to think about it.'

'Get your bloody hands off her!'

Chapter Thirteen

Kadlin turned her head to see Gunnar standing just across the front room at the end of the passageway. He wore one of the furs he'd arrived with around his shoulders as a cloak. It was long enough that it dropped almost to the floor, obscuring the heavily wrapped leg and almost, but not quite, hiding the bottom of the walking stick lodged under his left arm. But she doubted Baldr noticed it, because the menacing sword Gunnar held with his right hand was currently pointed at him and demanded his full attention. The fur had fallen back on that side, revealing his naked shoulder and the muscle that had returned there. It was impressive how he managed to hold what was intended to be a two-handed weapon so steady with only one arm.

'I'd heard you had returned, nearly dead and

unmanned, Gunnar. Glad to see the rumours were only half-right. You're not dead. What a surprise to find you staying here.'

If she had looked back at Baldr, she knew she'd find him scowling at her. The fury from his gaze all but burned the back of her neck. He felt betrayed that she hadn't told him, as if she owed him anything.

'Get your hands off her,' Gunnar repeated, his voice tense and solid, but not loud or angry.

He was controlled and it was that more than the words that made Baldr's hands loosen. She quickly disengaged herself from him and moved away, but she didn't want the potential for violence to escalate so she stayed near enough. 'Thank you for the mead, Baldr. Please give my best to Father.'

There was absolute silence after she spoke, her words a plea for him to leave. She didn't want Gunnar to have to outright demand that he go. That was a challenge a warrior like Baldr wouldn't be able to resist. He wouldn't be able to leave without a fight then; he'd be forced to prove himself. Gunnar didn't appear to be at a point where he could handle the situation with tact. Baldr didn't look at her, but she stared at him, imploring him to take the easy way out.

Finally, he did. The tension in his shoulders eased just slightly, just enough that he could step back towards the door, his hand raising to open it. When he did, Gunnar let the tip of the sword drop so that it rested just barely on the floor in front of him, still at the ready should he need to use it.

Without a word to either of them, Baldr left, slamming the door in its frame and leaving a heavy and awkward silence behind him. Kadlin wanted to say 'thank you', she should have said 'thank you'. She meant to say it, but Gunnar hadn't taken his eyes from the door, even after the hoof beats of Baldr's horse had receded. And she couldn't take her eyes from Gunnar. He stood tall, every inch the powerful warrior that he had once been. Suddenly, it became clear what the strange noises coming from his chamber had been. The clamour of metal against wood, the clatter as the sword fell to the floor repeatedly, the groans of strain. He'd been getting stronger. At least in his upper body. She had noticed the change when she'd helped him back to his room last week, when he'd kissed her, but she hadn't fully realised how much he'd changed.

Gathering her wits about her, she realised how much the exertion must have taken out of him and rushed over to help with his sword. 'Thank—'

But he spoke at the same time, cutting her off. 'That is who you choose?'

'What?' His words were so unexpected that she had no idea what he meant.

'Baldr.' Finally taking his gaze from the door, he pinned her with it, making her stop. 'You would choose him.' It wasn't a question so much as an accusation.

'Did it look like I had chosen anything?'

'Aye, it looked like you were about to kiss him.'

'Have you gone daft in that chamber all alone? Have you forgotten what it looks like when a woman wants to be kissed?'

It was the wrong thing to say. The fire in his eyes shifted to something more dangerous than anger. 'Aye, I remember well. You showed me only a week ago.'

She sucked in a tortured breath. She didn't know why she was surprised that he'd use that against her, but she was and it hurt that he could treat that moment so callously. 'You're a brute. If you thought I wanted it, then why would you interrupt?'

His gaze raked her body, lingering on her breasts. When Baldr looked upon her that way, it made her skin tight and uncomfortable, repulsed. But with Gunnar it wasn't the same at all. His gaze made her warm, hot, even…achy, and aware of her body in the way that always happened when he looked upon her. She gritted her teeth to fight the idea that she felt anything and waited.

He was silent for a moment as he studied her, but he didn't make her wait long before his gaze returned to bore into hers and he answered. 'Because you are mine, Kadlin. You've always been mine.'

The words hung between them, making the air heavy with their weight. It almost crackled with the power of those words.

She had been his. There had been a time— most of her life actually—when she would have given anything to hear him say them, because she had been his. Pathetically his. Except now, after all that had passed, they rang hollow. Or too true. Or everything in between. Beating down the very visceral and illogical thrill they caused to shoot through her, Kadlin made sure to keep her voice steady and strong. 'I was yours. Once. You let me go.'

His fury deflated with those words as he let out a deep breath, but it didn't lessen the intensity of his stare. Whatever he might have said was lost when Avalt's babble reached them from her chamber and then his sweet voice called to her. It made her realise just what a dangerous line she was toeing, but now wasn't the time to tell him of their son. Not now when she was too raw to withstand his rejection. Or perhaps it was simply a sign of her cowardice. She didn't know and couldn't think about it now with him staring at her.

'Kadlin.' His hand moved to rest gently on her belly, staying her when she brushed past him to go to Avalt. His voice was softer than his earlier challenging tone. He waited until she looked up at him before murmuring, 'I only ever did what I thought was in your best interest. Nothing I did was to hurt you.'

She wanted to believe him. The earnest intention was there in his eyes, but there was too much pain. She'd given herself to him and he'd abandoned her. Didn't he understand how that had crushed her? How could he claim that she was his when he had never really fought to have her? How could they possibly move forward when she knew that he hadn't ever cared enough to fight for them? All the questions she had tumbled through her mind at once, weighing down on her.

'Gunnar...' Silence stretched taut between them, everything they needed to say heavy in the air. It frightened her how easily she could feel herself wanting to give in to him, to accept any excuse that he gave her just so that she could be back in his arms again. But if that was because it was so right or simply because it felt too good, she didn't know. She'd never been so adrift in her own emotions before.

Avalt's sweet voice reached her ears again, calling for her from the confines of her chamber. It forced herself out of her own head and she pushed against Gunnar's light hold. 'I have to go,' she whispered.

'Can I meet your son? Avalt?'

Those were not the words she thought he would

say. For the life of her, she didn't know what had prompted them. Had he guessed or was the request his way of making peace? Was he telling her that he wanted to try to win her back? She had no idea and right now it didn't matter. She was too confused, too hurt, to consider either.

'Another time.'

His expression didn't change, but his arm dropped back to the hilt of the sword he'd placed against the wall, leaving her free to hurry to her chamber and close the door behind her.

Gunnar watched her walk away with a mixture of pain and anger warring for dominance. There were countless reasons for his anger: his father's rejection, the fact that Kadlin had married someone else, had a child with someone else, that he'd never be able to fight like a warrior again. Oh, the list was endless. But the one thing that stood out above all the others, the one thing that made his blood boil beneath his skin, leaving it itchy and tight, was that she was right.

He'd had her and he'd lost her. The knowledge burned deep within him and made him want to sink his sword to the hilt into something alive and breathing. It was too bad Baldr had run. He could use a fight just now.

Fighting had always been his outlet for anger, frustration and pain, but now it wasn't an option. There was Vidar, but he would beat the boy too quickly, even with his lame leg. The only option with Kadlin was to face their battle head-on. She didn't want to admit that she had any feelings left for him, but she did. He'd seen them when she'd talked to him after his father's visit, he'd felt them when she had so sweetly kissed him back, he saw them in the pain in her eyes just now. He wanted to take that pain away and soothe the hurt he had caused her. He wanted her to look at him the way she had in the past and admit to her lingering feelings for him. But he knew she wouldn't and he couldn't blame her.

You let me go.

The accusation stung no matter how many times he turned it over in his mind. His obvious response had been: *You didn't wait.* But he'd let it die on his tongue because it was unfair. He'd told her to move on. Besides, it cut too close to what had wounded him the most. She had just moved on so easily while he had still longed for her. He was still longing for her. By the gods, he'd seen the longing in her as well and something within him needed to fulfil that longing in her.

He clenched his jaw and grabbed the sword to make his way back to his chamber, her words still echoing in his mind. His leaving had hurt her more than he realised. For the first time, he wondered if something had happened to force her to marry someone else, if maybe she'd been forced to move on. The blow when he'd realised she had married had sent him into a dark mourning that had allowed for nothing but his own self-absorbed pain. In his mind, it had been inevitable that he would lose her, so he hadn't even stopped to consider what had made her do it. He had simply assumed that she had found someone she loved more than she claimed to love him. Seeing her pain now had him wondering if that was true. Had his leaving her made her feel so rejected that she had moved on or had there been something else?

Tossing the sword to the floor, he dropped the fur across the foot of the bed and eased himself down on top of it. The ever-present throbbing in his leg had grown worse from his exertion and even his shoulder was beginning to ache from holding the sword. It should have been enough to send him to sleep, the only escape he had, but it wasn't. His mind kept churning over his conversation with Kadlin and then settling on the question of why she had married. Had her hand been forced?

Avalt's squeal of pleasure reached him through the closed door and he pushed himself up to rest on his elbows. Gunnar had been doing everything in his power to avoid the child up to now. His request to meet him had in part been as penance for the way he'd behaved and to prove to her that he regretted his part in what had happened between them. In part, because he was curious about her life that had moved forward without him, as he was obsessed with all things Kadlin. Her son was a part of that life, a part of her, and Gunnar still had a deep-seated need to know everything about her.

His thirst for her had never been quenched. It never would be. What had been between them was still there. Touching her, kissing her and then seeing her with Baldr had driven that point home better than he could have imagined. She'd run from him after their kiss because she'd also realised that whatever was between them wasn't dead. She was running scared, afraid to confront it. Aye, afraid to confront him, afraid that he would hurt her again. Except this time they were both older. He wouldn't hurt her because this time they both knew that their love could be nothing more than physical. He could give her pleasure, show her his love in the only way that he could. He couldn't marry her, couldn't spend the rest of his life with her as he wanted, but he could demonstrate his love with his touch.

She was his just as he would always be hers. It had been that way for as long as he could remember. She didn't realise it, because he'd made sure not to let on, but he'd heard her greeting to Baldr and the words they spoke before sitting down to eat. He knew that she wasn't married any more and nothing was stopping her from being his for a little while. Now that he was here with her, so close to her, he'd have her again. It infuriated him that she hadn't bothered to mention her lack of a husband to him, but he saw it now as the only shield she could carry against him. He despised the need for shields between them.

If the past few nights were an indication, she was having as much trouble sleeping as he was. He'd find her tonight when she couldn't sleep and he'd make her admit that she wanted him still. The flame that burned between them was brighter than ever. The future was still a black wall that he couldn't see through, but for now, he could show her pleasure to help atone for all the wrongs he had done to her. She was the only one who had ever cared for him. It was a paltry offering, but it was the least he could for her.

Chapter Fourteen

Kadlin flopped on to her back, anticipating another sleepless night. Her body was tired, yet her mind wouldn't be still for sleep. It was filled with Gunnar. Always Gunnar—she was growing tired of the constant thoughts. Her life had been good for the past year. She'd made a home that she was proud of and raised a child whom she adored. There had been whole days when she hadn't even thought of Gunnar. She had more than proven to herself that she didn't need him. Or any man. An argument she'd had to remind her father of numerous times since learning of Dagan's death.

It didn't stop her from wanting Gunnar, though, and that was the crux of her problem as well as the source of her disappointment. If she couldn't stop her madness, then she would allow him to hurt her all over again. It couldn't happen. The pain before had been almost unbearable and now she had Avalt to consider. She couldn't let herself fall into the black hole Gunnar's rejection had cast her into the first time. She didn't have the luxury this time around, not with her son needing her. It wouldn't be fair to him.

Besides, she had more to consider at the moment than her failed affair. Baldr posed a very real threat to her. If Jarl Hegard was actually deranged enough to give Baldr the farm, then she would have no home. As a matter of fact, Jarl Hegard might cast her off the property himself, since Eirik had fallen out of his favour. The jarl had been indulgent of her thus far, but she had a feeling that his charity would end soon. Perhaps it was time that she returned home to her parents. She'd enjoyed her freedom, but she'd known that it had only been a temporary break from responsibility. It was time to consider Avalt's future, which meant that it was now seriously time to consider another marriage for herself, even as the mere thought made her heart ache. Somewhere deep inside, she'd known that her days alone were coming to an end. Closing her eyes, she took deep breaths until the pressure in her chest eased. She wasn't a girl any more, so it was time to give up fanciful daydreams.

If she was rational, there was only one thing to do. With Vidar and Harald's family so near, Gunnar hardly needed her to see him well. She'd begin making preparations to move home. Once there she'd allow her father to arrange a match for her, someone who would accept Avalt. It was the right thing to do, the only thing to do. Before any of that, though, she had to tell Gunnar that Avalt was their son.

Anxiety churned in her belly at the thought.

'Stop this madness,' she whispered to herself. 'It doesn't matter. He can't hurt you more than he already has.'

With a sigh, she sat up in bed and pulled the blanket up over Avalt's small frame. Easing from the room, she passed the alcove where Vidar usually slept and noted that it was empty. He was probably at Harald's, attempting to lure Ingrid out into the night to have her alone. Kadlin had already spoken to the girl about Vidar's attentions, but whether she would heed her warnings, Kadlin didn't know. On silent feet she crossed the

front room and added a bit of wood to the fire
to combat the slight chill and then lit a few candles. She'd need a proper inventory of her supplies if she was planning to move. Some of it she
would take, but the rest could go to Harald's family. Might as well start tonight since she wasn't
sleeping anyway.

As she sorted the sacks and jugs, her mind
drifted from the task, and no matter how she tried
to stop them the questions swirled of their own
will. She groaned in frustration and blinked several times to clear her mind. It didn't matter. Of
course it didn't matter. Gunnar was a part of her
past, at least as far as her feelings went. That's
the way it had to be. It just had to—

A prickling heat along her neck was her only
warning before his voice cut through the surprisingly short distance between them.

'Turn around, Kadlin.'

How could she not? She spun and pressed herself against the table, her knuckles white from
gripping the table's edge so tightly. He stood just
before her, mere feet away.

'Gunnar…'

'Don't say it.'

'How did…how did you get here? I didn't even hear…' But she couldn't even form a rational thought, because he looked at her as if he wanted to devour her. She'd seen him admire her. She'd even seen desire in his eyes when he kissed her. The amount of heat the man was able to convey in his eyes alone was enough to dissolve her into a puddle of need at his feet. But this…this was more. This was raw hunger, a need that demanded as much as it wanted. He stood before her in his trousers, but nothing else. The fire at his back reflected in the deep red of his hair and made it so she couldn't even clearly see his face. Its flickering light played with shadows there, revealing only his eyes and the movement of his lips when he spoke. The play of darkness and light made him appear almost predatory, but the thought didn't fill her with fear at all. Not the fear that she should feel being in a house alone with him in the middle of the night.

She almost jumped when he moved, but managed to hold herself still as his hand came up to her chin. The backs of his fingers moved in a too-gentle-to-be-believed caress before his palm cupped her cheek. It took every ounce of her will to stop herself from leaning into his touch. But she did close her eyes when his thumb traced over her lips, settling on a slow back-and-forth rhythm that made tingles travel from the contact down to her breasts, tightening her nipples until she was sure he could see them straining beneath her nightdress, if he bothered to look. But when she opened her eyes, he was still holding her gaze.

'You're beautiful.' The rasp of his voice moved through her to settle deep within the cracks that she feared would never truly mend. His thumb moved to the corner of her mouth, pressing ever so slightly to gain access, so she bit him.

She thought he smiled, or at least his eyes crinkled in the corners, but he didn't draw back. So she released him with her teeth and sucked his thumb, her tongue laving over the tip to taste him just once before she turned her head away, releasing him. Instead of retreating, he shifted on his sapling and closed most of the distance between them, leaving only a breath of space. His hand trailed down her neck and breast without stopping until coming to a rest on her hip.

'Gunnar—'

'You can deny that whatever has always been

between us still exists. You can deny it all you want, but it doesn't make it go away. It's there, Kadlin, and it always will be.'

She closed her eyes again, willing the heat of his touch to go away, but it wouldn't. The ripples of pleasure that had begun in her belly spread lower with the heat, making her body heavy and pliant to his touch. When she didn't move, he dipped his head lower so that his lips brushed over her cheekbone and then even lower, skimming the edge of her mouth. She took a ragged breath when he moved down past the column of her neck to settle a kiss at the hollow at its base. He nuzzled her there, his lips moving against her skin as he whispered, 'I want to touch you, to give you pleasure.'

'Why?' It was a simple question, but her heart pounded in her head as she awaited the answer. When it came, he spoke against her skin, his voice rumbling through her while his fingertips bit lightly into the flesh of her hips.

'Because I took so much from you over the years and I want to give some of it back to you. Because we should have had so much more than we've been allowed and I want to relish every bit of you while I can.' His teeth scraped her flesh as he said that, causing her to tremble and goose-flesh to rise on her skin, the sensation pleasurable and wicked.

Then he abruptly released her, leaving her bereft without his warmth, his touch. She watched him, torn between the fear of accepting his touch and the fear that if she pushed him away that she would never feel it again. He moved a chair over to set it before her and she watched, puzzled, as he sat down so that his left leg had room to stretch out to the side. She couldn't fathom his intention when he quietly placed the sapling on the ground and straightened to look at her. She tried to meet his gaze, and now that he was low enough that the pool of candlelight from the table could light his face she tried to look at him. But it was too much. A blush stained her cheeks and she dropped her attention to his chest, solid and wide with muscle.

'Turn around and sit on my lap.'

Her eyes snapped back to his face at the command to find a challenge lighting his eyes and the corner of his mouth tipped up. If he had touched her first, if he had continued his delicious assault

on her senses, she might have made herself obey
by simply letting him do what he wanted. But
how could she when he sat there and ordered her
to do things that she knew she shouldn't do? How
could she go into the fire that was almost certain
to burn her alive with her eyes wide open?

As if sensing the battle that raged within her,
he took her hand in his. His fingers gripping hers
with just enough strength to be reassuring rather
than forceful, as his thumb trailed back and forth
across her knuckles. But then he leaned forward,
bringing the heat of his body into dangerously
close proximity to hers. His face was level with
her breasts and he gave them a thorough appraisal
that had them straining through the fabric of her
nightdress, before meeting her gaze. 'I can have
you this way, as well, if you'd rather.' He released
her hand and gripped the loose fabric, pulling the
hem up her legs.

'What are you doing to us? Are you mad?'

'Aye, I could be, but I don't care any more.'

His attention shifted back to her breasts, making her almost strain towards him so that his
mouth would find her nipple. Just when she was
on the verge of putting it there herself, she spun

around to save herself from the temptation. His grip on her hips tightened and he pulled her down to sit on his lap, her thighs straddling his right leg. Immediately, he resumed pulling up the hem, leaving her unable to move to halt him or to help him. She could only watch its progress up her legs until his strong hands were running up the sides of her thighs. But he stopped and moved his left arm around her waist, pulling her back so that she lay against his chest. When her head rested on his shoulder, he turned just slightly so that his lips nuzzled her ear before he lightly nipped the lobe. 'If I touched you now, would I find you wet?'

She groaned in the back of her throat and closed her eyes against the truth of his words and the throbbing that began in her core. It wasn't fair that he affected her so effortlessly. He'd barely even touched her. The hand at her waist moved up to gently cup her breast, his thumb circling around the nipple until she whimpered and arched a bit to make him touch the straining flesh. But he didn't and his right hand had begun a maddening rhythm of trailing up and down the inside of her thigh, his fingers so close to where she ached but refusing to touch her.

'Is this all only to tease me, so that I'm as mad as you are?'

He laughed, *laughed* against the curve of her neck and rubbed his stubbled chin against the tender skin. 'Do you want me to touch you, Kadlin?'

'You bloody well know that I do.'

'Then you have to tell me. I won't have you thinking I forced you into something in the morning.' Yet, he pinched her nipple after he spoke, eliciting a gasp from her as darts of pleasure bolted through her core. Then he retreated, his hand resting just on her ribcage, while his right hand continued its maddening stroking of her thigh.

With a groan, she grabbed his wrist and brought his fingers to her centre. 'There,' she whispered. 'I need you there.'

'Ah, Kadlin.' His voice was a sigh against her neck, not mocking or challenging, but full of reverence.

She closed her eyes as she savoured the feel of his fingertips dipping into her, exploring how aroused he had made her. Spreading the moisture, two fingers found their way upward to the swollen flesh pulsing in wait. When he touched her, circling the bud with the solid pressure of his fingers, she bit her lip to stifle another moan of pleasure. It had been too long since he'd taught her how good his touch could feel and her own fingers couldn't compare to the skill of his. It was as if he knew just how to touch her, just how much pressure, just the right rhythm, just when the pleasure was mounting too fast and he needed to back off. When he pulled away, she grabbed his wrist, afraid that the tease was only that and wouldn't lead to the explosive burst of release that she craved.

'Don't worry, love, I won't leave you.' Even his husky voice soft against her ear was a caress that left her body vibrating with wanting him. 'Pull the top down, I want to see you.'

Immediately, she raised her hands to the ties of her nightdress, unwilling to even consider denying his request. She wanted it as much as he did. But she wasn't prepared for the rush of pleasure that washed over her when she revealed her breasts to him and he groaned in gratification.

Just like that she remembered how pleasing him had brought her so much pleasure in return. 'So beautiful.' His thumb brushed over the sensitive tip, making her arch into his touch. 'You don't know how much I've dreamed of this moment, watching you writhe beneath my touch.'

She gasped, but mainly from the unexpected thrill that shot through her middle and centred at the throbbing apex of her thighs. As if his words carried their own magic, she found herself moving her hips to make his fingers move against her. She met his gaze, the hot amber scorching in its intensity, before he looked back down to see what his hands had revealed. The humour, the teasing, even some of the fierceness drained from his face. All that was left was the naked longing and it touched her more than any of his words could have.

She couldn't look away when he touched her, only this time it was his thumb that circled her swollen arousal. He looked back at her, as if more interested in watching the ecstasy on her face than whatever his fingers were doing. It was too much, too intimate, made even more so by the abject awe on his face when his forefinger sought her opening and pushed into her. But he didn't flash her a triumphant smile, as she had feared he might. His expression didn't change at all as he worked it in and out of her and then pushed a second broad finger inside, holding still as he waited for her body to adjust to the invasion. Her hips were restless, asking for more, before he relented and began an easy, steady rhythm within her, his thumb continuing its skilful stroking of her.

When the fingers of his left hand deftly began plucking her nipple, she cried out and finally broke eye contact when she closed her eyes and moved with his rhythm. He didn't allow her to savour it, though. His mouth covered hers, his tongue seeking hers out as if he wanted to possess every inch of her body with his. It was too much and not enough at the same time. Needing something to hold on to, something to ground her, she reached up and tangled her fingers in the hair at the nape of his neck. Her other hand flailed until it met the wood of his splint, which brought her back to reality, but only briefly before his fingers made her only aware of him inside her and her entire world narrowed to that, to him. She moved her hand to find purchase on the seat of the chair between his legs, but her palm found something else, something strong and hard pushing into the base of her back.

Gunnar fairly groaned as she pressed against him, squeezing to test the contact. His reaction caused a brief mew of pleasure to escape her before she clenched her bottom lip between her teeth to stifle it.

'Nay, this is about your pleasure, not mine.' His voice made her open her eyes to look at him.

'Perhaps it still is.' She smiled.

He grinned at her and thrust his fingers again, harder. Overwhelmed by a wave of possessiveness, Gunnar looked down at her body, beautiful and open for him. But it wasn't enough. Releasing her breast, he grabbed the cloth of her nightdress and held it up so that when he looked down he could see her better. Using his thumbs, he parted her again, revealing how swollen she was for him as he watched his fingers disappear into her silken channel. The knowledge that he was making her lose her carefully orchestrated control made him harden painfully in his trousers,

but he ignored it. This would be about her pleasure, not his. He wouldn't take anything else from
her, though he'd wring out every bit of pleasure
from her that he could. Even when her greedy
hand squeezed him, he forced back the rush of
pleasure that moved up his belly.

His thumb circled the swollen bud, making her
hips move with him, ride his fingers. She gasped
softly, a precious sound that he wanted to hear
again and again. So he did it again, only this time
he kissed her shoulder, raking his teeth across
the delicate flesh. She was exquisite. Perfect. Her
hips bucked up, wanting more, so he gave it to her
and drove deep within her. This time she couldn't
stifle her cry of pleasure and the knowledge that
he'd elicited it thrilled him.

His name whimpered past her lips and he
longed to hear her scream it out with his manhood
inside her, but that would have to wait. Curling
his fingers upward, he stroked her as a faceless
woman had taught him once long ago. The memory caused a pang of guilt to shoot through him
at all the women he'd had that hadn't been her.

'Gunnar,' she called again, wiping all thoughts
but of her from his mind. There was only Kadlin

writhing beneath his touch, moaning his name as he stroked her. What he wouldn't give to taste her, to have her come apart as his tongue stroked her, but it would be too much. For now. For now there was just her and her pleasure. He'd make her remember how much she wanted him and make her crave him again.

'Come apart for me, love,' he whispered into her ear. 'Let go.'

She responded almost instantly, gasping as he pinched her nipple and plucked, while his fingers continued their assault within her. Then she was lost and her body clenched him hard as it trembled around him, but he kept stroking her until her body relaxed into him, her fingers limp and her breath coming in long, shuddering breaths. He kissed her then, trailing his lips from her ear and down her neck to her shoulder. She kept her eyes closed, but snuggled into him, sated and sleepy from her release. Pulling his fingers from her body, he shifted so that he could hold her close to him. He'd set out to prove something to her, to prove that she couldn't run or hide from what was between them. He'd never thought that in doing so, he'd realise just how much he needed her and just how afraid he was that she'd never realise how much she needed him. Tucking her head beneath his chin, he buried his face in her hair and took a deep breath. Losing her wasn't an option he could live with, but even knowing that, he knew there wasn't a future for them. There was only now and the pleasure he could give her.

Chapter Fifteen

'Kadlin.'

Her eyelids fluttered when he repeated her name, but she refused to open her eyes. Gunnar tightened his arm around her and stroked his thumb across her cheekbone. She smiled at the pleasant tingle of sensation on her skin, but didn't stir otherwise. 'You can't be sleeping,' he murmured and brushed his lips across her temple. The soft and gentle touch made her shiver, her belly warming from the implications even as her mind was wakening from its pleasure-induced lethargy. Even the raspy cadence of his voice caused frissons of awareness to move through her, making her crave more than he had just given her.

'Nay, not sleeping. Simply prolonging the inevitable.' Her hand snaked up to curve around his shoulder and she buried her face in his neck, breathing in the spice of his scent, a scent she'd know anywhere. He was so warm, so real, and in this moment…hers. It wouldn't last, but she didn't want to think of that now.

He sucked in a deep breath and froze. Whether it was from her words or her touch, she didn't know. She only knew that she wanted to savour these final few moments in his arms without any thoughts or any words to distract her from how good it was to have his arms around her. The solid breadth of him against her, the heat of his body, the knowledgeable stroke of his fingers, all of it had been so much more than she had remembered. She only wanted to enjoy the last stolen moments with him before reality intruded and she had to think of all the reasons this was so wrong.

He slowly pushed out his breath and tension took its place, keeping the corded muscles of his neck and shoulders rigid beneath her fingers. 'What is the inevitable?'

The respite was over.

Sighing, she allowed her hand to slip down to her lap, and she blinked up at the concern on his face. A weight seeped into her chest bringing with it an end to the delicious euphoria that had left her languishing in the pleasure he'd brought her. 'The inevitable is the argument we're about to have. The one where I accuse you of using my girlish fantasies of you against me.'

He winced, closing his eyes briefly to process the accusation, but when he opened them they blazed hot and without a bit of remorse. 'No arguments here, love. Except for the girlish part. You're all woman. Those fantasies aren't girlish.'

Her mouth actually dropped open at his audacity, but she recovered quickly enough and straightened in his lap. 'You have no shame, but perhaps that's what I should expect from you.'

'There's no room for shame between us. Don't try to pretend there is.' He grinned and brought a hand up to absently brush an exposed nipple with the backs of his fingers.

The shock of delicious arousal that moved from her nipple to her belly and then farther down shouldn't have caught her by surprise. He'd caused that same reaction more than once with just a hot look across his father's crowded hall and the way she'd just come apart in his arms had proved that his touch was as potent as it had ever been. She'd thought—hoped—that with her need for him so recently met, that she'd be stronger. Grabbing his wrist with both of her hands, she forced his hand to his lap between them and held it there. It left her breasts exposed, but at least he wasn't touching her, making her ache again. 'Don't touch me.'

That was enough to wipe the maddening smile from his face. 'You think I had ulterior motives for this, for touching you?'

'Of course I do. You have ulterior motives for everything. Didn't you want to touch me to prove that I still want you? Didn't you want to prove to me that I can't escape that fact no matter what I do? I came apart just as you wanted, stripped of everything. But I already knew that I would, so you didn't accomplish anything. Except now I know you'll stoop to using this…this *thing* between us as a weapon.'

'Oh, Kadlin.' He dropped his forehead so that it rested against hers, but she didn't want to pretend that what had happened was anything more than it actually was. When she pulled back, he shook free of her hold and brought his hand to rest on her chest. As if on cue, her heartbeat increased to a pounding thunder. 'Aye, I wanted to prove to you that what you appear so content to deny is true. Whatever this is between us will never die.'

'Then you've succeeded. Congratulations.'

He continued as if she hadn't interrupted. 'You want me now as much as you ever have. I want you.'

Pushing free and dislodging his hand, she grabbed the ties of her nightdress to begin righting herself, covering her breasts. While he allowed that, he refused to relinquish his hold on her waist so she still sat perched on his right thigh. 'This wanting, Gunnar... It's only lust. It only means that you still have this hold over my body. Nothing more.'

'Is that all you think this is?' He laughed, a soft exhalation of breath that rustled the hair at her temples. His lips brushed her skin as he spoke. 'It's so much more. I can't remember a time when you weren't a part of my life. One of my earliest memories is looking down on you in your mother's arms and thinking you were the most beautiful creature I'd ever seen. Your hair was just curly wisps of nothing then, but your eyes were the same deep, clear blue that stare back at me now. Even then, I'd known that my purpose in life was to keep you safe and happy. It's all I ever wanted.'

The sudden lump that swelled and ached in her throat caught her unprepared. She wanted so much for those words to be true, but they weren't. He'd proven to her time and again how untrue they actually were by hurting her. How did hurting her keep her happy? Covering his lips with her fingers to stop anything else he might be thinking of saying, she shook her head. 'Don't lie to me. Please not now. I still want you. I've said it. Don't make this into something else, something more because we both know that it's not.'

His eyes flashed with wickedness just moments before he grabbed both of her wrists and pressed them to the small of her back, making her arch into his chest. 'It already is something else. I don't have to *make* it into anything. Don't you understand that the hold I have over you is the same one you wield over me? Don't you understand that for my entire life there's only ever been you there with me every night when I close my eyes?

'Aye, the night you gave yourself to me was

the best night of my life, but it's more. It's your voice I heard calling to me those days when my father raged so loudly I thought the world would end, it's your arms I felt after every raid when the rush of combat would die out and I'd fall hard—'

'Stop, Gunnar! Just stop.' Anger flared inside her that he would dare to use lies against her when he had shown her that none of it was true. The fact that he was looking at her without meeting her anger only made hers flare higher. It was as if he was humouring her anger and she wouldn't let him do that to her, make her into some object to be used for his amusement. 'I don't believe any of it. If you so wanted to keep me happy, then why have you only ever hurt me? I loved those nights when we were children and you'd come to my chamber, but you took them away. You simply stopped as if I meant nothing to you. And then you made it hurt more by ignoring me. I'd see you when we'd travel to your father's hall and you wouldn't even see me, or you'd look through me as if I didn't matter. Or worse. When we were older I'd see you with another woman, touching her, leading her back to your chamber. Sometimes I'd catch you watching me, but when I approached you'd barely say a word. You shut me out so completely and I could never do that to you.'

He dropped his forehead to hers again and this time she didn't pull away. Just closed her eyes as she absorbed his nearness, his attention. When he spoke, his warm breath caressed her face. 'Ah… you don't understand. Keeping you safe was even more important than keeping you happy. Do you remember that day when we were children, when Eirik and I were attacked?'

She nodded and his lips brushed against her cheek. She couldn't forget that day, even though she hadn't been there. The boys had been eleven or twelve years old, while she was two years younger. Criminals angry with Jarl Hegard had abducted Gunnar and Eirik, and while Gunnar had managed to escape to get help, Eirik had been brutalised until his father and his father's men had come to save him.

'I failed Eirik that day. And I knew that I'd fail you, too, eventually.'

'Nay, that wasn't your fault.'

'Shh…' He transferred her wrists to one hand, keeping a firm hold on them so he could put a finger over her lips. 'It doesn't matter. But there's more. It wasn't long after that your father found me leaving your chamber one morning and told me not to come back. He knew I didn't deserve you.'

This was the first she had heard of such a meeting and her instinct was to accuse Gunnar of lying, but she held her tongue. It wasn't an impossibility; besides, Gunnar's finger still pressed gently against her lips.

'He was right to demand it. By then we'd already shared many kisses. Do you remember?' At her nod, he dropped his hand and pressed his lips to the corner of her mouth. 'Do you remember how long we would lie there in your bed kissing? How soon before I kissed you somewhere else?'

Her face heated as she remembered those nights near the end. She'd been too young to understand the reason his lips stroking hers had caused those strange tremblings in her belly and limbs. She'd only understood that she liked it and liked it even more when he'd lie on top of her; his weight pressing her down into her blankets.

'If I had kept coming to you, it would have been

only a matter of time before I parted your legs and buried myself between them.'

'You could have told me.'

'Aye, I could have and perhaps I should have. But you were so perfect. You *are* so perfect. I'm not. I didn't want to wait around and see the light that lit your eyes when you saw me die out.'

'That doesn't make any sense.' She shook her head to deny his reasoning, but the stricken look on his face stopped her.

'Of course it doesn't to you. Everyone loved you. And I don't begrudge you that. *I loved* you. But...' His voice trailed off, as if he couldn't say the words.

So she said them for him. 'But everyone who was supposed to love you...didn't? Your mother abandoned you to marry and have another family without you and your despicable father couldn't bring himself to see past Eirik.' He didn't agree, but he didn't argue, either. 'But I did, Gunnar. *I did*. Why did you have such little faith in me?'

'Because I didn't know how to have faith in you.'

It was an absurdly simple answer, but she believed him. 'And now? Do you know how to now?'

* * *

Gunnar stared at the face that would always haunt him. Her clear blue eyes stared up into his with an intensity that pierced his heart. She was so perfect it made him ache. Beautiful, kind, strong… She was all of those things. Everything that he was not. She was too perfect for him. All her life she'd only known love and acceptance. Though she could say the words, she couldn't understand how it felt to have those she loved desert her. But almost immediately, he realised that wasn't true. She had loved him and he had abandoned her. He was the one who had made sure she understood how abandonment felt. The realisation was like a knife twisting in his gut.

'Nay.' His answer was as honest as he could make it. She had married someone else. She had proven that she could move on without him. Was that what he had intended by not telling her to wait for him? Had it been some horrible, twisted test of her loyalty? He honestly didn't know and the thought sickened him. What sort of monster would use her love for him against her in that way? The knowledge that he didn't deserve her pounded through his skull. It was as true today as it had ever been.

She flinched in his arms and was about to pull away, but he caught her and gathered her close before she could. His thumb tipped her chin up so that she had to look at him. 'But it doesn't matter.'

Anger flashed in her eyes again. She was so angry with him that her skin was warm beneath his touch. He deserved her anger and he was willing to accept it if it meant that he could be close to her. Her lips parted, undoubtedly to tell him that it wasn't enough, and maybe it wasn't. Instead of letting her talk, he covered her lips with his own and stroked his tongue against hers. She moaned, a soft feminine sound in the back of her throat, but instead of pushing away she kissed him back. His arms went around her, crushing her to his chest. Having her in his arms was so right, he didn't know how he'd ever walked away from her. He lapped at her mouth, knowing that he'd never get enough of tasting her.

The click of the opening door was his only warning before Vidar chuckled. 'So this is how it is?'

Kadlin pulled away and fled before he could

secure his grip on her. Her hair streamed out behind her as she hurried down the passageway to her chamber and disappeared inside, leaving Gunnar with an aching heart and an aching erection. Neither of those left him in a good mood to face his brother. 'Bad timing, Brother.' Gunnar turned the ferocity of his gaze on the boy. 'What are you doing out at this time of night?'

'Same as you.' Vidar grinned and nodded towards Kadlin's chamber.

'Ingrid's only a girl. You should slake your lust with a woman able to prevent consequences.'

'That's profound, coming from you.' Vidar laughed, but sobered when he saw the look on Gunnar's face.

'What is that supposed to mean?'

Vidar shook his head and pulled the latch closed on the door behind him. 'Ingrid isn't the only reason I was out. Oddr, Harald's eldest boy, returned from visiting Father earlier tonight.'

Gunnar shrugged and leaned heavily on the table to get to his feet and balance with the bloody stick. 'I don't care to hear what the old man has to say.'

'He's dying. Oddr claims that he isn't well, that

he lies upon his deathbed.' When Gunnar didn't reply, the boy pressed him. 'Aren't you even concerned?'

'Nay, but *you* should be. You'll be the jarl when he's gone. I'll be gone once this bloody leg allows me to go.' The words were easy to say, but difficult to imagine. Where could he go? How could he bring himself to leave Kadlin again?

'What do you mean? You're next in line.' Vidar crossed around the hearth, coming to stand before him.

'Ah, you missed his visit. It seems I'm out of favour, along with Eirik. You're the next one now.' Gunnar almost felt a pang of sorrow for the genuine look of distress that crossed his brother's face. He looked so like Eirik, blond and broad, but without the ferocity Eirik carried. Gunnar had been told more than once that he shared that ferocity; their main similarity. Vidar was the youngest brother, so he'd escaped the near-constant pitting of son against son that their father had so enjoyed.

'Nay!' The boy spat out the word like it had bitten him. 'I don't want that. I'll earn my ship in a few years and travel the world. I can't be jarl yet.'

Gunnar envied him the lackadaisical attitude, the freedom to wander and know that his place was secure. Gunnar would have happily given his eyeteeth if he'd been told at Vidar's age that he'd become jarl. Becoming jarl was the only way he'd known to prove to everyone—including himself—that he deserved Kadlin. It had always been about deserving her. Nothing else had mattered. 'Don't worry, little brother. I think the old man has a few years left. He wasn't sickly when I saw him.' Though he hadn't looked well.

When Gunnar moved to go past him, Vidar held out his hand. 'Wait. There is doubt amongst the men. Without Eirik here they're not sure who will take over.'

A smile curved Gunnar's lips, but it was humourless. 'The old man isn't as smart as he thinks. He bet everything on Eirik and now can't deliver on his vow. That instability is bound to cause dissension. It'll blow over, but if he really is ill then I think your travelling days might be over.'

Vidar shook his head. 'It won't blow over. Baldr is there.'

'Baldr? Jarl Leif's man?'

'Aye. Father's man now, it seems. They say he's working his way in, that he plans to take over.'

'And how will he do that? Why would he risk Jarl Leif's favour?'

Vidar shrugged. 'Since we've been gone, he's been a second to Father even as he's worked under Jarl Leif. He could have the support of them both, but the men don't like him.'

Kadlin. Her face swam before his vision, followed by the sight of her in Baldr's arms. Once Baldr became jarl, particularly if it was at the discretion of her father, then there would be nothing standing in his way of having her. He shook his head to clear it and then took a deep breath. 'Rumours can sometimes just be rumours. They could mean nothing. Go home and see what you can discover. You should have gone home already.'

'Couldn't. I had to play nursemaid.'

Gunnar pushed his shoulder as he started back towards his chamber. 'Nursemaid to Ingrid, perhaps. I don't need you.' He grinned and tossed back over his shoulder. 'Go at first light and stay a few days. Come back and let me know what you find.'

'And whatever will you do to pass the time while I'm away?' Vidar laughed.

Gunnar ignored him as he made his way back to his chamber, sparing a glance at the closed door to Kadlin's chamber. Tonight had gone well…until it hadn't. Kadlin was afraid and he had to be patient, but that didn't mean leaving her alone. It appeared that she needed many more reminders of how good they were together.

Chapter Sixteen

Harald arrived early the next morning to check the limb he stubbornly insisted on calling a leg. Gunnar had long since given up on it ever being that again, but he allowed the older man his poking and prodding because he seemed to enjoy it. Lying back with his hands folded under his head, Gunnar watched as he unwrapped the bandages, smiling. It was the same every week; Harald would alternately smile and frown as he examined the limb before wrapping it back up again. Only this time, he wasn't frowning.

'You seem happy, old man. It's healing?'

'Aye, looking a might better.'

Gunnar sucked in a breath when he rubbed a bony finger across one of the broken areas on his shin. It hadn't really hurt, but the phantom pain had almost been as bad as real pain.

Harald laughed and moved his fingers over the spot again. There was a raised area where the bone must have fused.

'Another fortnight, maybe a bit more, and these splints can come off.'

'They come off now. I can't wear them a fortnight more.'

'Nay, Gunnar. The heal is good, but it's still too fresh. You could fall and break it clean in two again.'

But Gunnar was already pushing himself up and shaking his head. 'No more, old man. It's time I start getting back to myself, as much as I can. Those splints keep me abed too much. They're too awkward to move around. I can't wait any longer.' Not with Kadlin hanging in the balance. She'd seen how good it could be between them. For some reason he couldn't fathom, he needed her to understand that he was still a man, still a warrior, though he had no idea how that was even possible.

Harald sighed, but realised that argument would be futile. Raising a hand to urge Gunnar back down, he said, 'I'll rewrap the bandages tight. That, at least, will give the limb some stability.'

Satisfied that his wishes had been heard, Gunnar lowered himself back down to the bed and listened for Kadlin. She'd been in the front room when Harald had come in, but the man had brought over fish so she'd taken them outside to clean. Vidar had already left for home so there was no one else for the task. A knot of anticipation churned in his gut, but he refused to let it run havoc. Tonight they would be alone in the house with no chance of interruption for the first time since he'd been delivered to her door.

She'd been suspiciously quiet all day, leaving his breakfast at his door rather than face him. Whether she was angry at him still, or simply uncertain of her own thoughts, he didn't know. But it didn't matter. Tonight he would confront her again and make her feel everything that was between them, whether she admitted to those feelings or not. It was the only thing that he could give her.

As Harald wrapped his leg again, they spoke of the gossip Oddr had heard while visiting Jarl Hegard's hall. It was nothing that Vidar hadn't told him, but he reassured Harald that Vidar was up to the task of jarl.

'That's not the feeling amongst the men,' Harald argued. 'He's a boy.'

'He's not a boy any longer.'

'He's not a warrior. Warriors won't follow a man who hasn't proven himself in battle.'

'Then we should all wish my father long life.'

'That's not likely, boy.' For the first time, Harald narrowed his eyes at him in disappointment. 'He won't last out the season. You can't tell me you haven't spent your life wanting to be jarl. You could step in…take your father's place.'

Gunnar grinned. 'I could try, but I fear that would only hasten my father's demise. He doesn't agree with you.' Even in the unlikely event that he did, his men wouldn't follow a cripple. Gunnar couldn't bring himself to say those words aloud.

Harald nodded and tied off the end of the bandage before rising to his feet. 'Aye, but I recall a boy with flame hair who was as likely to spit in his father's face as follow his orders.'

There had been a time when he'd held on to the hope of earning his father's approval, but when it had always gone to Eirik, Gunnar had stopped trying. Even then, he hadn't realised the depths of his father's hatred for him. Failing to save Eirik had only been the last straw. Earning the jarl's endorsement wasn't possible and with his men across the sea fighting the Saxons, Gunnar didn't have the means to take the position. With a shrug, he sighed and shook his head. 'That boy is long gone, my friend.'

The older man stood there for a while staring down at him, before nodding and turning towards the door. 'That's a pity' was his only remark as he shuffled out the door.

Gunnar watched him go, his leg dragging on the floor with each step. His gaze automatically went to his own leg lying across the bed. Now that the bulky splints were gone, it looked more like a leg with a misshapen knee and a calf. He twisted it slightly, grimacing at the tightness and the persistent ache. Resting his weight on his hands, he moved slowly to the edge of the bed until he sat with his right foot on the floor and then moved his left leg to join it. A smile curved his lips as he accomplished that without a problem. Carrying the heavy splints around had helped his muscles to stay strong, but they couldn't help his knee, which seemed determined to never bend again.

Clenching his jaw, he put weight on his heel and tried to force himself to his feet, but the knee still refused to work. With a curse, he grabbed the ever-present sapling and pulled himself up on to his feet. Just like Harald's, his knee wouldn't bend, wouldn't support him like it should. It wasn't a surprise, just another disappointment. He sighed and moved forward, gratified that he felt much lighter with the splints gone. The small victory would have to be enough.

Hesitating at the door, he pushed it open and looked down the passageway. The front door of the sod house was open and Harald's voice drifted through it. Undoubtedly recounting the state of Gunnar's leg. Silently willing the man to leave, Gunnar made his way down the hall towards the front room. He was impatient to have Kadlin to himself. After last night, he didn't know how she would feel towards him, but he was eager to look upon her again, to talk to her, to touch her.

The moment he sat down in the very same chair he'd occupied last night, his thoughts took a different path. The mongrel came in through the open door and trotted over, tucking her muzzle under his hand where it rested on his thigh as she begged to be petted. With a laugh, he obliged her, burying his fingers in her grey-and-black fur. Her tail twitched back and forth in ecstasy. 'If only your mistress was so easily tamed,' he mused.

A movement near the door caught his eye. Thinking to see Kadlin standing there, he smiled and glanced up. But, though Kadlin's blue eyes stared back at him, it was not her staring at him.

Avalt studied him with the solemn scrutiny only a very young child was able to manage. The breath left his chest and the skin at the back of his neck prickled and tightened as he stared back at the boy. Though he possessed Kadlin's eyes, his full head of hair was the same as Gunnar's, not the light auburn that some of the other men possessed, but a dark red that Gunnar had only seen on one other person besides himself—his mother. When he could finally draw breath, he forced himself to glance down at the dog, drawing air into his lungs and moving his lips to make words come out, but it took a couple of attempts. 'She's a friendly mongrel.'

The boy slowly stepped forward, clearly uncertain of the man petting his dog. Gunnar moved just as cautiously, afraid of frightening him, but wanting him to come closer. 'Come, show me where she likes to be scratched.'

Avalt obliged and reached out to scratch her behind her ears. He followed suit, earning a grin from the boy. In the small face he recognised the almond shape of his own eyes and the nose that was a bit too strong for a child so young, but would sit fine and strong on the face of a warrior. He almost smiled, his heart twisting in his chest.

He had a son. *They* had a son.

There was no doubt that the perfect child before him was a product of them both. Kadlin was present there, too, in the shape of his brow and his long lashes. Instinct guided his fingers to rest on the soft baby cheek, earning a smile from Avalt. His skin was so incredibly soft and fine. Gunnar tried to imagine Kadlin round with his child and an ache tightened his throat. Had she been frightened to realise that his seed had taken root? Joyous? Nay, that was too much to expect. What woman would be happy to know that the man who had left her with child was across the world? A stab of guilt so harsh and raw that it was almost painful ran through his body, making him close his eyes to fight it down. He should have been more careful. But when he opened his eyes to see those blue eyes gazing at him curiously, he couldn't find it in him to be regretful or ashamed. They were always meant to have children. If life had been just, they'd have had many more by now.

Nothing that had created such a perfect creature could be a mistake. The mistake had been in leaving her to face the consequences on her own. The mistake had been his own actions, not hers. If only she would have sent someone to him, he could have come back and…

His mind went blank when it came to what would have happened next. Marriage would have been a certainty, but what then? He would have had to leave her to earn their way. Or perhaps her father would have given him a position beneath Baldr. Could he have accepted such a position? Nay, he knew the answer without even thinking about it. Had she not told him because she hadn't wanted him to give up what he wanted? He'd always demanded so much of her without giving anything in return. She must have chosen marriage so that their son wouldn't be a bastard. A bastard like his own father. Gunnar despised that she would have to make that choice.

There had been so many things that he'd done wrong, he didn't know if he could ever make them up to her. Shaking his head, he focused on the boy.

'My name is Gunnar.' He kept his voice low, unable to pull his gaze from his face.

The boy smiled, revealing tiny, perfect teeth before looking down at the wounded leg propped on the hearth. He must have had some idea that it had been Gunnar who had been residing in his home all this time and that he'd been injured. Gunnar searched his memory, trying to determine if the child had seen him in the early days, but those memories were too fogged and clouded with pain and the laced mead for him to be sure. He probably looked different anyway. Before he realised what Avalt meant to do, the boy reached out his chubby hand and patted his injured knee. Gunnar smiled and swallowed the sudden ache in his throat. 'Aye, I'm the one you've been hearing complain about my leg, causing your mother grief. You have my vow that I'll stop now. She doesn't deserve any more grief from me.'

'Avalt!' Kadlin's voice called from outside. The boy turned, but made no move to leave.

Panic rose within him, rushing the blood through his veins. Torn between confronting her with the truth and his need for her to tell him about the child herself, he froze. Neither of those could happen right now. 'Avalt, you should go to your mother,' he urged just moments before Kadlin stood in the doorway.

Gunnar sitting there with Avalt was not the sight Kadlin had expected to greet her. Gunnar always stayed in his chamber until they left for the river. Always. It was their unspoken agreement that he not intrude on her life with her son. She was angry, perhaps unreasonably, that he had broken that truce; yet even as she acknowledged the anger, she realised that it was so wrapped up in her own guilt for keeping Avalt from him that it was impossible to tell how much of one grew from the other. Gunnar met her gaze across the small space, but it was shielded. Had he guessed that Avalt was his? Of course he had guessed. When his own face stared back at him in miniature form, any man would guess. Wouldn't he? Was he angry?

Freyja trotted over and nuzzled her hand, giving Kadlin an excuse to break his stare as she looked down at the eager face staring up at her. She swallowed repeatedly, desperate to relieve the tightness in her throat, all the while despising the distraction for the cowardly act that it was.

'Avalt was just showing me how Freyja likes her ears scratched.' She glanced up to catch his adoring gaze settle on Avalt. 'He's a brave boy, Kadlin,' Gunnar added in a reverent voice.

Clearing her throat before she could speak, she nodded in agreement. 'He is. He's a strong son.'

Avalt beamed at her with a smile so like his father's rarely seen one that her breath hitched. Holding out her hand to him, she waited for him to come over and take it in his smaller one before returning her attention to Gunnar. This time she noticed that his leg was merely wrapped in linen. 'Your splints are gone. Did Harald say you had healed?'

He shrugged, but his eyes were assessing and cautious as he looked her over. 'Healed enough.

The knee won't bend still, but I suspect that it never will.'

He wouldn't press the issue of their son. She didn't know if she should be relieved or angry, so she tried not to be either one and let numbness settle over her. 'I've put the fish in the ashes in the hearth outside to smoke. Could you tend it while we go to meet Ingrid at the river, if you feel up to it?'

'I thought I might attempt a trip to the river myself, without the splints hindering me.'

He grabbed the sapling and was tensing to push himself to his feet, when the panic overwhelmed her. The need to escape him was foremost in her mind. It was too soon after finding such unspeakable pleasure in his arms last night, too soon after having him lay eyes on Avalt, for her to be around him. She needed time to understand what had happened, figure out their relationship now, and she couldn't do that with him so near to her.

'Not today, Gunnar.' She couldn't keep the panic from her voice.

He paused midway through rising, a flash of disappointment, maybe even pain, crossing his features before they smoothed out again and he let himself drop back down into his seat. He inclined his head once. 'I'll check the fish for you.'

'There's porridge and honey if you're hungry.' She nodded towards the earthenware pot near him on the table. The same table she'd been working at the night before when he'd touched her. The memory made her cheeks flame, so she turned towards the door to hide it.

'Tonight, Kadlin.' The words came out strong and deep. A command. Her heart must have stopped for a moment in her chest, because she couldn't breathe, couldn't do anything. 'You won't avoid me then.' A quick glance back over her shoulder confirmed that his gaze was every bit as hot and fierce as his tone. Butterflies swam in her belly and anticipation prickled up her spine. There was no doubting that he was right, so she fled. It was the only thing she could do.

Chapter Seventeen

Kadlin stepped to the door of her chamber and stopped with her hand pressing against the cool wood. Night had fallen long ago and yet she had lingered after putting Avalt to bed because she was so afraid of what would come next. If Gunnar had meant to keep her anxious and unfocused all day, he couldn't have chosen better words for the task. She spent the day dropping everything she touched and even burning the honey cakes she'd hoped to serve with the fish for their supper. She'd served them anyway, reasoning that it was Gunnar's fault that she had burnt them so he should have to eat them. Not that she'd actually had the enjoyment of watching him choke them down. She had left his food at his door without giving him a chance to join them for the meal, though even that act of defiance had left her guilt-ridden.

He had every right to confront her about Avalt. He'd been capable of discussing the truth about their son for weeks now, so she should have done the right thing. She should have swallowed her anger with his abandonment and told him…for Avalt. Yet the way he had summoned her… She couldn't determine if his words had been meant as a warning or sensual promise. The man was a mystery to her now as much as he had ever been.

She was afraid of the power he held over her, even as she craved its effect. He could so easily make her turn to him again. Deep in her heart, she realised that she could never rid herself of the love that lurked there. Her only choice to shield herself from it was to run. He'd all but told her that they still couldn't be together in any way except physical, but even knowing that she found herself walking out into the passageway and making her way to his door. Heart pounding in her throat, she raised a hand and knocked. It wasn't latched closed and swung open with the rap of her knuckles.

Gunnar stood with his back to her. The light

from a few candles illuminated the muscles in his shoulders and back, flexing under his golden skin with each turn of his sword as he swung it back and forth at shoulder level. The movement was meant to make him fall off balance, but he was doing a remarkable job of keeping his weight balanced on his right leg while his straightened left leg pushed him out at an awkward angle. The exertion must have been extraordinary if the harsh breath he took with each swing was any indication. The answering tug deep within her belly to each sound made her shift uncomfortably and she would have left had he not stopped and turned to face her. One side of his mouth tipped up in a knowing grin and his eyes pinned her in place, deep and mesmerising despite how tired he must be. Her pulse faltered for a beat before she could gather her wits.

'I didn't mean to interrupt. I can come back.'

'You didn't. I've been waiting for you to put Avalt to bed.'

Kadlin took a deep breath and stood firm under his scrutiny. She had lingered in bed with Avalt much longer than usual, almost to the point of thinking that he might come for her. Turning back, he placed his sword in the corner and leaned heavily against the wall as he limped to the crude table holding a basin of water. She dug her fingernails into her palms to keep herself from helping him. With his independent streak, he wouldn't appreciate her assistance. Instead, she forced a lightness in to her tone and changed the subject. 'You haven't forgotten how to swing a sword, I see. I knew the warrior in you would overcome the challenge of your leg.'

'Perhaps,' he said as he splashed water over his face, the droplets sluicing down his shoulders and back. 'But it's not nearly enough.' He glanced at her before reaching for his wadded-up shirt on the bed and wiping the sweat and water from his face.

'That's only for now. You'll get better.'

Straightening, his smile returned. It was surprising that the bitterness that so often coloured his eyes and voice when they spoke of his injury wasn't present. This was the smile she loved and it moved through her, warming her in all the places that had gone dormant when he had left. 'You truly think so, don't you?'

She nodded and he grabbed the sapling to make

his way towards her. 'Of course I do.' A delicious tingle snaked its way through her body with every laborious step that brought him closer to her. That feeling as much as anything had made her seek him out tonight. Her cheeks flamed at the silent admission.

'You're the only one who has ever believed in me. Thank you for that.' He came to a stop before her, close, but not touching.

Her gaze caught on a droplet of water that worked its way from his broad shoulder to the hard muscle of his chest. 'You don't have to thank me. It's the truth.' She believed in him because she knew what he was capable of doing, not because she needed his acknowledgement.

Catching her under her chin, he tilted her chin up and waited for her to meet his gaze before he spoke. 'I know that I don't. I want to. There's much I want to make up to you.' Then he fell silent, leaving her to gaze up into the depths of his amber eyes.

Was that an apology for leaving her behind? Her bottom lip trembled, so she bit the inside to stop it. 'Is that an apology?'

His thumb traced along the edge of her mouth,

leaving a slow burning fire in its wake. 'An acknowledgement that I could have done better by you. I should have.'

Her breath trembled in her chest, stuck there because she was too afraid to learn the answers to her questions. Last night had been wonderful. Last night had been a piece of what they might have had without everything coming between them. Was it horrible of her to want to have that again before it got taken away?

It was easier to change the subject. 'How is your leg without the splints? Does it still pain you?'

He blinked at her abrupt change of subject, but that was the only indication that it might have thrown him off. After a moment, he nodded and followed her gaze down to the appendage. 'Aye, there's still an ache. I suppose there always will be.'

'What does Harald say?'

Raising his hand again, he gently pulled her chin up so that she would look at him. 'Kadlin...' But whatever he saw in her face made him grimace in pain and press a light kiss to her forehead. Then he snaked an arm around her waist and pulled her against him. Her hands went to his shoulders, naturally, as if they belonged there, as if her hands already knew just how broad they would be. As if he was hers.

He sighed into her hair. 'Harald doesn't know. There are no certainties.'

'Go lie down.' The words were a whisper, but she repeated them so they came out a bit stronger. 'I'd like to take a look at that leg.' When he paused as if to argue, she stepped back to gently break his hold before taking his hand and leading him to the bed, mindful of his slower progress. It gave her time to savour the warmth of his larger hand surrounding hers.

Once he'd settled with his left leg outstretched on the blanket and the wall at his back, he raised a brow at her. 'Do as you will.'

Without a word, she took a seat on the bed and began unwrapping the bindings. They were tight enough to keep the bone and muscle confined while still giving him more mobility than the splints. When she finally pulled the last of them away, she ran her fingers over the red markings left from the cloth and then moved a finger across the shin. It was obvious that his left calf was a bit smaller than the right, probably from muscle loss, but it wouldn't be long before at least some of that came back, if he had his way.

'Harald mentioned that rubbing the muscle can sometimes ease the ache of healing.' Without waiting for permission, she moved both hands to the flesh beneath his knee and moved them down with slight pressure on each side of his calf to end at his ankle. The dusting of dark red hair abraded her palms in a way that threatened to distract her, so she looked up to his face to make sure it was helping, but that was a mistake.

He wasn't watching her rub his leg at all. His gaze was firmly fixed on her face, stroking as palpably as if he was using his fingertips. A pleasant warmth lit in her belly and spread outward, making her breasts tighten in awareness of him. Those amber eyes were a deep gold now, mesmerising, warm. They made her want to climb inside them until nothing hurt any more.

'How does this feel?' She couldn't manage more than a whisper.

For a moment she thought he wouldn't answer and his stare deepened somehow, darkening until only a thin sliver of gold remained. When he did speak, his voice was harsh, raspy with need and want all rolled into one. 'Come here, Kadlin.'

Her hands faltered for a moment before resuming their stroke down his leg, but only after she managed to jerk her gaze from his. 'I'm afraid,' she answered truthfully. Afraid of losing herself to him again.

'Aye, I know that you are.' Leaning forward, he took her wrist and pulled it to him, placing a soft kiss on each finger. 'But I won't hurt you again. You have my vow.'

His lips were soft as they brushed each finger, making each one tingle in turn. His fingertips stroked up and down the tender inside of her wrist, spreading the tingle up her arm, weakening her.

'Gunnar…there's so much that's happened…'

His kiss moved to her palm where he lightly scraped his unshaven face over the sensitised skin, causing her to shiver as she took a deep breath. 'There is much to be said and we'll talk all night if that's what you want.' He paused and gave her a meaningful look. 'But I don't think you want to talk tonight.'

Nay, she didn't want to talk tonight. She wanted

him. She wanted to make everything go away so that it was just them and the love that ached to bloom between them. A taste of what had been, after the years of drought. There was no future to worry about and no past to hurt them. Her body moved of its own accord, pulled to him and everything that he was offering. Slowly, as if he wanted to make her aware that the choice was fully hers to make, he dropped her hand to his chest and reached up to pull out the silver fastenings holding her hair up. Then he gently released her braids, running his fingers through the strands until her hair was flowing free down to her waist.

'Does it make me a coward if I confess that you're right?' Her voice was barely a whisper.

'We need each other just as we need the air to breathe. To deny that is to deny a part of ourselves. I can't deny it any more, no matter what has happened.'

'And what of tomorrow?' She breathed the words, afraid to know.

'There is no tomorrow where I am not yours.'

Delving her fingers into the damp hair resting at the nape of his neck, she pulled his mouth to hers, opening for his kiss and savouring the hot stroke of his tongue against her own. The allure of calling this man her own, even for just a little while, was heady and too powerful for her to resist. He had always been hers and claiming him was only natural. With a whimper of need, she moved to straddle his lap, as he wrapped his arms around her, pulling her flush against his chest. They kissed, his tongue moving against hers, stoking the heat inside her until her lungs burned and she had to break free to catch her breath.

He brought a length of her hair to his face, closing his eyes as he breathed in her scent. 'Do you know I took a lock with me when I left you? So that I could stroke it every day and remember how it felt splayed across my chest.'

Biting back a smile, she nodded. 'I suspected. Did you…did you really…?' But the question fell away. Now was not the time to question him.

'Think of you every day?' he finished for her. 'Aye, love, every moment of every day for as long as I can remember.'

For the first time she allowed herself to believe that perhaps that was true. Giving in to the allure of his warmth, she moved her palm over the dips and planes of his chest, savouring his heat and the beat of his heart beneath her hand. It was the first time she had touched him, explored him of her own volition, since that night so long ago. 'One night with you wasn't enough. It wasn't nearly enough,' she confessed, raising her eyes to meet his again. There was that look again, so heavy and deep that she could happily drown in it.

'Kadlin.' He paused, and her heart paused with him. 'I want you to know that there hasn't been another woman since that night.'

'What do you mean?' Her heart refused to allow her to believe what her mind insisted those words meant.

'I haven't had a woman in over two years, not since our night together.' He cupped her face in his large palm. 'You've always been the one I wanted. I've never imagined another wife in my future. Every woman I ever had in my bed left me imagining what it would be like to bed you, hold you, love you. After our night together there seemed to be little solace to be found in the arms of another. She would never be you. She would never compare to you.' Leaning forward just slightly, he brushed his mouth over hers so his next words were spoken against her lips. 'I couldn't stomach the thought of her not being you.'

The urge to call him a liar was on the tip of her tongue, but when he pulled back and she met his eyes again, they were the earnest gold of the boy she had loved, though a man looked back at her now. They were the eyes that had gazed at her with trust and honesty all through the nights of their childhood; the eyes of longing that had occasionally met hers across his father's fire; the eyes of the warrior who had battled for so long he didn't know when or how to stop. All coalesced into the perfectly flawed man before her.

'Gunnar...' She blinked to fight back the ache of tears. 'I didn't know if you...if it had meant anything to you. I thought I knew, but then you spoke so harshly, and then you left....'

'It did, Kadlin. I vow to you that it did.' He kissed a corner of her mouth, the tip of his tongue tracing her bottom lip and leaving a burning trail of temptation as he pressed a kiss to the other side. 'I've always been yours.' He moved his wrists, wrapping her hair around each of them until she was tightly secured to him. His stare never wavered. 'Leaving you that night was the hardest thing I've ever done. I could only do it because I knew I was doing what was best for you. But I'm taking you tonight, reclaiming what is mine.'

Her lips parted on a gasp, but instead of taking advantage, he dipped his head and took her bottom lip between his teeth. The light scrape was so quick and unexpected, that she gasped again, but it turned into a sound in the back of her throat that she didn't recognise when his tongue stroked over it. Only then did his mouth claim hers in a hungry kiss that left her arching into him, parting her lips beneath his to take everything that he wanted to give her. But when she stroked her tongue over his lower lip, he retreated, his breath harsh as he looked down at her.

'Kadlin,' he whispered her name over and over as if he couldn't get enough of saying it. His lips brushed her cheekbones, her chin, her ear, leaving a path of heat in their wake. He growled against her neck, making her smile as gooseflesh prickled her skin. Closing her eyes and moving her head to accommodate his hot, open-mouthed kisses, she groaned softly when his teeth scraped across her skin. Her hands went to the hem of her dress, tugging it up along with the wool of her overdress. His hands were there to help, pulling the garments roughly over her head so that they soon joined his discarded shirt on the floor.

Then his hands were on her breasts, framing them between his palms as his thumbs stroked across the sensitive tips. Her whole body clenched from the pleasure of that touch. An involuntary whimper escaped her throat as she opened her eyes, surprised to find his gaze on her face instead of her body. The knowledge that he preferred to watch *her* as she revelled in the pleasure he gave her was more powerful than any words he could have said. Any lingering barrier to having him inside her that night crumbled beneath the power of that look. Of their own volition, her hips moved against him, bringing her into deliciously harsh contact with the erection straining against his trousers. Knowing his effect on her, he pushed his hips against her, pushing his hardness up against her aching centre. She bit her lip to stifle the cry that begged to be released. But he only did it again, this time stroking his tongue across her nipple before sucking it into the wet heat of his mouth.

Her cry rent through the air in the room, but she barely heard it as she arched into him, her hips moving in rhythm to his tongue on her body. It wasn't enough. Moving herself against his hard length had only made her want more, crave more of him. She wanted him inside her, stretching her, moving within her, filling her until she couldn't think of anything but him. 'Gunnar…' Her voice trailed off on a gasp as he moved to her other nipple, laving it with the same heated attention. Yet it didn't stop the ache that was only growing worse within her.

Her hands moved between their bodies, trembling as they brushed against his impressive erection before working at the fastenings of his trousers to release him. Finally the fabric gave way and she pushed a hand inside, groaning in pleasure when she palmed his swollen manhood. She'd almost forgotten how he felt there, so hot and incredibly hard she couldn't imagine how he'd fit where he was meant to go. But he would fit and her body trembled with the remembered pleasure of him moving within her.

Testing her own effect on him, she squeezed, smiling when he released her nipple with a wet pop and turned his head to the side, eyes closed tight from the pleasure. When she released the pressure only to squeeze again, his eyes flew open, staring at her with a fierce hunger that might have been frightening if she didn't want him so badly.

'Don't tease me, Kadlin. I've been too long without you.' The words tore from his throat in a growly rasp that caused an involuntary shiver to vibrate through her.

She exhaled a shaky breath and moved her hips forward. 'We can't risk another child.'

There was a pause, an infinite hesitation as he processed her request. 'Aye, I can be careful.'

'Then it's not a tease. I want you inside me.'

Before she knew what was happening, she was on her back, watching him push the trousers down to free his length. Then he was pushing her thighs apart to move between them. But he paused to look down at her, and it brought back a memory of their first time together so clearly that she blinked back tears. He'd looked at her then, too, there between her legs where no one else had ever seen her. Just like now, the look on his face had been full of love and reverence, as if looking upon her was some great gift she was bestowing on him. At that moment she realised that was exactly what he thought. That *she* was the only one giving. He didn't understand that he was giving just as much to her.

'Come to me.' She reached for his shoulders, pulling him over her until he was seated in the cradle of her thighs. 'I need you.' Brushing his lips across her temple, he made his way down to her mouth. When she tasted the salt on his lips mingled with the sweetness of his tongue, she realised she was crying. His arm hooked under her right leg, presumably to keep her from accidentally jarring his injury, but it had the effect of opening her up to him. The head of his manhood stroked across the sensitive flesh of her sex. 'Please, now,' she urged against his mouth, pulling him down to her.

Chapter Eighteen

Gunnar watched her face as he nudged her opening with the head of his shaft. She was so incredibly wet; he only wanted to sink into her with mindless oblivion. Anticipation thundered through his veins, but he forced himself to go slowly, to savour every moment of her. She bit her lip and her eyes widened as he pushed forward, breaching her silken channel with the head of his erection and pressing inside. By the gods, she was tight. Though his arms were shaking from holding back, he moved slowly, allowing her time to adjust to his invasion as he sank to the hilt without withdrawing. The pinkening of her cheeks and her sigh of pleasure when he filled her was almost enough to make him push harder, but not quite. He wouldn't rush this. Pushing in that last final bit so that their bodies were fully joined, he finally allowed himself to revel in the heat of her embrace.

She was so tight, felt so good squeezing around him that he could find his release in only a few strokes, but it wouldn't be enough for her. Closing his eyes, he buried his face in her neck until he could get a grasp on his control before he dared to move within her. When he finally mastered himself, he pulled back again to look at her. She clutched at him eagerly, her fingers tangling in his hair as she lifted her hips up for him. Her eyes were pools of liquid blue, her tears wrenching his heart in his chest. He vowed that he'd only make her smile going forward.

Holding himself off her with his palms flat on the blanket and using his one good knee for leverage, he dipped his hips and pushed into her…hard. The movement jarred his aching calf, but it didn't matter. Nothing mattered except her pleasure and the way she cried it out as her tight, hot passage gripped him. Everything about this was right. Her smell surrounding him, her taste on his tongue, her cries in his ears, her hair clinging to the sweat of his body as he rode her. This was everything that should have been all along.

This was everything that would be in the future as long as there was breath in his body.

Her eager hands clawed at his back, eventually settling on his buttocks, pulling him into her with each thrust. He bared his teeth in a grimace, fighting against the need to take her savagely until he came within her. The way she urged him on told him she would enjoy it just as much as he would, but he fought the impulse, intent on respecting her wishes. Even though the very idea of her round with his babe made him want to keep her in his bed until his seed had taken root.

But it wasn't to be. He couldn't be the husband she deserved, so he pushed the provocative thought aside.

Tonight was about her pleasure. He kept his eyes fixed on her face, watching each flicker of bliss that swept over her precious features. Her fingernails dug into his flesh with a sweet pain. When she closed her eyes, his name spilled from her lips, torn from them with a cry of pleasure so raw and true that he felt his own release building despite the ache of his leg. Just as the tremors of her body were subsiding, he pulled out of her with a hoarse groan of his own, spilling his seed against her thigh.

He fell heavily on to her, only managing to pull himself off after taking a few gasping breaths. Even then he only moved his torso so that it fell to the bed beside her, his shoulder still pressing her down. His leg throbbed, but he could barely feel it he was so exhausted. She must have felt the same, because she surprised him by curling herself into him, pulling a blanket over them before putting her arms around him and burying her face against his chest. Cupping her cheek, he ran his thumb over the blue shadow that marred the perfect flesh beneath one eye; evidence of how exhausted she was. He was to blame and the guilt chafed.

We can't risk another child. Did she even realise what she had said? *Another child.* She'd all but told him that Avalt was his, but somehow had managed not to say the words. Pressing a kiss to her forehead, he vowed to give her time, to make everything better for her so that she would trust him enough to confess all. It was the least he could do; the least he planned to do. Before he was finished she'd admit how good things were between them.

* * *

Some time later, Kadlin awoke to a large, muscular arm around her. It pressed against her belly, pulling her back against a chest and body that was just as solid and firm. Gunnar. Letting her eyes slide closed, she remembered everything that had happened and savoured the warmth the memory lit inside her. Or maybe it was the man sleeping behind her and not the memories making her feel so warm. Slipping her fingers between his, she lightly squeezed his hand where it rested against her. How did it feel so perfect to lie with him after so many years had passed? She'd awakened to his arm around her countless times when they were children and could still recall the wave of contentment that would sweep over her before she fell back to sleep. It was the same now, only more because he was hers, at least for the moment.

She wanted to look upon his face until she had memorised every crease and contour, just as she had memorised those of the boy he had been, but she didn't want to chance waking him by turning in his arms. Instead, she contented herself with relishing the solid press of him along the length of her body. As she snuggled closer, she became aware of the insistent press of a certain part of him, hard against her bottom. That had never happened when he'd come into her bed years ago. A smile curved her lips and an answering heaviness seeped into her limbs, while a pleasant thrumming began at her centre, that part of her he had filled so completely just hours ago. He was a man now. A warrior who was as magnificent as any warrior had ever been. And he was hers.

He was Gunnar. The man who had made her eschew all of the warriors her father had presented to her for a husband. The only man she had ever dreamed of marrying. The man who had fathered her child. The man who would hold her heart in his hand for ever.

'Tell me about your life, Kadlin. What have I missed?' His sleep-roughened voice caressed her ear, just before he placed a kiss on the shell.

The fingers of pleasure that stroked down her neck from the contact made her smile. She wanted to tell him everything. It felt wrong to not share how afraid and happy she had been to discover her pregnancy. But she couldn't think about that now, not yet. For once, she just wanted to be happy and enjoy that happiness. Instead of talking about it, she shook her head. 'Nay, you know my life. Tell me of yours. I haven't really known you since we were children. I barely knew you after you began travelling with your father. Tell me of your adventures. I want to know of the places you've seen. I want to hear your voice.'

'Do you want the tales of pillaging and fighting?' he teased.

The rumble of his voice seeped through the bones of her back to settle in her chest. She closed her eyes to savour the feel of his lips moving against her temple. 'Aye,' she whispered. 'Tell me everything.'

'Bloodthirsty wench.' He chuckled, but obliged her with tales of the adventures that had occupied him over those years when he was caught between boy and man. As he spoke, she could pick out the lingering excitement he had felt in travelling to new places and experienced a pang of jealousy that she hadn't been a part of that life. When he spoke of his more recent time in the Saxon land, the pride in his voice was evident as he recounted how he had led his men to victories and, though he never said the words, how he had earned their respect. The boy she had known was still there, hiding beneath the hurt and disappointment that had been his life.

How would their lives be different without that hurt and disappointment? It was a question that haunted her. When he fell silent, she turned in his arms and stared at the shadow of his face. Light was just starting to come in from the front room, but it barely penetrated this deeply into the house. She wanted to see more of his face, but was loath to rise and light the candles that had flickered out. 'Is Eirik truly happy with Merewyn?'

He paused, probably wondering at her change of conversation, but he answered, 'Aye, Eirik's content with his choice.'

'I'm glad of that. You realise he owes that happiness to you?'

Even in the pale darkness, she could see that he shook his head. 'Nay.'

'Aye. There are two reasons that's true.' Her fingers brushed over his cheek, unwilling to be this close to him without stroking him in some way. 'I heard what your father said to you. He had commanded you to bring Eirik back home without her. You could have done it, but you didn't.'

His laugh filled the small space between them, but it was without mirth. 'I thought about it, had even made a plan to take him during the night on my ship. I kept thinking that if I brought him back, then my father might reward me with land so that I could finally claim you. But it's you who kept me from acting. I knew that you would be disappointed, so I didn't. He owes his happiness to you, love.'

Her fingertips came to a rest on his bottom lip. 'Do you have no shame in admitting that?'

'I have no shame with you.'

Silence stretched taut between them, filled with all of the things that hadn't been said. It was only broken when he kissed her fingertips, one by one. He cupped her breast in his palm and his thumb circled around her nipple, causing a tremor in her belly that she vowed to ignore until their conversation was finished.

'What is the second reason?'

'Eirik told me that it was you who found Merewyn hiding in that cellar during the Northumbrian raid. It was you who brought her up.' When he held his silence, she prompted, 'Is that true?'

His thumb stilled its fondling of her nipple. 'Did I want her for myself, do you mean?'

The hint of bitterness in his voice twisted something in her. She moved her hand to tighten her fingers in the hair at his temple. He wanted to lump her into the group that included his father, those who always expected the worst of him. Who would accuse him of taking a woman against her will. She suspected it was his way of keeping himself closed off. If no one cared for him, then he didn't have to care for anyone and everything would be so much easier. But they had come too far to go back to that now. 'I'm not like the rest of them, Gunnar. I know who you are.'

He breathed out and the sudden tension drained from his body. His turned his face to nuzzle her palm and his hand closed around her breast. 'I found her, aye. I brought her up so that we could use her in bargaining.'

It wasn't until his admission that she realised she had been holding her breath, awaiting his answer. She let it out in a huff too unplanned to be subtle, so of course he heard it. It wasn't that she thought he would have forced his attentions on a woman, it was that he had wanted her at all.

He chuckled near her ear and this time it was real. 'You were jealous,' he accused and nipped her earlobe.

Closing her eyes and arching into his touch, she laughed, too. 'Of course I was jealous. I don't want you to want any woman but me. Do you know how it killed me to watch you with those other girls when we would visit your father, walking hand in hand into the dark to do all the things that I wanted to do to you? I'm still so angry with you for that.'

'You don't have to be jealous any more. I've told you there hasn't been a woman since you. You've ruined me for any other. I'm all yours.' For now. The words lingered, but remained unspoken so she shoved them from her mind. His teeth scraped her neck and when he would have pushed her on to her back, she resisted and pushed him on to his.

'Then I'll take what is mine,' she teased and moved to sit astride his hips.

His strong hands grabbed her hips to pull her on to his length and she eagerly obliged, already slick with wanting him. As she sank on to him, she leaned forward to kiss him, absorbing the purely male groan that came from the back of his throat when he was fully seated and pulsing within her. She tried to move, eager for the friction of his hardness within her, but he held her tight.

'I've only ever wanted you.' His whisper caressed her lips and filled the air in the room. It was exactly what she had said to him their first time together.

Squeezing her eyes closed to fight the ache in her throat and the tears threatening to fall, she took a deep, shuddering breath. Though it was dark, when she opened her eyes they rested on the shadow of his face and she knew that he was watching her.

She raised her hips and he brought her back down, hard. Her breath caught on a gasp as pleasure rippled through her. He didn't give her time to catch her breath before his mouth plundered hers and he pulled her down hard again, impaling her on his shaft. She kissed him back, her body clenching him tight with every stroke of his tongue against hers. Only then did his hands move from her hips to cup her bottom, giving her leave to take over and rock against him as he squeezed her tight.

It wasn't slow and gentle like he had been with her earlier. It was fast and full of all the need that had accumulated between them over the years apart. With one hand fisting tight in his hair, she rode him hard until the first tremors of her release snaked through her, stealing her strength so she moved against his chest. Then he took over, his strong hands moving back to her hips to bring her down on to him over and over again, while his teeth and tongue tortured pleasure from her nipples. It pushed her over the edge, so that she was falling to her release, coming apart at the seams as her cries filled the room. Even then, he didn't stop. Holding her tight on him, he thrust his hips, pumping into her until his own gruff cry of pleasure reached her ears and he pulled out of her.

Kadlin lay sprawled on his chest, struggling to catch her breath as an incredible peace swept through her. His hands moved up and down her back in soothing strokes that made her feel cherished.

Curling her arms around his shoulders, she held

tight and whispered into the warm skin at the hollow where his neck met his shoulder the words she knew would be true for as long as she lived, 'I love you.' The words were too soft for him to hear and a gentle exhale of his breath was his only reply, except that his arms tightened around her, causing warmth to bloom within her.

When Kadlin awoke later it was morning. Avalt would be awake soon, so she gently disentangled herself from Gunnar. He grumbled, but soon his deep breaths assured her that he slept as she rose. She couldn't resist turning back to look at the man who had taken her so thoroughly. There was enough light streaming in through the open door to see him, showing her that, even tousled in sleep, he was beautiful. The light caught the red of his hair, turning it to flame, and even caught the hints of red in the dark hair sprinkled across his chest, between his legs and down his long, strong legs to his ankles. She blushed when she recalled how good it felt to have that hair abrade her softer skin, everywhere. There wasn't an inch of her left that he hadn't touched.

Bringing her wrist up to her nose, she realised

with delight that she even smelled like him. It was a wholly masculine smell: sweat and linen mixed with his own spice, a scent she could pick out with her eyes closed. She'd never fully realised how much more satisfying it would be to sleep beside him now and have his solid strength keep her warm all night. Picking up her clothes from the floor, she turned towards the passageway with a smile.

Freyja picked her head up from her spot on the bed guarding Avalt when Kadlin stepped into her chamber. Kadlin stopped to pet her, her gaze falling to the dark-red curls of her sleeping son. The sight made a tendril of doubt creep its way into her heart. How long would Gunnar stay with them this time? She was certain he loved her, but she knew that wouldn't be enough to make him stay. The wounds he'd inflicted before ran deep, deep enough that she would remember to take their time together for what it was…an indulgence. It wouldn't be permanent. It wouldn't be more than a few nights to hold him.

Chapter Nineteen

Gunnar sat straight up in bed when he awoke, jarring his leg and cursing as he did. The bed was empty and for one dreaded instance he wondered if the night that had passed had been a dream. But the smell of her was in the room, on his skin, the slight weight of her body lying against his still fresh in his memory. Every moment of it had been real and more precious than he'd imagined that it could be. More gently than he had sat up, he lay back down and let the memories of the night before hold him before the lure of her voice in the front room dragged him to his feet. He was anxious to see her again.

Steaming wash water had been left just inside his door, so he made use of it before donning his trousers and making his way cautiously down the passageway to the front. He was uncertain of her mood and if she would embrace what had happened between them or if she would hide as if it hadn't happened at all. Either way, he would overcome her reservations.

He paused at the threshold, uncertain of his welcome, his gaze following her movements as she drizzled honey into a bowl filled with porridge and then placed it before Avalt. Instead of following her again, his gaze hung on the child and his head of dark red curls. The boy eagerly accepted the porridge and spooned some into his mouth. The skin on the back of Gunnar's neck tightened and a weight settled in his heart. He watched the boy's tiny lips as he smacked the sweetness and then his equally small tongue as it came out to lick the honey from his spoon. Gunnar was taken aback at how this boy was so different than the child he'd been expecting. He'd been expecting the blond hair of Kadlin's late husband or perhaps even the silvery tint of Kadlin's own hair, but not this. Not the perfect match of his own red hair, a colour he'd seen on no other person aside from his own mother. Not his own child.

Once caught, Gunnar's attention couldn't leave

the boy. He moved forward, gaze tracing the perfect face, his every feature, again looking for signs of himself mixed with traces of Kadlin as if they could have changed since yesterday. They were both there, mixed perfectly in the boy. If he had dared to let himself dream that a child had resulted from that one night, this is what he would have conjured. The beautiful child who sat before him. An ache squeezed his chest, threatening to choke off his air, so he looked away to the boy's mother to find her gaze on him.

She seemed taken aback for a moment at his presence, but then she smiled. A halting smile, but it allowed hope to spread through him that she wouldn't shut him out and pretend that nothing profound had happened. 'Good morning,' he managed, though his throat had become almost unbearably thick.

'Come, take a seat and have breakfast with us.' He hadn't realised that he'd stopped until she nodded to the stool at Avalt's side. 'You don't mind if Gunnar sits with us, do you?' This she directed at the boy, who only spared Gunnar a grin and went back to attacking his breakfast.

'He looks to be a hearty eater,' he said and took his seat, awkwardly because of his leg.

'He is,' she agreed and placed a bowl before him before sitting with her own food across the table. 'He's very strong and healthy. Always has been.'

Gunnar nodded and took a bit of porridge, but he couldn't seem to tear his attention from the child at his side. Every move the boy made was fascinating in a way that he couldn't explain. They were just chubby hands grasping a spoon, tiny fingers covered with honey and porridge, but Gunnar wanted to touch each one, look at each impossibly small fingernail and feel if the pink skin of his cheeks was as soft as it looked. He'd seen children before, but had never been fascinated as he was with this one. But then, none of them had ever been his… Kadlin's. That made all the difference.

'Did you sleep well?' Kadlin's voice interrupted his thoughts, drawing his attention back to her.

He smiled as he took in her features, the blush staining her cheeks. 'Aye, very well once you let me sleep.'

She blushed and bit her lip to stop a grin before

taking a bite of porridge. His gaze strayed to her mouth, her tongue as she licked a stray bit of it from the corner of her lips. A wave of tenderness, of protectiveness, welled within him for both of them. It was amazing how natural this felt, as if he'd spent every morning having breakfast with her and their child. He still couldn't believe it and let his eyes dart to the toddler again, as if to make sure the features he recognised as his were still there: the exact same shade of hair, the nose, the shape of his eyes. The truth was that Gunnar wanted it to be true so badly that he had to make sure he hadn't fabricated the similarities. But they were there and no one could say they didn't exist.

He wanted to be upset that she had kept the boy from him, but he couldn't feel anything past the strange happiness that was seeping through him now. They had a child and it seemed the most natural, most perfect thing in the world, except he needed to hear Kadlin say the words so that it would be true. He needed to know why no one had told him. 'Kadlin…' The question was on the tip of his tongue. 'Tell me—' Before he could say the words, the door swung open and Ingrid burst through with one of her myriad of brothers, full of excitement about puppies some mongrel had given birth to.

The moment was lost. Gunnar turned his attention back to his porridge and cursed the bad timing, at the same time conceding that the girl had saved him. Above all, he needed to tread carefully with Kadlin. The last thing he wanted was to scare her and drive her away. If he wanted her to confess the truth to him, he needed to earn her trust and have her come to him. He knew that. Understood it. Trust wasn't something he could force.

But it wouldn't be easy to wait for the words.

After breakfast, it was decided that the group would go to the forest to pick bilberries. This time Gunnar was prepared to force the issue if Kadlin was determined to keep him away. Now that he knew about Avalt, he wanted to spend every moment with them. A child with Kadlin was a dream he'd had for so long and one he had been certain would be left unfulfilled. The fact that it had come true left him eager to soak up their presence for as long as he had them. With no home to call his own, the future was murky, but for now they were his.

Avalt ran outside as fast as his tiny legs could take him, squealing his delight to be out in the sunlight. Ingrid and her brother followed, leaving Gunnar standing near the door waiting for Kadlin to collect the baskets they would need. A possessive need tugged at him as he watched her movements, so fluid and graceful as she moved around the kitchen area. His eyes could touch her every day for the rest of his life and not get tired of her. As she passed near him to leave, it seemed that she was avoiding his gaze and he found his fingertips reaching out to touch her before he even knew that he had moved.

'I'm going with you.' The pad of his thumb brushed lightly along her cheekbone, letting him savour her soft skin. Though the words sounded confident, he braced himself internally for her rejection.

Instead of arguing, she nodded, but still didn't look at him. He allowed his hand to drop back down to his side and followed her outside. He despised the distance that lingered between them, but understood it as something he would have to overcome. It had been his own actions that had created it. It was foolish to expect one night to take it away.

Breathing again because it seemed she would accept his presence, he followed her at a slower pace. He'd wrapped the top end of the sapling with a blanket for extra padding and tied it off, but manoeuvring for any length of time was a task he had yet to master. The bilberry bushes were just across the clearing at the edge of the forest. It was the same clearing he'd been determined to cross on his own that night that seemed like years ago now.

Now he was crossing it with an entirely different feeling growing in the pit of his stomach. He wouldn't go so far as to call it happiness, but as he walked, his gaze kept going to the red hair of the tiny boy running through the high grass and the feeling that passed through him could be close to that. Nay, it *was* happiness, if only he could allow himself to forget the future existed. The smell of the springtime grass teased him as he took a deep breath and allowed his gaze to move to the land around him. The deep blue of the sky with only a few puffy clouds scattered about, the rolling hills that made their way down towards where he knew the river would be—if he squinted he could see the sun glinting off a ribbon of silver, then back to the tall, green forest looming before them. This was home and the only people he wanted to spend his life with were there with him.

Aye, perhaps this could be happiness.

Kadlin watched Gunnar with their son from a spot just along the path. She had just walked Ingrid and her brother to the path to bid them goodbye as they left with a basket of berries to take to Ingrid's mother and Kadlin had returned to the tender scene before her. They were on the blanket she had brought along and spread out on the ground. Avalt was lying down and laughing as he fed berries to Gunnar, who leaned propped on an elbow beside him. Gunnar would pretend that he was going to bite his tiny fingers with each one, sending the boy into peals of laughter.

The sight of their heads pressed so close together, the identical shade of their hair, their enjoyment of each other, the utter adoration on the strong warrior's face, all of it brought tears to her eyes. She found herself wiping them away before she'd ever even known they were there. Her other hand pressed tight to her chest to combat the ache growing there.

This. This is all she had ever wanted in the world. It seemed cruel that she would be given a taste of it to enjoy for only a little while before it would be gone again. Though Gunnar seemed to still long for her, he hadn't spoken of the future. Even if he had, she didn't know that she could believe his words. He had left her before and, if she was being honest, nothing had changed. He'd made no plans for a family and, as far as she knew, he had nowhere to take them once Jarl Hegard demanded they leave. Where would they go? He was as without a home now as he had been before.

Wiping the last tear from her cheek, she took a deep breath and vowed not to think any more of the future. Whatever time they were given now... she would accept and enjoy. That would have to be enough. A cool breeze rustled the leaves of the ancient trees, drying her face and bringing a smile to her lips as she walked to the blanket and sank down on to her knees. They both looked up at her and smiled, causing her heart to slip right down to her stomach.

'Have a berry.' Gunnar pressed the dark purple berry between her lips, much to the delight of their son.

Kadlin chewed the sweet flesh and let her gaze move from Avalt to the intense gaze of his father. Gunnar's smile had changed from one of joy to one of hunger, as his fingertip traced the curve of her mouth, promising so much more than she imagined he was willing to give. To distract them, she turned her attention to Avalt and ran her hand lightly over his belly to give it a tickle. He squealed, drawing Gunnar's attention back to him. They played with him for a while, each trying to draw a laugh from him until he spotted some tiny yellow flowers growing in the grass at the edge of the blanket and went to pick them.

'You're a wonderful mother to him. He's lucky to have you.'

She glanced at him, but Gunnar was watching their son with that same look of adoration she had noted before. Aye, she determined, he must know that the boy was his. 'Thank you.' She wondered if he thought of his own mother, whom he had hardly known. The silence stretched between them until Avalt came back, gifting them each with a bouquet of the weeds before running off to hunt for tiny rocks at the edge of the small clearing.

'Kadlin…' Gunnar opened his mouth to speak, but then swallowed as if turning the words over in his mind. A brief moment of panic gripped her that he might ask her now. Though she wouldn't lie about Avalt's parentage, she had no wish to open that wound just yet. She needed a few days to just be with him. 'Was his birth a difficult one?' he surprised her by asking.

'It was long. It started one morning and he came the next morning just at sunrise, but there was never a hint of danger.'

He nodded, a look of relief coming over him. 'And you weren't alone with the pain, even for a moment?'

There was an earnestness in his gaze that stole her breath for a moment, then it made her want to reassure him. 'Nay, I wasn't alone. Not even for a moment.'

He nodded again and turned his attention back

to their son, though his hand moved to rest on hers, drawing her gaze to that point of contact. After a moment of silent debate, she gripped his fingers with hers and felt a tug on her heart when he squeezed.

Chapter Twenty

Over the course of the next few days Gunnar's patience began slowly to unravel. Every day that passed he told himself that he deserved her silence. Every meal they ate together, every night that she fell asleep in his arms, every time Avalt's laugh filled their home, the need to hear her confession ate away at him. It wasn't that he needed the reassurance that the child was his. That truth was obvious to anyone with eyes. It was that he needed her, all of her, with no boundaries between them. He'd been foolish to think that he could have only a small piece of her and not crave all of her. He was a fool to think that he could ever walk away from her again. As the days passed, he'd been having a difficult time imagining any sort of future without her. How was he supposed to walk away from her again? How was he supposed to leave his son behind?

He'd spent the past days thinking of the future. His only option was to return to Eirik's and finally take him up on his offer to rule one of the manors he had helped to overtake. He was loath to bring Kadlin and Avalt along, though, because they were all outlying positions still vulnerable to Saxon attack. That was changing, though. Before his injury, Gunnar and his men had planned to spend the summer solidifying their hold on the region, and by next summer or the one after, he could be firmly established. Certainly by then a home could be safe for them. In the meantime...

He shook his head. None of it mattered. It all hinged on his men accepting a lame master and Eirik accepting his ability to lead his men with only one leg. That was only likely to happen if he'd already established himself as a jarl, if he had already assumed a command position that didn't involve leading his men on raids to gain territory.

A future for them was murky at best, but that didn't stop him from wanting all of her. Perhaps that was selfish, given that he could make them no promises, but her silence about their son was a boundary that kept him from having every part of her as completely as she owned every part of him, and it kept him from being Avalt's father.

She never tried to waylay his attempts to get to know the child. Every morning they ate breakfast together and then they played with the wooden horses Harald had carved for the toddler. Avalt had warmed to him already and seemed to bask in the attention Gunnar gave him. But the boy never called him Father. Gunnar conceded that perhaps he hadn't earned the title yet, but it wasn't because he didn't want it. It was simply because he'd never known of the child's existence. Kadlin's continued silence on the subject seemed particularly harsh.

Every night he held her, loved her, brought her to pleasure again and again, hoping to breach the chasm between them, only to have her withdraw come morning. He never awoke to her in his bed. The first day hadn't bothered him, but each morning that passed without her there brought with it the knowledge that there wasn't any going back for him.

They couldn't come this far only to lose each

other again, but she was slipping away from him. While he could have her smiles and her kind words during the day, she refrained from touching him. It was as if their intimate moments could only be given free rein in the night. But that didn't stop him from touching her. His fingers found their way to her every chance they got. A stroke against her shoulder, a touch of her hand, a kiss against her temple. He wanted to take her every time he found her alone, but he held back, determined to allow her to set the pace and understanding that what he felt wasn't exactly fair to her. He understood her reluctance with him, but he wanted to talk to her as he had all those years ago with nothing between them. Most of all, he wanted her to tell him about their son.

He wasn't a patient man. Not with Kadlin. Finally, his patience came to an end as he eased down beside her on the grassy banks of the river, trying to figure out exactly how to say what he wanted. He enjoyed watching Avalt frolicking naked in the shallow pool Kadlin had made of rocks at the river's edge. Today they had brought along the small wooden boats Jarl Leif had sent to his grandson and the boy squealed with delight as one of Ingrid's brothers held it under before letting it go so that it popped above the surface of the water.

Kadlin laughed, but it was in that soft, distracted way that meant she wasn't with him. His eyes caressed her profile, stopping to linger on the pink shell of her ear before he leaned up on an elbow and placed a kiss on the soft skin just below where her ear met her neck. She smiled and turned her head. 'Stop or they'll all see you.'

He didn't care. He wanted them all to see him kiss her, but he leaned back on his elbow and took her hand with his. 'Do you think they haven't realised that you share my bed?'

'I haven't given it much thought, I suppose.'

His thumb traced circles on her palm as he willed her to look at him. She did, but it only verified that her eyes were shuttered, not open and hot like they were at night when they were alone, though she shivered from his touch. Bringing her hand to his mouth, he placed a single, open-mouthed kiss on her palm, letting the tip of his tongue trace a slow circle there before pulling away. The sound of her breath hitching was gratifying, but then he'd never questioned the effect his touch had on her body. *I love you.* He wanted to tell her daily, but he held back because it wasn't fair. Instead, he said, 'I love the sounds you make when I touch you.'

Her lips parted to speak, but at the last moment she turned her head to look back at the river.

A knot of dread settled heavy in the pit of his stomach. 'Am I only allowed to say pretty words to you when I'm inside you?'

'Gunnar...' It was an admonishment. She closed her eyes.

'Or is it only under the cover of darkness that we can talk?'

She shook her head and gave him a pleading look. 'Please...can't we just enjoy what we have now without pushing it further?'

Now. However long *now* ended up being. The one certainty was that their time at the sod house was coming to a close. His father had already given him notice to leave and he doubted Kadlin would be welcome to stay after harbouring him. *Now* wasn't very long at all. The uncertainty of it only heightened the anger that had been brewing deep within him; the anger that he'd been trying to dispel in favour of keeping peace *now*. But it spewed forth. Perhaps if it hadn't, he could have chosen his words more carefully. Instead, they came without tact and fell into the chasm growing between them. Avalt squealed again, drawing Gunnar's attention to the hair on the baby's head, so soaked it almost appeared black except for the glint of red in the sunlight.

'Why haven't you confessed to me that Avalt is my son?'

This time her voice was stronger, though her cheeks had lost their colour. 'This isn't the time. Not yet.'

'When?'

She sucked in a deep breath, the pain it covered up almost slicing his heart in two, but he couldn't back down. Every day he felt her slipping away. There would be no better time.

'It hurt me so badly when you left, Gunnar. I can't just forget that.' She had closed her eyes tight against him to speak and he wanted to grab her and hold her close. He wanted to reassure her, but he couldn't. He wouldn't leave her like that again, with harsh words and lies, but he couldn't have her. Not yet. Not when he couldn't even figure out where they would live if he kept her. Not when his lame leg made his position so uncertain he couldn't promise her a future.

'I didn't do that to hurt you,' he whispered. 'It nearly killed me to leave you.'

'Aye, but that was the result, wasn't it? You chose to go fight and you left me behind to marry someone else.' She opened her eyes to look at him and the blue irises burned with pain.

He reached for her, intending to bring her close, but a movement through the trees across the river caught his attention and his hand dropped.

'You left us...'

The rest of the words she spoke were drowned out by the beat of horses' hooves against the dirt, matching the heavy pounding of his heart in his ears. There was more than one horse and they were coming too fast to be bearers of good tidings.

'Someone comes!' He clawed his way to his feet and reached for his sword, calling the children away from the river just as two men on horseback broke from the trees on the other side. They were leading a third horse, but it appeared to be vacant a rider and they were still too far away to identify. 'Get everyone inside.'

Kadlin scrambled to her feet and nodded as she took Avalt into her arms. Despite how fast the men were riding, Gunnar had just enough time to get them home and inside before turning to meet the men as they rode into the field in front of the house. For one brief moment he relived the feeling of helplessness as those men had ravaged Eirik. What if he once again failed to protect those that he cared about? His grip on his sword tightened and he vowed to battle them to the death if need be.

'Gunnar!' a slightly familiar voice called to him.

After a moment they had ridden close enough that he could identify them as his father's men, which meant that Vidar should have been with them. One of them carried the reins of an extra horse, but there was no sign of the boy. Lowering his sword, but keeping a firm grip on it, Gunnar nodded a greeting to them both. 'Dom, Flein. Good day to you.'

Though a few winters younger than his father, Dom had been in charge of training his father's warriors for as long as Gunnar could remember. The man had spent many hours teaching him the finer points of wielding a sword and beating an enemy with his fists when the sword failed. Dom was usually rather long-winded with his stories, but the fact that he didn't even offer a greeting was further cause for alarm.

'You must come with us, Gunnar.'

'What's happened? Where is Vidar?'

Flein was only a few winters older than Gunnar and rarely said a word. His role had been to guard Jarl Hegard and blend into the background. It was a job he performed admirably, for a man built as stout and strong as a rock wall. 'Those whoresons got him is what happened,' he spat.

'Vidar,' Dom supplied before he could clarify. 'He was leaving to come back here two days ago and Baldr and his men took him.'

Alarm tightened in Gunnar's gut. Gunnar had been the one to send Vidar back home. Into a nest of vipers, apparently. He shouldn't have brushed off the boy's concerns so casually. Perhaps he should have dealt with the issue himself, but he hadn't bothered to care. By the gods, had his selfishness earned them more trouble? 'He's alive, then? Where do they have him?'

'They're holding him in one of the storerooms.'

Dom glanced at Flein, who nodded once. 'Gunnar… Your father… He only has days left. His health has been failing for a while, but the past fortnight hasn't been good. He's in constant pain and hasn't left his chamber in days. This is the end.'

From somewhere deep inside him, a store of anger erupted. Gunnar thought that he'd been past any feeling at all except pain, but he was wrong. Guilt and now anger tore at him, each as vicious as the other, clawing their way out. 'Baldr wants my father's place and is holding Vidar to ensure his succession.'

'Aye.' Dom nodded. 'He took Vidar so the boy couldn't rally support.'

'And what of me? Has he not seen fit to put an end to me yet?'

'With Kadlin here, Baldr couldn't risk Jarl Leif discovering his ploy too soon. Besides, you're cut off from the world here. He's had men posted in the forest. I'd bet anything he'll come for you soon.'

'It doesn't make sense. Why would Baldr risk Jarl Leif's ire on such a ploy? The jarl is friends with my father. He won't stand idly by and allow this to happen.'

'He won't stand by and let a jarl's second take over after his death? Why not? Happens all the time as long as he has support,' Dom argued.

'Then the men support this? Flein?'

'The men don't know who to support. No one likes the way Baldr has taken over, but with Jarl Hegard in bad health, no one can afford to speak against him. Baldr has amassed his own following since you've been gone.' Flein shrugged.

'The men would follow Baldr over their jarl's own blood?' Rage churned in Gunnar's belly.

'Nay, Gunnar, but Vidar is no warrior…not yet.' Flein dismounted and walked to stand before Gunnar. 'Who would you have them follow? There is no one unless you offer yourself for the task. That's why we're here. We may have a chance of turning this without bloodshed. You make your stand and the men make their decision. There will be too much bloodshed if Baldr has his way. He'd have war amongst the men so he can come out on top once they've fought each other. Come back with us now, while it's still early enough to stop.'

Gunnar stared at Flein and then looked to Dom. Both men had been trusted allies at one time, but that had been long ago. Had their loyalties changed in the years he'd been gone? 'How did you bypass Baldr's men in the forest?'

'I know this forest better than Baldr. We went north the day Vidar was taken and cut down southward again. Baldr wasn't watching for someone to come from the north,' Dom stated, though his jaw firmed. 'What are you asking, Gunnar?'

'I'm asking if you want me to come back with you because the men will follow me or because Baldr has sent you for me. He's a coward. He wouldn't come for me himself.'

Silence was his answer. Flein looked stricken. The question sat in the air heavy and thick until Dom cleared his throat and nodded towards the distance. Following his direction, Gunnar could see three distinct figures moving along the edge of the forest, just making their way towards the tall grass of the field. His gut clenched, readying for battle.

'Baldr's men. If we were on their side, they'd

stay hidden, but they want to know why we're here. What we're telling you.'

Flein walked back to his horse and put his hand on the hilt of his sword, ready to draw it at a moment's notice. 'What do we tell them, Gunnar? Do we keep them from talking of this meeting to their master? Do you come with us?'

The mere thought of those bastards watching the house turned his stomach. The thought of them watching him and Kadlin while they played with Avalt outside, watching them by the river, was enough to make his blood boil. Lame leg or not, he'd kill them all. The intensity of his anger surprised him.

What they were asking wasn't certain. It was distinctly possible that he'd be cut down as soon as he showed his face in his father's hall. But then that had been a risk he'd always been willing to take. This is what he was good at; this is what he knew. He was a warrior. He'd die a warrior. 'Aye, I'll go back with Dom. But after we're done here, Flein, I want you to take Kadlin and her son home to her father. Today. I won't risk Baldr trying to use them as leverage.'

Flein looked at him as though he was mad.

'Nay, Gunnar, I go back with you. We have to kill that whoreson and all those who would dare oppose the jarl's bloodline when he isn't even dead yet.'

Gunnar shook his head without taking his eyes from the assassins making their way across the field. His heart pounded with each step that brought them closer. The thundering in his ears almost drowned out Flein's words and he took a breath to steady himself. He could see how the fight would go down before it even started. The one on the left was already cutting around, hoping to come from behind, but they were too stupid to be coordinated. Their timing would be off. The two in front would strike early and against the three of them they didn't stand a chance. Gunnar would wager he could take them out himself, but he didn't have the time to waste on them.

'I won't go unless I know they are protected. Your job is to see them safely home and inform Jarl Leif of the situation. You've guarded my father well these years, now I'd ask that you guard Kadlin and my...' The word tripped him up. He'd never referred to Avalt in that way, but it felt right. 'Guard Kadlin and my son.' This time he levelled his gaze on the large man just in time to see his eyes widen in surprise. Flein would follow whatever order Gunnar gave him, he had no doubt about that now that he'd been reassured of his loyalty, but knowing that Avalt was his son, his blood, would ensure that the man followed the order to his death if needed.

'Aye, I'll see them home, on my life.'

Despite Gunnar's certainty that Flein would offer his vow, the words made relief flood his body. It centred him, lightening his chest and allowing his blood to settle. Gripping the hilt of his sword, he raised it, all the while knowing that the action would spur the assassins to faster action. It would make them careless. Flein and then Dom followed suit, drawing their weapons with the ease born from years of battle, so that when the two finally entered the clearing they were facing three swords. The one in back hadn't even made it to the house yet, just as Gunnar knew he wouldn't.

He was a warrior. This is what he knew.

Chapter Twenty-One

Kadlin waited until the sounds of battle had faded before she moved to press her ear to the front door. She had made everyone else lock themselves in her chamber while she waited in the front room, knife at the ready. She had no idea who had attacked them or who had won the battle until she heard Gunnar's voice just before he opened the door. Relief like she had never known came over her when he stepped into the room. Before she could remember that she wasn't supposed to feel all that much for him, she threw herself into his arms, only belatedly realising that he was marked with blood.

She pulled back, but only enough to look up into his face and reassure herself that he was whole. 'Are you injured? Tell me you're all right.'

He smiled, his gaze turning from ferocious to

tender in an instant as an arm went about her. 'I'm fine, winded but fine. The blood is not mine.'

Closing her eyes as she let out her breath, she dropped her forehead against his chest and relished the brush of his lips against her temple. 'Who were those men?' she asked when she could find her voice.

After he told her about Vidar, his father and Baldr's plan to take command, he took her hand and rubbed the pad of his thumb along her palm. It was a move that never failed to make her tremble, but this time she got the feeling that there was something more to come. Finally, he took a deep breath and spoke. 'Flein is taking you and Avalt home to your father.'

'Nay, Gunnar, I don't…' She had almost confessed to not wanting to leave him, but that wasn't really her choice. There wasn't an outcome of their current situation that she could imagine would leave them happy and whole. She should know because she'd spent the past days trying to figure it out, turning words over in her head, trying to find the right ones that would keep them together. But she hadn't found them.

There were no words that could convince her that he wouldn't leave her again.

Oh, she had tried to shut down that tiny voice of doubt. When he had made love to her and proclaimed his love in every way but the words, her heart had felt so at peace, so full of him that she thought that what had happened in the past didn't matter any more. Except that the doubt hadn't gone away. His touches made her forget, made her brain fuzzy so that she didn't think it mattered, but in the clear light of day, when Avalt stared up at her with his solemn, trusting eyes, the doubt became louder until she could only hear that voice in her head reminding her that Gunnar had left her before. Even though she was sure that it had been love shining in his eyes as he'd joined his body to hers, he had left just hours later. As much as she wanted this time to be different, she couldn't trust that it was.

She couldn't trust him. And when he left this time, he would hurt Avalt, too. Now she knew that she had been right. This was him leaving her again. It shouldn't hurt so much considering she'd expected it, but the words were like a knife's blade to her chest, cold and sharp, leaving nothing but a burning chill in their wake.

She nodded and moved back to disentangle herself from him. 'Then this is how it ends this time.'

'Nay, Kadlin.' He touched her face with his free hand, his other supporting him on his sapling, and traced his thumb over her bottom lip. 'It's not safe for you here. I don't trust Baldr not to use you somehow. You'll be safer with your father. I have to go free Vidar so I can't stay to protect you.'

'I understand.' Pulling back even farther so that she was just out of his reach was one of the hardest things she'd ever had to do.

One of the men called his name from outside and he dropped his hand to his side as he turned towards the sound before looking back at her. 'Kadlin.'

'I understand,' she repeated. 'Of course you have to go.' Even though she meant the words, she knew that she wouldn't see him again. There was no part of her that thought he would come back. 'Goodbye, Gunnar.'

'This isn't—' His words bit off with a curse and he raked his fingers through his hair.

'Don't pretend this is anything other than it is. You never promised me anything, please don't start lying to me—'

He growled as he flung the sapling to the floor and stepped towards her, knocking them both a bit off balance so that her back pressed against the wall and he pinned her there. Before she could react, he forced her chin up and pressed his lips to hers. It was a scorching kiss that ignited into something wild as soon as his tongue swept into her mouth. Her hands came up to push him away, but somehow only managed to fit themselves to his broad shoulders and pull him closer. He ate at her lips, taking every bit that she allowed him to have until he forcibly wrenched his mouth away, his breath coming in harsh gasps as he stared down at her.

'This isn't over,' he promised and then stepped back.

She was so far gone, she didn't even notice that Ingrid and the others had come out of her chamber until he allowed her the space to breathe. Gasping for breath, she watched as he gathered his sapling and limped over to brush his lips against Avalt's wet hair and whisper something to their son.

Then he left them. Only then did she allow the tears to fall.

One by one the fires of the night began to light up the houses of the village in the valley stretched out below him. It was his home, or it had been until he'd left over two years ago with Eirik and the harsh words of his father ringing in his ears. *Bring Eirik home or don't return at all.* Gunnar had known when he'd set sail that he wouldn't be coming back, that his home had been taken from him. Looking down on the familiar houses with the jarl's longhouse in the distance, he should have felt…something. There should have been some gratification from seeing the place again. There should have at least been some sense of well-being, some sense of belonging now that he had returned to the place that had borne him. But there wasn't. Or if there was, he was too numb to feel it. The euphoria of the fight had long since worn off in the day-long journey from the farm to the village. The three assassins had been dispatched too easily. They barely had a sporting chance.

In some ways it was worse than his time fighting the Saxons. Then, he'd welcomed death with each fight, but he'd always imagined Kadlin's face before battle, remembered the way it had felt to hold her, to sink into her body as she clung to him. Those thoughts were still there now, but marred because he'd hurt her and potentially lost her. Again. The pain in her eyes as she'd watched him leave was still with him. There was no pleasure, no escape to be found in those thoughts, so he closed his body and mind off to everything. Some part of him was aware of how the endless jarring of the horse's steps for the past hours had hurt his leg, but the pain was only a minor tug in the back of his mind. It didn't mean anything.

A footstep sounded at the bottom of the slope and Gunnar dug his fingers into the grass, ready to push himself to his feet at a moment's notice to meet the enemy. The gentle snicker of recognition from one of the horses in the forest behind him told him it was Dom, so he relaxed and got to his feet more leisurely. They had arrived earlier in the afternoon and Dom had gone down to assess what was happening. The village moved lethargically, getting ready for the night ahead. There were no signs of strife or even a skirmish. 'Vidar is alive. Jarl Hegard still lives, though barely.'

Gunnar nodded, though he hadn't expected the boy to be harmed yet. Baldr would need Vidar to pledge fealty to the new jarl. He'd only be harmed afterward; killed for refusing to pledge, or killed in a convenient accident after pledging, for assurance that he wouldn't go back on his word and rally men to his side.

'I talked to some of the men about you...'

'And?' Gunnar prompted.

Dom looked down, unwilling to say what Gunnar had already anticipated.

'Out with it.'

'It's been years since you were home, Gunnar. You didn't leave under the best circumstances and...' his gaze flicked to Gunnar's leg '...and they've heard about your injury. Most don't think you can stand, much less wield a sword.'

Gunnar nodded again. He'd already gone through the likely scenarios in his head and every time he had come back to this one. He wouldn't put his support behind a man who hadn't come to ask for it, a man he didn't know could bear the weight of that support, so he couldn't expect his father's men to, either. 'Then we go in alone.'

'I didn't think to ask you earlier, but…can you? I saw you wield your sword with Baldr's men, but can you stand, fight for any length of time?' Dom shook his head, already assuming the worst. 'Give me a day or two. I'll make the rounds of the farms. I'm sure I can find men to come in with us. Flein will be back then, too, and I've no doubt Jarl Leif will have committed men.'

'You didn't *think* to ask me that earlier?' Gunnar laughed, already limping back to the horses. 'I'll fight until I can't, but we go now. We can't wait for Baldr to get reinforcements. If what you say is true, my father could die at any hour. I won't allow Vidar to face that risk.'

'It's madness. At least wait for light.'

Nay, there would be no waiting. Aside from the fact that Vidar's life hung in the balance, Gunnar recognised that so did his life with Kadlin. This was his only chance at a future with her. If he could take his father's place, then he might finally deserve her. He might finally be able to offer her and their son a home. He closed his eyes briefly as he saw the pain on her face again—pain he had put there. He'd caused enough pain in the past by leaving her. It was time to fight for her.

'They're warriors, Dom, they gossip worse than women. By first light every one of them will know I'm here hiding like a coward. What's wrong? Afraid to die tonight?' Gunnar grinned and grabbed the reins. 'Stay here if you'd rather. Someone needs to live to tell the tale.'

'Daft bastard.' But Dom was smiling as he walked over to mount his own horse.

Chapter Twenty-Two

They rode down the hill to the edge of the valley where he slowed his horse to gauge the distance to his father's longhouse. His gaze lit on several of the men, recognising most, but noting some new faces. Faces of men who likely belonged to Baldr. Whether they had come with him from Jarl Leif's land or had been acquired from lands farther away, he didn't know. Instead of riding the horse to his father's door, he dismounted with his sword strapped to his back, determined to walk the distance even though he'd have to use the hated sapling. It was best for the men to see that he was still capable of walking, still capable of fighting, still a man. He was dimly aware of Dom dismounting, following him just off to his side, as he made his way through those who had lingered outside during the evening meal.

Some had stopped to watch him and, now that they were closer to the house, more were turning their heads. A murmur had begun, as they recognised him and wondered at his presence. In his borrowed trousers and plain tunic, he didn't look like a jarl coming home to claim his place. At least he'd removed the bindings from his leg so that his injury was disguised, even if his limp was not.

The outside kitchen was bustling with activity, but even that came to a halt as he approached. The women who worked there glanced up, either afraid to be admonished for halting their work or afraid that his presence meant a confrontation. 'Lord Gunnar!' The voice belonged to Hilla, the slave in charge of the kitchens. She had practically raised him. The fact that she'd hushed her voice midway through his name told him that this would go badly. He was firmly in enemy territory.

'Hilla.' He paused and nodded, noting that her face appeared pale, strained.

'Your father…' She walked over to him, shaking her head with despair.

'Aye, I've been told. Is Baldr inside?'

The woman nodded, but cast a worried, disdainful glance at the front door of the longhouse. 'Inside with his men. They sit at the dais as if they belong there while your father rots in his bed.'

'Think I'll go remind him of his rightful place.'

'I knew you would come, Gunnar. I'd heard of your injury, but I knew it wouldn't keep you away for long.' She reached out to touch his arm and he briefly covered her fingers with his own before pulling away.

'Go now, back to work before one of his men has reason to question your loyalty. You need to keep yourself safe, no matter the outcome tonight.'

The woman harrumphed but backed away, though not before whispering, 'If it comes to it, I'll kill him myself.'

Grinning, he continued towards the house, but the smile faded at the glares coming from the two men guarding the open door. One he didn't know, but the other he did. A younger son of a farmer who had joined up with Eirik years ago to seek his fortune, but had married and stayed behind rather than fight the Saxons. He was decent, honest, but Gunnar couldn't tell from his expression if he could count on his support. Instead of the sounds of revelry that generally accompanied the evening meal, the sounds coming from the large front room of the house were hushed, sombre. Their jarl was dying. That in itself was enough for the lack of merriment, but Gunnar had to wonder how much of that was due to Baldr's presence. Did the men really want him there or was Dom right? Only one way to find out.

'Good evening, Geir. It's been a while.'

'Evening.' The younger man nodded, but didn't crack a smile, instead casting a quick glance at his counterpart on the other side of the doorway.

Gunnar made to walk between them through the open door, only to be stopped when the other guard stepped in his path.

'Who are you?' the unknown guard demanded.

'Let him pass,' Geir urged. 'He's come to see his father.'

The man looked to Geir and then back at him, and his face turned in a sneer. 'I don't like the looks of him. Baldr won't, either.'

Gunnar curled his hand into a fist, aching to pound the sneer from his face, but forced his fingers to uncurl. A fight now would be a very bad idea. He'd save it all for Baldr if the man was foolish enough to put his face that close to his fist. 'If he can tolerate *you*, I can't be that objectionable.'

The guard all but growled, but Geir stepped in and pushed him back. Outraged, the man brought up his hand to push his arm, but Geir wouldn't be put off so easily. He shoved and the guard stumbled to the side and Geir followed, clearing the doorway. Gunnar stepped inside with Dom at his heels. The ceiling soared to an arch high above them, held there by the thick timber posts placed at even intervals around the room, scraped bare and polished to a golden shine. Benches lined the walls, and tables laden with food filled the floor around the centre stone hearth, though its fire was banked now since it was warm and the cooking was being done outside. It didn't feel like coming home, but Gunnar could appreciate the grandeur of the long hall. It had been designed to be impressive, intimidating, and it had succeeded. He'd always felt a sense of pride walking through the door. Even now, the sight made a heavy warmth begin to spread through his chest, but he stifled it before it could start. This was not his home yet, and he held no illusions about walking through the door into enemy territory unnoticed.

Already the men at the tables closest to him were putting down their bowls and staring. Soon their stares were accompanied by murmurs that led the way to the raised dais on the right, where Baldr and his cohorts sat smiling and drinking his father's mead. Hatred, cold and deep, ran through his body, settling like a vice around his heart. The whoreson had no rightful claim to that seat, yet there he sat, though the smile had been wiped from his face. The man's eyes immediately darted to the guards at the door before latching on to the men seated nearest Gunnar, searching for allies and protection. *Coward.*

'Bold of you to show your face here, Gunnar,' he called out, making sure that the entire room heard him.

'Bold of you to sit your arse in my father's chair.' Gunnar surveyed the room, but it was impossible to read the men. Most of them were his father's men, which meant they were well-trained warriors and they wouldn't give up their secrets until they had to. Right now they waited to see what he planned, to see how Baldr would react, before making a decision. Aware of the need to prove to them all that he was worthy of their support, he walked the last few yards holding his head high and meeting the eye of every man who dared to meet his gaze. 'Looks as if we're both feeling reckless tonight.' He grinned up at Baldr as he came to a stop before the dais.

Baldr laughed, though it didn't reach his eyes. It was for the men in the room, a ploy to show them that he was in charge. 'How's the leg? Still dragging it behind you, I see.' The two men on either side of him chuckled, but Gunnar shut them both down with a cutting glance. They twitched and glanced to Baldr. 'And Dom. I have to admit I'm a bit disappointed to see you with this mangled excuse for a warrior. I thought you were smart.'

Gunnar didn't give Dom time to respond. 'You have my brother. I've come to set him free.'

'Your brother is comfortable. He'll be free to leave soon. Unfortunately, I cannot say the same for you.' Picking up his tankard, he took a drink while gesturing to the men nearest Gunnar and Dom that they should be taken.

Gunnar glanced around. A handful of men stood and he nodded at each one to acknowledge them. The rest stayed seated to watch the confrontation unfold. It wasn't a good sign, but it wasn't bad, either. When the two men nearest him began to get to their feet, Baldr's men intent on following his order, Gunnar turned his attention back to the man. 'You want me? Come take me yourself.'

Baldr laughed and swung his tankard in the air. 'I'm busy.'

'Busy? Is that what you are? Looks more like insolent cowardice to me. The only thing you're busy doing is drinking mead that doesn't belong to you and sitting in a chair to which you have no claim.' Gunnar spat and cast another glance over the room. All eyes were on Baldr now. Good.

'Get him out of my sight.'

'A true leader isn't afraid to face a challenger.' His words echoed in the stillness of the room.

'Are you challenging me, Gunnar?' Baldr threw his tankard to the floor at Gunnar's feet, so angry now that his face was turning red.

The two men had moved to either side of Gunnar and Dom, but they hesitated. It was now or never. If they tried to take him, the action could turn the tide of the room and the few followers he'd found would be no match for the rest. 'You're a coward. If you can't take a lame man out, what sort of leader can you call yourself? Do you follow a coward?' He raised his voice to ask the room. Murmurs rose throughout the tables. The two men who had stood to take him in hand moved back to their seats. It wasn't an endorsement, not yet, but it meant he'd get to prove himself. Gunnar grinned.

Baldr rose and walked slowly around the long table before jumping down from the dais. His insolent gaze raked Gunnar from head to toe and Gunnar realised that he'd never expected to face him. He'd never expected Gunnar to come and challenge him. The man was an imbecile as well as a coward.

Shrugging out of the sword sheathed diagonally across his back, Gunnar held it out to the side with his right hand. 'I'll make it easy for you. Without swords. We'll fight like men were meant to fight.'

'Aye, I'll kill you with my bare hands and then I'll take Kadlin as my whore.'

Baldr lunged for him, barely giving Gunnar the time to drop the sword to the ground and brace himself for the impact. He just managed to stay upright, but Baldr took the advantage and kicked the sapling out from under him before landing a hard blow to his gut. Breath whooshed out of him. The second blow came hard and he couldn't withstand the impact and keep his balance. The added pressure on his leg caused pain to slice through the limb and he crumpled beneath Baldr's weight. But he went down laughing. Baldr didn't know how many wrestling matches he'd fought with Eirik, or how many fights he'd initiated over the years, trying to get himself pounded into oblivion so that he could forget Kadlin. He excelled at fighting on the ground and when the men all got to their feet, standing on tables and grappling to get a better view, their energy moved through him.

Baldr rose above him, glaring down at him as though he was mad for laughing. Perhaps he was, because he only taunted him. 'One punch to my face. That's all you'll get. Take it.'

As if he'd been waiting for permission, the other man pulled his arm back and let his fist fly. It connected with the ridge of his cheekbone, just below his eye. It was a solid blow and the pain of it vibrated through his entire face. Pain he understood. He'd lived in it for so long that it was a source of strength. He used it now, absorbed it until it mixed with the energy of the room and he erupted. Grabbing a fistful of Baldr's hair in each hand, he pulled him down and drove his head into the bridge of his nose. Blood spurted and the man howled, his hands instinctively going to his face. Using the power of his one good leg to propel them over, Gunnar swapped their positions so that Baldr was on the floor, still holding his nose, blood seeping through his fingers. Gunnar didn't give him time to assess the damage before laying into him, landing a few solid punches to his gut, before the man could even try to defend himself. When he did finally lower his arms to counter the blows, Gunnar just changed the direction of his blows to the man's face.

Each fist landed with satisfaction. This was real. The crunch of bone along with the pain he was dimly aware of throbbing through his fist with each blow told him that. This was something he could control, unlike protecting Kadlin's heart, or the ache gripping his chest when he thought of her—this was pain he could manage. Though it wasn't enough. He wanted someone who would fight back more. The bloody coward wasn't even trying!

A shooting pain suddenly bloomed throughout his side. It was so sharp and unexpected that he realised immediately the whoreson had somehow got his hands on a blade. Gunnar reared up on to his knee on instinct, his hand going to the wound that was already sticky and warm with blood. Baldr quickly shuffled out from under him and rose to his feet, a grin on his lips, though his teeth were as bloody as the rest of his face. He wielded the knife that must have come from his boot, and he looked far too pleased with himself. Satisfaction made Gunnar grin when Baldr frowned and worried a tooth with his tongue, before spitting it to the floor, leaving a gaping hole in the front of his mouth.

A movement from the circle of men that had gathered around them to watch caught his attention. A man he faintly recognised made a move towards Baldr. It seemed the tide had turned in the room, but Gunnar held out his hand to stop him. 'Nay, the bloody whoreson is mine.' He growled the words. They were pulled from deep in his chest where the ache for Kadlin lingered.

Baldr laughed and twirled the knife in his hand. 'You always were a jealous one. You were jealous your father chose your brother and now you're jealous he chose me.' Baldr lunged, swiping the knife towards his throat, but Gunnar pushed back to avoid the blow. 'Even your woman chose me. I'm going to fill you with my blade and make you scream the way your whore screamed when I was inside her.'

Gunnar barely listened to the words. They were a poorly veiled attempt at distraction. Nothing more than the taunts of a desperate man who knew he would be beaten. 'She would never let a disgusting piece of filth like you touch her.' His gaze never wavered from the weapon as Baldr started to circle around him. Impatience for the man to strike gnawed at him, but Gunnar forced a calm he wasn't even close to feeling. He wanted to pummel Baldr some more. And he would, but first he needed to wait for him to strike to catch him off balance.

'Perhaps after I beat you, I'll take her right here

and we can compare. The screams of a cripple and the screams of a whore. I'd be hard pressed to say which I liked better.'

The idea of Kadlin at Baldr's mercy was enough to spur him to action. He shouldn't have, but he lunged with a punch to the coward's leg. It opened him up and left him vulnerable so that Baldr could swipe with the knife, narrowly missing his throat and leaving a stinging cut where his shoulder met his neck. Then the man swung back out of his reach. 'Coward! Come and fight me like a man!'

'You're not a man.' Baldr sneered. 'You're a waste of life. *I'm* the one your father chose.'

It was the only taunt that Gunnar couldn't deny. It shouldn't have held any power to wound him, yet it did. He'd been told to leave while Baldr had been invited to his father's dais, to Gunnar's old seat. He hesitated for a heartbeat. That was long enough for Baldr to risk kicking him, his booted foot landing on Gunnar's shoulder. He'd seen the blow coming an instant before it connected, long enough to brace himself for it and then grab the boot in both hands and twist. He might have heard a crack as the ankle twisted, but

Baldr yelled as he lurched to the ground to ease the pressure from his leg, covering the sound. The knife clattered to the floor, giving Gunnar the opening he needed to pounce on the man's back. Digging his fingers into Baldr's dark hair, he pulled his head back to ram his forehead into the floor, then let loose a torrent of blows. He pounded the back of his head in a blur of rage. It wasn't until Dom was pulling him away that he realised Baldr was unconscious and not fighting back.

Blood whooshed through his ears, his entire body alive and pumping with it, numb to the pain in his fists, leg and side, that would surely come later. As Gunnar rose to his feet, Dom pressed the hilt of his sword into his hand and he automatically turned towards the two men left on the dais. They were standing with their own swords in hand, ready to fight him, but a roar filled the room. It took a moment for his thoughts to clear, for Gunnar to realise that the roar was a collective cheer from the men. It was followed by the sounds of metal and wood clashing in a chorus over and over again. Shields piled high on the floor as one by one the men laid down their weapons, offering him their fealty.

Only the two on the dais dared to oppose him. His gaze swung back to them. 'You can fight and die tonight, or live out the rest of your life in exile. The choice is yours to make.'

They stared at him, hatred, fear and humiliation robbing them of their reasoning. As one they lunged from the dais, but didn't get far before a wall of warriors stopped them. The skirmish was brief. The warriors were still riding the energy of the fight they had just witnessed and itching for one of their own, and they didn't go easy on them. Subdued and beaten, they were brought before Gunnar, but he barely spared them a glance. 'Take them to the hold and free my brother. Take this waste of life with you.' He nudged Baldr's boot with the tip of his sword.

'You should kill him.' Dom spat on Baldr's unconscious body as someone grabbed him under the shoulders to lift him.

'He'll die a slow death knowing he failed. We'll ship him to the Saxons and Eirik will hear of his deeds. Everyone will know. He'll not have the reputation nor the gold needed to ever have warriors under his command again, so he'll die a labourer. That's enough.'

As Baldr was carried out, cheers went up around the room and Gunnar allowed himself a moment to take them in. This was the moment he'd dreamed about as a boy. The moment when he would hold his head high in this very hall and hear the warriors he'd fought beside swear allegiance to him. It felt like acceptance, like everything he'd ever worked for was finally coming together. It almost felt like coming home. Almost, because this wasn't his home and he wasn't jarl, no matter that they seemed to think so. His father was still jarl. Still, a stirring of hope began in his chest that perhaps he could have Kadlin and Avalt after all.

With a nod of acknowledgement, he took the sapling Dom held out to him and rested his weight on it while raising his sword high in victory. The cheers went up again and he finally allowed himself a smile to savour the moment. It was only when he lowered the sword that he winced from the sharp stab of pain in his side and remembered Baldr had stabbed him. Dropping the sword to the floor, his hand found the wound sticky, still oozing warm blood. He cursed.

'We'll get Hilla to sew it.' Dom smiled and walked away to find her, just as Gunnar's father's voice filled the room.

'Your jarl's not even dead yet and you offer your loyalty to this misbegoten cur!'

Tending to his wounds would have to wait. Gingerly taking his shirt off over his head, Gunnar wadded it and pressed it to his side. Now that the heat of battle had died out, he could feel the wound throbbing along with his hands. Together they almost matched the ache and shooting pains in his lame leg.

The room quieted as the crowd parted and all eyes turned to where the man stood just outside the door to his chamber. 'I should skewer you all with my sword and be done with the lot of you.'

'Quit your barking, old man. I just rid your house of a viper.'

His father gave him a fierce stare, but Gunnar couldn't say what was in his eyes. They were bloodshot, sunken into their sockets, and filled with bitterness even as he stood on the edge of death.

'In my chamber, boy.' Certain that his authority would be obeyed, the man turned and disappeared through the doorway.

Gunnar almost turned the other way. He almost walked out of the house without looking back. There was nothing for him here while his father lived, but then his gaze went back to the men in the room, moving over each one in a slow study. Each one of them looked back at him, meeting his eyes head-on with looks of acceptance, maybe even pride.

'Welcome back, Gunnar.' One of them spoke and clasped his arm as he walked by to leave, in pursuit of other entertainments now that the fight was over. Others joined in with a clasp of his arm or a slap on the back as they left the house or went back to their meals at the tables. No matter what happened with his father, they had already made up their minds about him.

His mother had left him, his father had rejected him and his own guilt about his past had held him down for too long.

He had finally been accepted. Nay, not finally.

Kadlin had accepted him long ago. Taking a deep breath, he smiled and let it out as his gaze took in the great room once more. It was time to bring her home.

Chapter Twenty-Three

After the last hand had been clasped, Gunnar made his way to his father's chamber. Gritting his teeth through the pain of his wounds, he paused at the door. His father lounged in his chair before the hearth, eyes staring blankly into the fire and hands limp on the arms of the chair. He didn't look like the image of the larger-than-life jarl that Gunnar had stowed in his memories. The fire in him had waned, leaving him slumped in his chair and defeated. The plain, linen tunic he wore reached his ankles, showing his bare feet.

This was not a jarl. This was a mere man meeting his death. All of the anger Gunnar held for the man fled, leaving him hollow and aching. None of it mattered any more. Kadlin was his future and the men had accepted him. Nothing this man thought or did could affect him.

'You coming in or standing there all night?' His father's gravelly voice drew him into the chamber.

The smell in the room was horrible, made only worse by the stifling heat from the fire. It might have turned his stomach if he hadn't already had numerous other ailments taking his mind from it. 'Just making sure you're not changing your dress.' He managed the wry comment as he stepped inside.

The man turned his head and gave him a scathing look that took in his bare chest and then the wound at his side. 'You've gone soft lying up in bed at that farm fostering that lame leg. The boy I taught to fight wouldn't have let him pull a blade on you.'

His father had never taught him to fight. Dom had taught him, demonstrating holds and how to exploit known weaknesses, having him spar with opponents and correcting his errors. His father's version of teaching involved pitting a boy against a warrior over twice his size and watching the entertainment while he drank his mead on the dais. Not that it mattered any more. Gunnar shrugged and pulled the wadded shirt away from the wound to examine it. The linen was almost completely saturated with his blood and it stuck to his skin a little when he shifted it. The wound burned like someone had lanced him with fire, but at least the blood flow was slowing. 'It appears we're both losing our touch. Why would you get sick and allow a scoundrel like Baldr to take over?'

'Who are you to question me? You're nothing but the bastard I was too stupid to send off with your mother when she left me to marry that farmer. A thorn in my side since the day you were born.'

'Aye, you've always made that fairly clear.' Walking around to stand next to the fire and face his father head-on, Gunnar sucked in a long, quiet breath before asking the question that had always lurked in the back of his mind. 'What did I ever do to displease you so?'

His father answered without hesitation, 'You had my eyes. Eirik was my true son and he didn't have my eyes. What makes you think you're entitled to them?'

Those words made no sense. Either the man was truly close to death and running off at the mouth with nonsense, or his words hinted at something more. Determined to smother any flicker of pain, Gunnar grinned. 'What's this, Father? Complaining because your seed runs true?'

The jarl had already turned his attention back to watching the fire, seeming to get lost staring at the flames before he spoke again. 'You looked like Finna, except for your eyes. Those were mine. Everyone knew. Eirik's mother—*my own wife*—knew. If not for those bloody eyes we could have passed you off as the son of some other man.'

'My apologies for ruining your plan of keeping your wife's sister as mistress under her own roof. I'm sure it was disappointing for you.'

'Quiet!'

Clenching his jaw, Gunnar turned his attention to the fire, determined to allow the old man to say whatever he needed to say and then leave him to rot. It didn't matter.

'You don't understand. When I walked into their father's home to meet my future wife, Finna was the first person I saw. I wanted her immediately. I even asked her father to allow me to have her instead of her sister. He refused, claiming she was too young for marriage. She wanted me, too, but even she couldn't sway him. So I married as planned and I convinced my wife that she should bring her sister home with us.' He paused as if lost in the memory before continuing. 'Finna was able to hide her pregnancy until after Eirik was born and there were whispers then, except no one had seen me go to her bed, no one could say for certain. But then you were born.' He huffed at the memory and shook his head. The momentary spark that had returned snuffed out again. 'It was the longest day and night of my life. She was so young, so small... I was sure that I had killed her. That *you* had killed her. It was a much tougher, longer labour than Eirik's. You always were disagreeable. My Finna was strong, though. She made it through and later...after all the others had found their beds...I went to her. She was exhausted, but she presented you to me with more pride than I had ever seen in anyone.'

Lost to memories, his father's words tapered off and his heft slumped down in the chair even farther. Was it possible that the man had actually loved her? The thought had never crossed his mind before. It seemed impossible that the hard man who had never cared about anything except leading his men could have stooped so low as to lose his heart to a woman. Gunnar couldn't bring himself to believe it, but he'd also never heard him talk about anyone this way. Perhaps what the man had felt had been some distorted version of love, but it hadn't been what Gunnar felt for Kadlin. It hadn't been anything like his *need*, his absolute knowledge that she was his. Guilt had been the more likely emotion his father had felt.

The jarl sighed and began again. 'You had my eyes and my wife had her accusation. I ignored her as long as I could. Her father had died by then so she had no one to which to voice her appeal. You were my son after all, no matter her feelings. But then she began taking her jealousy out on your mother until even she was asking to go, begging me to allow her to marry. I was weak back then. I thought her happiness would absolve me of my crimes against her and I allowed it to happen. She married and begged me to keep you here. She wanted no reminders of me.'

His only knowledge of his mother, aside from the brief snippets of memory he had, was learning of her death years ago. The moment he was told hadn't even been very noteworthy, just a simple declaration by his father one evening before they had retired to bed. There had been no mourning or explanation. He'd felt nothing then aside from a strange, hollow ache. That ache was back now and growing larger. Gunnar couldn't look away from his father. He'd always assumed his mother had abandoned him like the unwanted bastard he had been. He had no memory of her leaving, just that one day she was gone from his life. But to hear the awful truth stated aloud, that he had merely been an inconvenience unwanted by both of his parents... The pain grew until it sucked the air from his chest.

It was no wonder that he had clung to Kadlin, the only constant source of love and approval in his life. It was no wonder that he had sought her out when everything else around him had been so horrible. Yet, instead of protecting their love—instead of protecting her—he'd been obsessed with protecting himself. And then he had thrown her love in her face. He'd taken everything that she had given him and turned it against her.

'I was wrong,' his father continued. 'Her happiness only fed my misery.'

He'd always thought of his mother as nothing more than a convenience for his father. The man was notorious for his fickle affections when it came to women. There had been no reason to suspect that she had been anything other than a momentary distraction for him. Nothing more than a challenge or another conquest. Could it be that she had been more? 'You loved her.' The idea was so unfathomable that he could barely get the words out and when he did they were more of an accusation.

The old man flinched, but didn't shift his gaze from the fire. 'It wasn't a sentiment in which I could indulge. I had my duty and the rest didn't matter. Finna knew that. She had known that from the beginning.'

It was so easy for him to cut people out and pretend they didn't matter. It was what he had done to Gunnar's mother and what he had always done to Gunnar. Gunnar stared until he realised his fingers were wet. The shirt was completely red with his blood, so he tightened his grip and pressed it hard to the wound at his side. It burned and throbbed, but he made himself ignore it. 'She knew that she didn't matter because you had other things to do? What sort of man—'

What sort of man allowed the woman he loved to think she didn't matter?

He'd been as horrible as his father, only in a different way. The blood drained from his face, leaving him slightly dizzy and as disgusted with himself as he was with his father. Kadlin had thought that very thing and he'd done nothing to make sure she knew it wasn't true. He'd abandoned her without a promise for the future and with his child to raise alone. That wasn't any better than what the defeated old man before him had done. Making her decisions for her hadn't protected her at all. Neither had trying to make it up to her, but then, she'd wanted so much more from him than just the pleasure he could bring her body. She'd wanted all of him. Every piece of him that he kept hidden away because he'd spent his entire life being afraid.

Not any more. Nothing mattered without her.

He was not his father and he refused to repeat the man's mistakes. He also refused to live under the weight of his family's rejection any longer. Kadlin was his family and she had given him a son. He'd spend every day until his death letting them know how much he valued them, how much he regretted every moment he had spent away from them.

'I put what was right for my men before what was right for myself. I am jarl. You'll do the same.'

'I will.' That didn't mean sacrificing Kadlin. It never had. His own fear had guided him in that. Fear that she would one day look at him and see what everyone else saw. She'd never believed what they had seen and for once he was beginning to suspect that she had been the one who was right. Or at least he could strive to be that man she saw.

The weight of his father's stare settled on him again. 'Aye, you will.' Then he rose to his feet, his hand shaky on the chair as he pushed himself up. Gunnar moved forward, but the old man put his hand up to stop any assistance and stepped slowly towards the bed almost as if the conversation had taken the last of his strength. After he sat, he looked up again and their amber eyes clashed. 'You were not my first choice, Gunnar, but you are a solid choice. You have my support. I will make sure the men know that. Go, and send Dom in.'

Gunnar could only stare at the man and see the future that he'd been headed towards. Without Kadlin, this is how he would meet his end. He'd live out his life knowing that he had never fought for the woman he loved. Just as his father had done. Giving his head a shake, he acknowledged that he deserved more than that. *Kadlin* deserved more than that. She deserved to know that he wanted her, needed her and would do anything to keep her. Anything. Nothing mattered except what she thought of him. Not her father, his father, no one mattered except for them and the child they had created. Right now, she despised him and he couldn't blame her, but he'd not let that stand.

He turned to leave, but stopped at the door to look back at his father. Though his anger with the man had died, he couldn't summon any stirrings of tenderness, only pity. It was shameful that the man had wasted his life in bitterness. He could, however, thank him for finally letting him know what he had kept quiet for so long. The knowledge wouldn't change the past, but he'd make sure that it would alter his future for the better. 'Thank you, Father.'

His father glanced at him and something

passed between them in that quick look. It wasn't acceptance or love, but a small glimpse of understanding. In that look, Gunnar understood what his father had never been able to articulate. His severity had never been about Gunnar, but about his own disappointments. There had been nothing Gunnar could have ever done to overcome that. It was too late for them, but not for Kadlin. Not for Avalt. He had a lifetime with them ahead.

Gripping the door frame with one hand and the sapling with the other, he pulled himself from the room. He was exhausted. His muscles all but shook with fatigue. The limp was even more pronounced. Spying Dom and Hilla across the hall, he threw himself down on to the nearest bench, too tired to make the trip. They both rushed over, making him think he must look as horrible as he felt. As Hilla *tsked* over his wound and began the agonising process of cleaning the blood away, he leaned back against the wall and let his thoughts wander to Kadlin and Avalt. It wasn't over. He wouldn't allow the mistakes of his father to rule his future any more. They were his and he would claim them.

* * *

Kadlin awoke the moment an arm went around her waist, pulling her back against a broad chest. Even in the darkness, she knew that it was Gunnar. His scent enveloped her as completely as his arm held her secure to his chest. She closed her eyes and allowed herself just a moment to revel in the comfort of his hold and the knowledge that he was safe. His lips brushed her neck before he buried his face in her hair and took a deep breath. It didn't really surprise her to awaken in her childhood chamber to find Gunnar there, but she hadn't expected him to come. She'd spent the past days certain that whatever had been between them was over for ever.

She had come home only to realise that it didn't feel like home any more. Home was the farm. Nay, home was Gunnar. The farm had been a sanctuary, but never a home until Gunnar had made it so. Home was here in his arms.

'How do you keep getting in here? I'm beginning to doubt the strength of my father's fortifications.'

He laughed and kissed her neck again. The harsh rasp of his short beard made her shiver and sent a thrill of pleasure to her belly. It was so easy for him to do that to her, to reduce her to a puddle of need without even trying. 'Don't fear, love. This time I'm here by his consent.'

That made her eyes shoot open and she sat up so quickly he had no choice but to relinquish his hold on her. 'What?'

The sounds coming from the house outside her chamber assured her that it wasn't very late in the evening. A glance assured her that Avalt hadn't come to bed yet, which meant that her mother hadn't relinquished him yet. She'd left them playing outside in the twilight, going to her chamber because it seemed to be the only escape from her family's constant prodding about what had happened between them on the farm. Also, it was the only place she was safe to indulge her own fear that something terrible had happened to Gunnar. Flein had relayed the information about Baldr to her father once they had arrived and he'd been so alarmed that he had gone with a group of his men to aid in the fight, but hadn't returned yet.

Gunnar shifted, leaving the bed, and in moments a few candles flickered to life. It wasn't much light, but enough to make out his form and bring colour to his face when he returned to set a candle on the bedside table.

'Oh, Gunnar, what happened to you?' Rising to her knees so that she could reach him, her fingertips brushed near the swollen flesh above his cheekbone and then the cut above his eye. 'Did you fight Baldr?'

His large hand, a strip of linen wrapped around the swollen knuckles, caught hers and brought it to his lips before dropping it and moving slowly to sit on the bed. He winced and her attention moved to the side he seemed to be favouring. Her hands were already on the linen pulling it up, before his fingers intercepted her. 'It's merely a small cut, nothing to worry yourself over. Aye, there was a fight, but Jarl Leif is safe. He arrived after everything had been settled and has stayed behind to pay his final respects to my father.'

'I know that I should say I'm sorry for your father. Flein mentioned that he is sick, but I cannot. He caused so much—'

'It doesn't matter, Kadlin. That's over.'

His eyes were so clear and warm as they looked down at her that her breath caught in her throat. Then he smiled at her and it was a true smile untouched by bitterness or anger, and it made her see anew just how handsome he was despite the injuries. 'What happened with Baldr?'

'Defeated. He'll be exiled.'

'Oh.' His explanation seemed like a brush off, but then, she hadn't really expected that he would not defeat Baldr and the specifics really didn't seem to matter as long as Gunnar was safe. She wanted to ask if he was staying, if the defeat meant that he could take the jarl's place when the time came, or if he was planning to leave. Then she realised the only question that mattered right now was why he was in front of her. She opened her mouth to ask, but just as she did, the pad of his thumb brushed across her bottom lip, stealing her breath yet again.

'My father has given me his favour and his men have sworn their allegiance to me.'

'That's wonderful. It's what you've always wanted.' She meant it, but even she knew that her enthusiasm hadn't reached her eyes.

'I've come to take you home with me to be my wife.'

He said it so simply, as if it could be the easiest thing in the world. Perhaps it could be if she wasn't still hurting inside. The intensity of his gaze was too much, so she dropped hers to the blanket. He moved slowly and sat on the bed beside her, his knee brushing her thigh. 'I'm not sure what to say.'

'Fair enough. I'll talk. There are things I should have said to you long ago and I'll say them now. I've always loved you, Kadlin. That much you must have suspected, but you don't know how much I struggled with knowing how to love you. I didn't know what it meant. I didn't know how to take care of you. I only knew that no one believed in me, believed that I could be a warrior, a man worthy of you.' When she looked up at him, ready to point out that she had, he took her hand and nodded. 'Aye, I know that you did. You were the only one, but I couldn't be that man until *I believed* that I was that man. There was so much that I needed to learn to deserve you. If I could go back and do it all again I would make sure that you knew how I felt about you. I would have asked you to wait for me. I love you, Kadlin. I should have told you back then. I should have given you the promise to come back to you because it was there inside me. I just didn't know how to say it. There will never be another person I love as I love you. Never. I know that I haven't been worthy of your love, but I will do everything that I can to deserve it. I know that I can't demand your trust on that, but I will earn it going forward. Come back with me. Give me a chance and I'll prove to you that I'm the man you deserve, the father Avalt deserves.'

Her breaths had become short because she couldn't get air past the ache in her chest. He was saying all the things that she had ever longed to hear from him, but she couldn't quite believe the words. 'I'm afraid,' she whispered. 'You don't know how much it hurt me to watch you leave and then to later find out that I was with child. Gunnar...it was the most wonderful and terrifying time of my life. I'd only ever wanted to be your wife, to bear your children, but to do it alone was terrifying.'

'Kadlin...' Her name came out as a breath filled with pain. It threatened to break her heart. 'If I had known, I would have come to you. Why didn't you try to reach me?'

The ache in her chest moved up her throat, stealing her ability to speak until it finally receded, but her eyes had filled with tears. 'You told me you didn't want me, Gunnar. What was I to do, send for you and trap you into a marriage you didn't want?'

He moved closer, his lips brushing across her cheeks and eyelids as he kissed the tears away. 'Kadlin… Kadlin…don't cry. I'm here now and there hasn't been a day that I haven't wanted you. Your dreams are mine, as well.' His voice was strained so he cleared his throat before speaking again. 'Our children around us, a fire in the hearth and the winter raging outside. Every time I ever dared imagine the future, that's what I saw. I saw your beautiful face and our children. It's what's meant for us. Let it be now.'

Closing her eyes against the ache of tears, she pushed the imagery away so that she had a hope of continuing with what she needed to say. Even without seeing it, the weight of his gaze touched her. 'But how can I trust you again?'

He sat back just enough to look down at her. 'I have faith that you can and I'll keep proving myself to you until you do. In another life, we could have had this all along. I'd never have been apart from you. Our friendship as children could have been nurtured to grow into something powerful and consuming. This is the life we have and, despite all that's happened, what we have has grown into something powerful. We are so much stronger together than we could ever be separately. You'll see that when you come home with me.'

'You say that as if it's a foregone conclusion.'

He smiled, a hint of desire shining through. 'I have to return tomorrow and I want to take you and Avalt with me. I won't force you to be my wife or to stay with me. All I want is for you to give us a chance. If you choose not to return now, then I'll come back every day to remind you that I love you. I don't want a day to pass that you don't hear those words from me and I don't want Avalt to ever grow up thinking that I don't love him or that I regret his birth.'

'It's too far for you to come every day.' She couldn't resist the tease.

'Then I'll make camp and wait for you.' His smile had vanished as if he was serious about that.

He spoke as if what he declared was easy, as if there was nothing to lose. Perhaps he didn't understand how it had almost destroyed her when he hadn't returned for her. 'I'm afraid of giving us a chance. You hurt me before, Gunnar. I can't just brush that aside.'

His arms wrapped around her waist and he pulled her closer to him until her hands settled on his shoulders. 'We can't change the past, Kadlin. We can only move forward. You only have to believe that I'll do everything in my power to keep you happy, just as I believe you will do the same. Do you believe?'

'I want to.'

A grin spread across his face and his arms tightened around her. 'You and Avalt mean everything to me. I won't let you down again. You have my vow and my faith. I promise that I will earn yours. I'm just asking for a chance. I've gone without you in my life for as long as I can. There's not a future for me without you.'

Before her was the man that she had always caught glimpses of, but could never see clearly in him. He'd come into his own and the transformation was breathtaking. She was nodding before she even knew what words she would say. The light in his eyes glowed brighter. 'Is that an aye?' he whispered.

'Aye.' With her hands on either side of his face,

she pulled him down to her. His mouth claimed hers in a fiery kiss as his fingers clenched her nightdress, pulling her even tighter against him until he winced and she pulled back just enough to gauge his pain. 'You're wounded. I almost forgot.'

He chuckled and pulled her back to him. 'That won't stop me. I've waited too long for you.' Before she could brace herself, he gently toppled her so that she landed on her back on the bed. He followed her more gingerly until he was lying upon her, staring down into her face.

She gasped at the pleasurable shock of the weight of his muscled body pressing down on hers. 'You really don't know what's good for you, do you?' she teased and tangled her fingers in the hair on the back of his head.

'Aye, I know exactly what's good for me. You, love. Only you.'

* * * * *

MILLS & BOON®

Why shop at millsandboon.co.uk?

Each year, thousands of romance readers find their perfect read at millsandboon.co.uk. That's because we're passionate about bringing you the very best romantic fiction. Here are some of the advantages of shopping at www.millsandboon.co.uk:

* **Get new books first**—you'll be able to buy your favourite books one month before they hit the shops

* **Get exclusive discounts**—you'll also be able to buy our specially created monthly collections, with up to 50% off the RRP

* **Find your favourite authors**—latest news, interviews and new releases for all your favourite authors and series on our website, plus ideas for what to try next

* **Join in**—once you've bought your favourite books, don't forget to register with us to rate, review and join in the discussions

Visit **www.millsandboon.co.uk**
for all this and more today!